WEIRD SISTERS

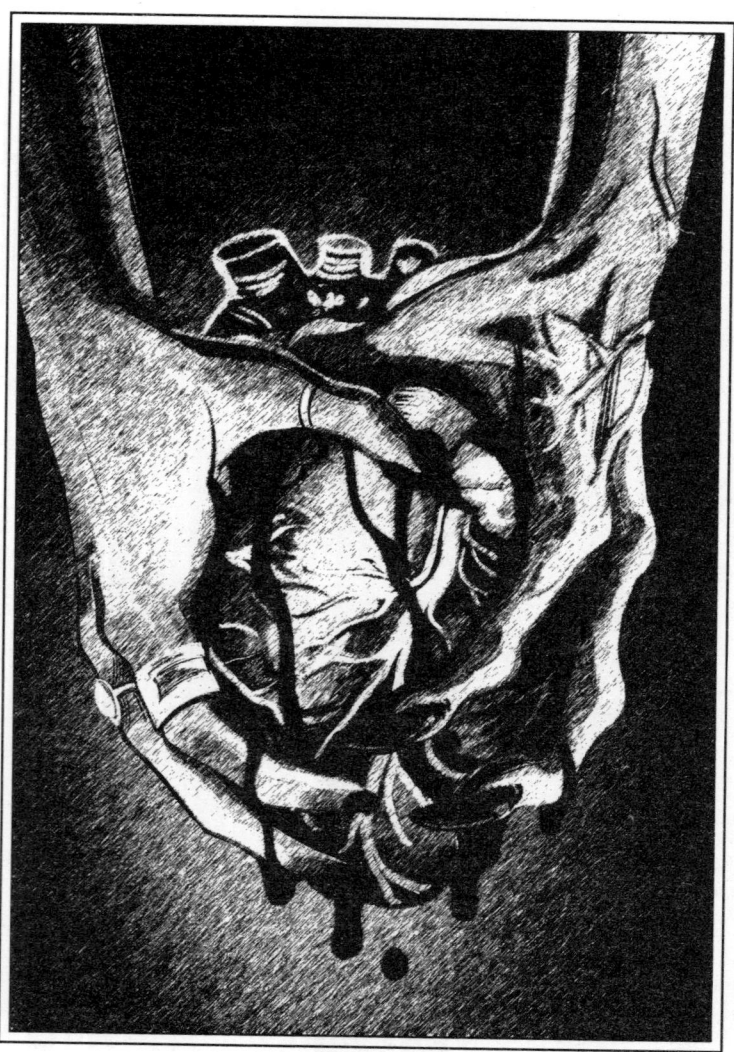

WEIRD SISTERS

Tales from the Queens of the Pulp Era

Edited by
MIKE ASHLEY

First published in 2025 by
The British Library
96 Euston Road
London NW1 2DB

Selection, introduction and notes © 2025 Mike Ashley
Volume copyright © 2025 The British Library Board

"Daemon" © 1946 All Fiction Field Inc., renewed 1974 by C.L. Moore.
"Brenda" © 1953 by Margret St. Clair. Renewed in 1981 by Margaret St. Clair.
Reprinted with permission of McIntosh & Otis, Inc.
"They That Have Wings" © 2011 by Debra L. Hammond as literary heir of
Evangeline Walton Ensley. Reprinted by permission of the copyright holder.
"Mirror, Mirror" © 1994 reproduced with permission of the estate of Tanith Lee.

Every effort has been made to trace copyright holders and to obtain their
permission for the use of copyright material. The publisher apologises
for any errors or omissions and would be pleased to be notified of any
corrections to be incorporated in reprints or future editions.

Cataloguing in Publication Data
A catalogue record for this publication is available from the British Library

ISBN 978 0 7123 5522 3
e-ISBN 978 0 7123 6858 2

Cover design by Mauricio Villamayor with illustration by Sandra Gómez.
Frontispiece by Sandra Gómez.
Illustration on page 288: detail from *So-called Hours of Philip the Fair*, f. 280v (c. 1495).
Text design and typesetting by Tetragon, London
Printed in England by CPI Group (UK) Ltd, Croydon, CR0 4YY

CONTENTS

Introduction	7
A Note from the Publisher	11
The Rat Master GREYE LA SPINA	13
The Withered Heart G. G. PENDARVES	37
Leonora EVERIL WORRELL	67
Ode to Pegasus MARIA MORAVSKY	83
Mommy MARY ELIZABETH COUNSELMAN	93
Daemon C. L. MOORE	107
More Than Shadow DOROTHY QUICK	137
The House Party on Smoky Island L. M. MONTGOMERY	153
Forbidden Cupboard FRANCES GARFIELD	167
The Underbody ALLISON V. HARDING	181
Brenda MARGARET ST. CLAIR	205
They That Have Wings EVANGELINE WALTON	221
Foxy's Hollow LEAH BODINE DRAKE	247
The Crying Child DOROTHEA GIBBONS	259
Mirror, Mirror TANITH LEE	271
Story Sources	283

INTRODUCTION

The American pulp magazine *Weird Tales*, which appeared in March 1923, was the first English-language magazine to specialize in tales of the supernatural, bizarre and fantastic. There had been a few earlier attempts that didn't quite make such a memorable impression, including *Black Cat*, which ran what were called "clever" stories and included as many mystery, adventure and romance stories as it did weird tales, and *The Thrill Book*, which concentrated mostly on adventure stories. There had also been a German magazine, *Der Orchideengarten*, or "The Orchid Garden", which ran from 1919 to 1921 with many stories of the weird, surreal and erotic, but never left its mark outside central Europe.

Weird Tales, on the other hand, established itself as a significant market for strange stories, and though its sales were always moderate, its influence was huge. Examples of three authors who contributed to the magazine will give some idea. It was in *Weird Tales* that H. P. Lovecraft established his reputation and was able to develop his cosmic horror stories which became known as the Cthulhu Mythos and to which fellow writers also contributed, thus helping build their careers. Amongst them was Robert Bloch, famed author of *Psycho*, who cut his teeth on *Weird Tales*, and Robert E. Howard who had established himself creating strong but cunning barbarian heroes, most notably Conan of Cimmeria.

Although it nearly folded after its first year, *Weird Tales* struggled on and helped develop a market for stories of the bizarre and unusual. Its very existence prompted other publishers to produce their own magazines, amongst which were *Strange Tales*, *Strange Stories*, *Unknown* and *Famous Fantastic Mysteries*, but *Weird Tales* outlived them all. It ran for 279 issues until September 1954 and has since been revived four times with upwards of another hundred issues, and is still appearing today. Its early issues are highly collectible and, depending upon condition, extremely valuable, and it has become something of a legend amongst the devotees of pulp magazine history.

I mention all of this because, thanks to *Weird Tales*, and subsequently its rivals, a market developed amongst the pulp magazines which welcomed women writers as much as men. Most of the contents of those specialist pulp magazines publishing westerns, crime stories, science fiction and sports fiction, were dominated by men. The romance magazines were a more significant market for women but it was also a fairly formulaic field. Not so *Weird Tales*. Its second editor, Farnsworth Wright, who replaced its inaugural editor Edwin Baird after the first year, whilst being somewhat cautious with one eye on sales, also enjoyed stories that were out of the ordinary, and a fair number were by women. What's more, when Farnsworth Wright retired, the new editor, who saw the magazine through from 1940 to the end in 1954, was a woman, Dorothy McIlwraith, and under her control the magazine published some of its most original and unusual stories—many by women.

This volume celebrates those female contributors. It's difficult to be certain about just how many women appeared in the magazine since the purchase records were destroyed and it's possible some women contributed under male pseudonyms or appeared simply with initials instead of first names. So far as I can tell there were 123 women contributors, with 356 stories which represented about a seventh of the fiction contents of the original pulp issues. There were also many poems, articles and illustrations by women, including work by the now legendary artist Margaret Brundage who painted 68 covers—almost a quarter of the original pulp run. They became notorious for their often erotic illustrations of voluptuous naked young ladies and certainly helped sales, though they also led to the magazine being banned for a while in Canada, and in some cases the covers were "adjusted" before publication!

I've included stories by fourteen of those 123 writers plus a bonus with a story by Tanith Lee who was one of the major contributors to the revived *Weird Tales*. The authors selected are amongst the leading contributors to the magazine including Mary Elizabeth Counselman, Catherine Lucille Moore, Margaret St. Clair, Everil Worrell and the mysterious Allison V. Harding, who was the most prolific female contributor. I've included a story by Lucy M. Montgomery, the famed author of *Anne of Green Gables*, who may seem a surprise contributor to a weird-fiction pulp, but she enjoyed ghost stories. Another notable one-off contributor was Signe Toksvig, the great aunt of comedian and television personality Sandi Toksvig. I haven't included her story, "The Devil's Martyr", from the June 1928 issue, because it is readily available in the Tales of the Weird volume *The Horned God*, edited by Michael Wheatley. There is also something of a mystery about the author Dorothea Gibbons, of which I say more in my introduction to her story.

In three cases I've selected stories from beyond *Weird Tales*. C. L. Moore's contributions, which made her one of the most popular authors, fell into two separate series featuring the female heroic equivalent of Conan, Jirel of Joiry, or the space adventurer Northwest Smith, both still widely available. Rather than select one of those, I have gone for a lesser known story she contributed to the glorious pulp *Famous Fantastic Mysteries* in 1946, a story which would have been well suited to *Weird Tales*. Leah Bodine Drake was primarily a poet and though she contributed a handful of stories to *Weird Tales* I have selected one from the short-lived rival *Fantasy Fiction*. Evangeline Walton's "They That Have Wings" was actually rejected by *Weird Tales* as being too gory but it survived amongst her papers and resurfaced in 2011 thanks to the industrious delvings of Douglas Anderson.

The stories are printed in the order of the author's first appearance in *Weird Tales*. Readers may draw their own conclusions as to whether the women writers in *Weird Tales* favoured any particular themes. To my mind, after having read so many of the stories in the magazines, it seems to me that there is an emphasis on personal relationships and especially children, who feature in several of these stories. But really, their treatment of themes and ideas is every bit as broad as those by their male counterparts—and often more memorable. See what you think.

MIKE ASHLEY

A NOTE FROM THE PUBLISHER

The original short stories reprinted in the British Library Tales of the Weird series were written and published in a period ranging across the nineteenth and twentieth centuries. There are many elements of these stories which continue to entertain modern readers; however, in some cases there are also uses of language, instances of stereotyping and some attitudes expressed by narrators or characters which may not be endorsed by the publishing standards of today. We acknowledge therefore that some elements in the stories selected for reprinting may continue to make uncomfortable reading for some of our audience. With this series British Library Publishing aims to offer a new readership a chance to read some of the rare material of the British Library's collections in an affordable paperback format, to enjoy their merits and to look back into the worlds of the past two centuries as portrayed by their writers. It is not possible to separate these stories from the history of their writing and therefore the following stories are presented as they were originally published with minor edits only, made for consistency of style and sense. We welcome feedback from our readers, which can be sent to the following address:

British Library Publishing
The British Library
96 Euston Road
London, NW1 2DB

1942

THE RAT MASTER

Greye La Spina

Greye La Spina (1880–1969) was born Fanny Greye Bragg in Wakefield, Massachusetts. She barely knew her father who was seventy at the time and who died four years later. He was a retired Methodist minister—apparently she was a "Child of Prayer". She married three times, the first in 1898 when she was only eighteen. She had a daughter, Celia. Her husband died in an industrial accident after they'd been married less than two years. She married again in 1905 to a pharmacist and they had a son, but it seems this was not a happy marriage as they divorced in 1910. Soon after she married Robert La Spina, Baron di Savuto, and so became a Baroness. Alas, money did not come with the title.

Fanny had the good fortune to come runner-up in a story contest run by Photoplay in 1921 which won her $2,500—the equivalent today of around £35,000. They invested this in a poultry farm in Windy Knoll, Pennsylvania but the Baron developed a debilitating condition, becoming an invalid. Both the Baron's private business and the farm fell victims to the Depression. Fanny became the primary wage earner, undertaking various jobs and even becoming a master weaver, designing tapestries.

Her first supernatural stories were for the legendary *Thrill Book* in 1919, which included the werewolf tale "The Wolf of the Steppes". She sold to several other pulps before her *Weird Tales* debut with "The Tortoise Shell Cat" (November 1924). Many of her stories involve shape-changers—werewolves, vampires, were-cats! Her first serial, "Invaders from the Dark" (April–June 1925), includes a seductive Russian shape-changer. Arguably her best werewolf tale is the novella "The Devil's Pool" (June 1932). Her final appearance was with a low-key ghost story, "Old Mr. Wiley" (March 1951). "The Rat Master" dates from later in her career, appearing in the March 1942 issue. It was apparently inspired by the many rats that lived near her Pennsylvania home.

The night was pitchy dark; the sky indigo. Black vaporous racks flitted across the moon that could be glimpsed only occasionally through rifts in the interlacing branches of the crowding trees. The rutty roadway had become a rude cattle trail, along which I urged Carry with ever-increasing anxiety, although upon what my apprehension was based I myself did not exactly know.

Once in a while I used the electric flashlight; oddly enough, not to make surer our panting way along the hardly-used trail, but to lighten my furtive glances into the creeping shadows that lurked about us, not only galloping fast upon our heels, but pressing closer on either hand while giving way with suspicious readiness ahead.

Carry, good little sport, leaned more and more heavily upon my supporting arm. Her high-heeled pumps (chosen for motoring, not for that scrambling, hasty flight over rough, rugged trails) continually tripped her; she turned her slender ankles more than once, with faint ejaculations of impatient dismay. That she was at the point of exhaustion I intuitively sensed, but I dared not let her realize my awareness of her condition; instead, I managed to jerk out occasional words of encouragement that would lead her to believe I thought her capable of far greater effort than yet remained in her fragile body.

That we must continue on our arduous, struggling way, Carry realized as well as I. Night in that thick, unfriendly wood was not to be contemplated save as the ultimate alternative. Yet we two, breathing in thick panting gasps as we willed our muscles to repeat, time and time again, the same expansions and contractions that resulted in our slow forward movement, were facing the fact that night had come on apace under cover of those thunderous and gloomy canopies of darkness which an approaching storm was hanging across the lowering sky.

Go back we could not if we would, for by now I knew that I could not have found my way back to where we had abandoned the car, when it refused to travel farther. Yet I would have been glad to have felt it possible to return; with plate glass windows properly fastened up, we would have had the semblance of a refuge about us, whereas now we knew not how long we must stumble forward in the fast-gathering darkness, ignorant of what lay before us, even while we fled from what we instinctively felt was pursuit closing in with inimical intent.

Most of all things terrifying to the human soul is the intangible. It is not that final terrifying apparition that freezes the blood in one's veins. It is the slow turning of the knob of one's chamber door in the eerily still hours before dawn, when one knows that he is alone in the house and that no other human being can possibly intrude upon his guarded solitude. So now those creeping, silent shadows drew ever closer upon Carry and me, while we clung to each other, slipping and stumbling along the narrow trail, lighted scantily now by sparkling fireflies that flashed more and more thickly as we went on.

"Jack—I—can't—go—farther."

Carry collapsed against me heavily, the faint words jerked from her panting lips. With difficulty I held her from the ground, clasping my arms desperately about her half-fainting body tightly, and trying still to urge her along. My efforts were vain.

"You *must* try again, dear. You can't stay out here all night. It is beginning to rain. You'll be drenched if we stay here. There must be a house of some kind nearby, or there wouldn't be this definite trail, poor as it is."

The pattering of heavy raindrops on the carpet of dead leaves had been faintly discernible while we were moving along. Now that we stood still we heard them more plainly, although after a moment they ceased entirely. In their stead there came from the murk about us a soft rustling, a faint stirring. Then I observed what had escaped my notice until that moment. The fireflies that had been flashing on either side of the trail were emitting their lights only in doublets, as it were, and none were flying higher than a few inches above the ground. Strange fireflies, these. Something about them struck a bizarre note that was highly unpleasant.

"Jack! The fireflies—?"

Carry had observed it also. Her frail body was trembling in my arms with an agitation not altogether that of physical exhaustion. All at once she pulled against my encircling arms with unexpected violence.

"Let us go on, Jack! Oh, we must go on! Fireflies emit a yellow light, and these are a livid green. *They are not fireflies.* What are they, then?" Her voice sank to a faint, scared whisper. "Jack—the rain—*it wasn't rain*, Jack."

Powers above! She was right. What we had taken for pattering raindrops had been the delicate drumming of feet, the feet of an innumerable horde of small animals, so tiny that their eyes, sparkling with strange green light, were but a few inches above the carpet of dead leaves over which they ran. *What could they be, that walked when we walked, stood when we stood?* My body twisted in a shudder of involuntary horror and distaste. My teeth went suddenly on edge. I could feel gooseflesh coming out on my skin.

"Courage, sweetheart! There must be shelter near at hand. Come, lean on me, and try again."

*

Carry withdrew from my supporting arms and once more addressed herself to the arduous efforts her exhaustion had but a moment since obliged her to abandon. Fear whipped her nerves and her muscles into momentary action. As she stumbled onward with me, she moaned under her breath.

"Jack—I'm—dreadfully—frightened."

"Nonsense, dear. Nothing to be afraid of," I lied boldly, but I was listening, ears suddenly keener for every night sound.

I heard that soft rustling and pattering all about us, *that was not rain*; my eyes shrank from the flashing of innumerable tiny sparks of green *that were not fireflies*. A shiver of nausea and distaste caught at my shrinking flesh and I had much ado to quiet it that Carry might not catch the contagion of that involuntary horror from me.

There was something afoot on another plane that had impinged somehow upon ours; this much I knew intuitively. There was a gathering about us in those dark groves of creatures that in some secret fashion were interested in us; whether their will was potent for good or evil only time would show. I felt a sickness within my soul, that bade me beware; it told me that the interest our strange escort had betrayed in the movements of us two night wanderers boded ill.

I could feel the body of my little sweetheart sinking more and more heavily. I caught her against me yet tighter, and heard her faint, despairing whisper.

"Dear—Jack—I told you—*he* would never—let me escape."

Her hopeless tone filled me with a fury that momentarily gave me fresh strength. Dwight Harkness should not have her body again, to use in his vile incantations; he should no more suck the lifeblood from her delicate arteries.

"He can have nothing to do with anything here, dearest. We have left him miles behind. He can hardly have learned yet that you have fled. Lean on me, little love. I shall be strong enough for two."

"I—cannot—take—another—step."

Carry went into a shapeless heap at my very feet, and I was obliged to stop and lean down in order to get that slender little body up into the shelter of my arms. As I stopped, and leaned, the sound of drumming feet about us died away, and it seemed as if it began to be quiet close to us, and then little by little grew quiet afar off, as if the escort of creatures in the shadows were indeed an army that stretched through the woods and into the far distance all about us.

"No use—Jack dear. Leave me. Save—yourself!"

(Oh, she would say that to me, my heart of gold!)

"And what would my life be without you, little love? If you cannot go with me, I stay here with you."

"Jack—dear—you are—truly good. For your sake—I will try—again."

I helped her to her tired feet. The soft rustle of her rising was echoed and prolonged all about us. As she staggered weakly up, I flashed the electric torch quickly to left, to right. Shadows. Black shadows. Thick, dark, ugly shadows. None else visible. Nothing moved but those portentous blots of night that lurked and seemed to leer on every side. Or was it not they which moved? Perhaps it was the owners of the eyes—?

"Don't try to talk, darling. Spare your breath for this last effort. We *must* find shelter of some kind near at hand."

As if the necessity behind my words had evoked an answer to my inward prayer, the path took a sudden twist. We rounded the curve, and oh! the joy of seeing dim lights ahead.

"Here is a house, dear. Courage! Only a few steps more and we shall be under shelter."

We gained the hovel. It was too mean to be termed a house or a cottage, but it was shelter of a kind; it had a roof and four walls, two blank and dirty windows that seemed to permit a pale light to filter through into the night darkness. I rapped at the door imperatively. At the sound of my knock, the rustling about us ceased and such a silence wrapped us about that almost I could have desired to hear once more that drumming and pattering of unseen thousands of tiny feet, the rustling and stirring of myriads of living creatures in the night about us.

Then, as if my knock had been a signal, the door flew open to us, and simultaneously the windows went blanker and the light that had seemed to emanate from within was gone. Carry dragged at me, unavailingly.

"No—no—no!" she was crying in terrified, choked gasps. "It is a trap. I tell you, *he* will not let me escape. Now he will have us both!"

Her exclamations died away suddenly. I picked up her slight, unconscious body and stepped across the threshold, at the same time directing the rays of the torch into the interior of the hut, for it was little more than a hut. It was entirely empty. I thrust the door shut with my foot, then stood holding Carry against my heart while I listened.

Silence. Heavy silence, thick with portent. A kind of panic seized upon me. Again I threw the brilliant ray of the torch about, to find nothing save a door opposite that by which we had entered. Reason told me it could only lead out of the hut again, for I had seen at a glance that it was but a rude shack. For the moment, then, I dared forget the slowly growing murmur without, as if millions of tiny animals were whistling and chirping and squeaking together in an ever-increasing, evil chorus.

I let Carry's body slip gently to the rough board floor, ripped off my coat and cushioned her dear brown head upon it. Then, standing the lighted torch upright beside her, I set to chafing her cold fingers between my own warm palms. I had taken the precaution to kneel in such a position that the door by which we had entered could not be pushed open, being blocked by my own body. As to the rear door, I dared not for the moment take time to see if it were secured or not;

first I must bring consciousness back to my poor darling who lay white and still upon the floor.

It was as her eyelids fluttered open that I leaped to my feet, seizing the torch from the floor, for it was my only weapon. Too late I remembered that I had left my automatic in the door-pocket of the car when we abandoned it. I stood before Carry and faced the opposite door now; turned the light upon it, my nerves jumping in an ecstasy of horrid anticipation. For I had caught the slight creaking of the rusty hinges. Now I saw the turning of the knob, and the inch-by-inch widening of the opening that would presently admit—*what?*

Behind me Carry cried out and struggled to her feet, that she might meet whatever was to come bravely, standing. My game little Carry! How my heart yearned over her.

The door slipped yet wider with reluctant creakings and then remained motionless, perhaps four inches open. My nerves (none too good after the tramp through those haunted woods in the attempt to snatch my little sweetheart from the man who called himself her guardian but of whose dealings with the Evil One she had for long had no doubt) could not brook that silent and ominous waiting.

"Whoever you are, enter!" I shouted furiously. "Either come in or go out!"

The door swung obediently wider. My heart almost missed a beat. Leaning against my left shoulder now stood my little love, breathing in short, quick gasps.

"You ask me to come in?" said a voice, with incredulous intonation. "I had hardly expected a welcome."

"Either get in or get out!" I snapped. "And be quick about it."

"I accept your kind invitation," said the voice, on a curious high pitch, somehow reminding me of the twitter of mice under the flooring.

"It's all wrong, Jack!" breathed Carry's soft whisper into my ear. "You shouldn't have asked—*it*—in. It is evil. I feel strongly that it is evil. Had it been good, it would not have waited for an invitation."

Hastily the voice repeated, "I accept your unsolicited invitation."

The owner of that high, squeaking voice appeared so suddenly in the narrow aperture of the doorway that almost I started back in consternation. A noisome odour made itself known as he came in.

"Shut that door behind you," I ordered, feeling that my own voice was not as even as I would have liked it to be. "There's something unpleasant abroad tonight, and there's no sense in asking it inside, too."

The only response of that ragged mantled, dwarfish creature was a shrill titter. At the sound of it Carry quailed; one of her delicate little hands took hold upon my arm so tightly that her fingernails pinched through my shirt and hurt me so that I winced involuntarily.

I stared at that strange visitor, holding the bright ray of the electric torch steadily upon him. The grey mantle shrouding his crooked, stunted body was drawn across his face as if to shield his eyes from the too-bright glare of the light; it effectively concealed from me what manner of man he might be. Unprepossessing, beyond doubt, if I were to judge from that wretched, shrill voice of his, so like—Powers Above, so like the high, twittering squeals of rats in their foul holes. As that ghastly thought possessed my brain, I turned my eyes cautiously in their sockets without moving my head, and met the frozen stare of Carry, leaning weakly against my shoulder.

"Who and what are you?" I demanded sharpening my tone as I once more focussed my gaze upon the intruder.

"A poor wanderer, seeking shelter from the storm and night," squeaked the newcomer. Again that high, irritating titter, for all the world like mice in the wainscoting.

"Jack! Let's go on! Anything would be better," began Carry, shrinking behind me.

"Hush, dear. It would be folly to attempt going on in the darkness, and with that army of creatures outside. Sit yourself down, stranger, on your side of the room. Carry, rest on the floor, on my coat, dear. I'll keep watch. This storm will pass, as must the night. And then the things outside will surely depart and we can go on."

Obedient, if reluctant. Carry sank down behind me in the corner.

The grey mantle of that other wanderer seemed to have grown wider and longer, for when he also sank to the floor against the opposite wall it was large enough to envelop him completely, so that to the casual eye nothing was discernible but a heap of dark cloth tumbled together in a raggedy huddle. Not so much as the faint motion caused by breathing could be distinguished when I turned the electric torch upon that heap of dark garments, and I turned it there occasionally during the next dragging hours, although most of the time I kept it in my hand, focussed upward so that it would cast its illumination over the entire interior of the hovel.

Carry slept well, from sheer exhaustion. I myself felt more wide awake than ever, for much might depend upon my wakefulness. I had looked at my watch and was just slipping it back into my pocket after noting that it was almost four o'clock, when a sound without the hut galvanized me into action, bringing me to my feet with a snap. I put the light on the third inmate of the hovel, but the pile of dark garments yielded no sign of life. The sound without was that of human footsteps that came unevenly as if the walker were uncertain, in the murky night, of his path.

No other sound had broken in upon the silence of the long night, save the soughing of heavy gusts of wind among the treetops and the occasional swoops of the gale bursting down upon our rough refuge. Once, indeed, when I had chanced to give a swift and unexpected glance at the huddle of garments in the corner, I could have taken my oath that from its midst a keen, bright eye peered sharply at me with a kind of constant watchfulness that made me grit my teeth together involuntarily with the shock. The intent, sly gaze of that misshapen being slumped against the wall held in it more than a suggestion of the unpleasantly bizarre and bordered all too closely on the furtiveness of some foul denizen of another plane which should never have ventured across its own border into material existence.

Again those uneven, wavering footfalls without, sounding distinctly upon my straining ears between the blows the swirling wings of the tempest hurled at the frail hut, that rocked and shuddered at each fresh impact. My harried gaze fell once more upon the third occupant of our refuge, and again I saw the glitter of a partially shielded eye, that gleamed like a wild creature's green reptilian orb out of a thick, black night.

The wanderer who shared the hut with Carry and me was alert, in spite of his huddled and shapeless appearance; his readiness held for me a hidden significance that I strove in vain to penetrate. That it carried a concealed threat I knew instinctively. I felt about it an emanation as of obscene, silent laughter at the impotence of creatures weaker than he. This stranger who had entered the forest cabin upon my inadvertent invitation was more than he seemed to be upon the surface. Twisted and deformed of body as he appeared to be, about him I felt the steady purposefulness of well-aimed and knowledgeful power, potent for good or ill as he might will.

Well had Carry's guardian planned, when he permitted her escape with me. We had been obliged to flee in the only possible direction, through those haunted woods, since his wild country habitation was so situated upon a rocky ledge that only by going through this thick wood could we eventually regain the highways of civilization.

Thus securely had old Harkness hidden himself and his vile magical practices from the cognizance of mankind. I told myself bitterly, as I listened to that groping footfall without, that Carry was right; I might have known it had I not chosen to be blind. That bitter and vindictive old man would not permit her to escape. He let her think she was escaping, so that her final recapture into hopeless slavery might destroy in her the last clinging vestiges of hope that her love for me, her faith in me, had so far maintained within her. By trapping me also, he would destroy her finally with devilish completeness.

In my mind I cursed the sheer nervous stupidity which had made me take the wrong turning, the fatal assumption on my part that my gas meter registered correctly. Had I been a bit more careful, we could at least have returned to the crossroads and there gained the right turning that led out of this thickly wooded wilderness onto the main road that would have taken us out of this strange and portentous country. We would have had enough gas to have lasted us to the nearest village. I blamed myself only, for Carry had clung to me with implicit faith in my ability to extricate her from her terrible position that she had given not a single thought to the details of her escape.

Yet—I threw a tender look at her quiet form, her dear brown head pillowed on my coat—she would be better off to die whatever death might face us together, rather than to perish in the midst of some vile incantation, soul-victim perhaps as well as body-victim, to that villainous old man who had been sucking the life and personal will out of her by his evil magic. As I looked down at her she stirred; her eyelids fluttered open.

Her face was still rosy with the flush of dreamless sleep. So great was her confidence in me that she had slipped off into heavy slumber without a misgiving. She met my gaze with a smile, a courageous smile that wrung my heart, for I knew we had only begun our struggle with powers and forces about which I could as yet make only faint surmises.

"Jack, dear, is it morning yet?"

My eyes jerked away from her, for the torch had reflected a sudden sliding and metallic beams of light from the huddle of dark garments across the room, and I knew that the stranger had moved at the sound of her voice. Without taking my eyes from the being which shared our refuge, I answered her in a cautiously lowered voice.

"Dear, someone is lurking outside. I've been hearing light footfalls in the pauses of the gale."

Carry sat up quickly, and I could imagine without seeing it the expression of dismay that was passing over her sweet face.

"Jack! Oh, dear God, it is *he!*"

"Nonsense! It is only someone caught in the storm, or lost, just as we and our friend over yonder were."

"No—no—I feel that *he* is near."

Her agitation stirred me. I would get that stranger outside, at least.

"Time you wakened and got out of here, my man!" I exclaimed. "The storm is dying away, and I'm not at all sure that we want more of your company."

The huddle of dark garments stirred into motion. The being within them got to its feet with a lithe but obnoxious synchronism of muscles that made my nose wrinkle in distaste, for it was more the easy movement of a wild creature than the balanced grace of an athletic human body. For a moment, as he arose, he rested on feet and hands like a beast, and there was something especially sickening to me in that momentary posture, although it almost immediately changed to an upright position. The slate grey of the ragged mantle still concealed the stranger's features, but two piercing and scintillant eyes glared fixedly upon Carry and me from that carefully maintained shelter.

"I am to go, eh? And why? You asked me in, didn't you?"

A sickening voice he had; a voice that went off into an occasional squeak; a sharp, uncontrolled animal sound.

"I rather fancy it is daylight without," I said irrelevantly, and gave Carry a hand to help her to her feet. "These windows are so soiled with dust and cobwebs that very little light filters in, but my watch says it is nearly five o'clock. The sun must be coming up by now."

A high tittering laugh filtered from behind the grey cloak.

"You are taking a high hand," said the stranger, his shoulders shaking as if in silent mirth.

"We were firstcomers here," I retorted sharply.

"Ho, ho, ho! But you see, this happens to be *my* house," explained he, and his sharp little eyes flashed and sparkled disagreeably.

I did not reply at once, but listened keenly for those groping footfalls that had affected me so unpleasantly a few minutes ago. Although the wind had died down with the closer approach of dawn, I heard them no longer.

Carry touched my arm timidly.

"Let's go, Jack. I—I'm afraid to stay here."

Our host laughed and chuckled to himself, or perhaps at her naive admission.

Then, "Outside," said he abruptly, "are all my children. They were called here. They are waiting now to be fed."

He stared at us, eyes glinting cruelly.

God knows, there was nothing in the bare words he said to make my flesh shrink, my lips draw back tightly against my teeth in sheer loathing, but Carry's fingers, squeezing into my arm, told me that she, too, had received the same horrid impression.

"Open the door, if you wish, my dear guests. Perhaps then you will choose to remain inside here."

*

I rubbed the filthy pane of one window vigorously with the sleeve of my discarded coat, which I had retrieved for the purpose, but without helping out the situation much, for the glass was scratched and marred as well as vilely dirty, and I could not see clearly through it. There was no help for it. In spite of that shrouded being's veiled menace, I must risk opening the door to see what threatened from without.

Cautiously I tiptoed to the door of our last night's entry, lifted the latch slowly and carefully, my foot behind the opening door that any sudden rush from without might not fling it wide. As I opened it a crack, I applied one eye to that small point of vision and stared. Then I jerked the door to, my hands trembling with the icy cold of nervous shock, and stood, back against it, breathing hard.

"Jack! Jack! What was it?"

"Carry, I am afraid I have dragged you into something as horrible as what you thought you were escaping from. My imagination fails to conceive what it may be, but you were right, my poor little love, about your guardian. He is a potent magician indeed, as well as a vampire and a devil," I cried out bitterly.

Carry's hands clutched at me frantically.

"But what did you see outside? What did you see? Was it—*he*?"

"No, he is not there. At least, I did not see him."

"Then what—what has so shocked and changed you, Jack?"

"Carry darling, outside this wretched hovel there are—literally thousands of rats sitting waiting everywhere I could see. Ugh!"

My teeth had gone on edge as my mind roved among the horrid possibilities of our situation. And like a fool, like a stupendous fool of fate, I had left my automatic in the car pocket! It would have offered us an alternative, at least, to whatever horror threatened us now. Oh, was ever a would-be knight errant more asinine, more criminal, than I? From the ghastly fate that had threatened my little love under the roof of her "guardian," I had snatched her, only to expose her to as horrid and disgusting a death as the mind could conceive and retain sanity.

Across the room the mysterious being rustled and chuckled and jeered and jerked in ugly, loathsome merriment.

"They will stay, will my guests. Ah, yes, they will stay—for as long as I will let them. Ho, ho, ho!"

"But we shall not be obliged to submit to suffering your presence here," I shouted suddenly moved to swift action, for it seemed to me that I could no longer breathe the same air that this vile creature was polluting.

I sprang across the room, throwing off Carry's small restraining hand as I leaped, and flung myself upon the disgusting huddle of noisome rags that shrouded that sneering being. I met the impact of my hands upon his throat only to feel his muscles tighten to an iron tautness that told me immediately that my strength was puny in comparison to that which I had so madly defied. The creature made no returning gesture of physical violence, but appeared rooted to the spot with a steady immovability upon which my own athletic fitness broke as a powerful ocean wave breaks and disintegrates upon an implacable cliff of adamant.

Carry's cry of dismay and despair gave the final touch to my mounting apprehension. I cursed myself for an impotent fool, as I felt my fingers slowly losing their grip upon that steel which they had grasped beneath a dwarf's rags. My eyes left the devilish keen contempt of that creature's shining orbs to see, the other door opening with a swift movement, and the entrance of a fourth human being into the hut. It was old Harkness himself, and as he entered my straining ears caught the milling from without of those thousands of rats that were waiting—waiting—waiting—with such hideously confident patience.

At his entrance, the being whose throat I had grasped gave himself a quick shake, and I slipped weakly from him, while he seemed to have expanded in potency so that the power emanating from him made his very physical semblance more lofty, straighter. He turned to Harkness, burning eyes that were still shielded by his upheld mantle, disregarding as if we meant nothing in the scheme of things, Carry and myself.

"So you have called my children," he stated rather than asked, and his squeaking tone held accusation.

Dwight Harkness wasted but a bare scornful look at Carry and me. He drew his form to its full height, and he had once been a man of noble and commanding mien before he had degraded mind and body by vile magical arts.

"You dare resent my action?" he said, scowling until his prominent hooked nose almost met the beard that clothed his chin luxuriantly in snowy white, giving him the false semblance of a noble patriarch.

"Resent?" Our host uttered a high, tittering laugh. "I? Ho, ho, ho! It is not *I*, it is *they*, who resent the calling. My children are hungry. They wait without. You called them for your own purposes only, to drive these—" —and he gestured indifferently in our direction— "—into your power again, that you might once more assume possession of a soul and body that you have found useful in your work."

"And if I have?" steadily replied the other, holding himself with high dignity.

"Ho, ho, ho! You omitted to provide food after the calling. My children are waiting, and they are hungry; *very* hungry," squeaked that voice with soft emphasis.

Carry's slight body slumped against my arm. I shook her a bit harshly to bring back active consciousness, poor child, for it was no time to lose one's wits when our fate was being decided by two as foul beings as ever drew God's fresh, sweet air into their polluting lungs.

Dwight Harkness threw out one hand in an impatient yet curiously placating gesture.

"I will send them away again," he said scornfully. "I need them no longer."

"And you really believe you can send them away? And you think they will go?"

The piercing orbs of the dwarfish creature lighted suddenly upon my face then, with a kind of devilish mirth a-dance within them.

"You, young sir, who have brought your sweetheart to this sorry pass, shall have a chance to atone for your indiscretion. The girl shall live. She shall return to her guardian's protection. But my children without must be fed, if they are to let her pass free among them."

A ghastly silence hung heavily upon the hut's grey morning murk. The meaning of those words was only too clear. Carry would be permitted to return in safety to her guardian's laboratory, if I would give myself to the famished vermin waiting with such devilish patience without. God, could a man contemplate such an alternative and not shrink from it?

I uttered an involuntary groan, for with the sacrifice of myself, Carry would be riven of all human friendship, cheated of all hope of human succour. It was this, I swear, which held me in bitter dread and resentment at that moment.

"Jack! No! Rather let us both go to face the rats!"

My brave girl! My lovely sweetheart! I took her outstretched hand firmly in mine. We met together, the eyes of that Evil Two.

"I cannot go, leaving her to that devil in human form," I protested, oddly enough to the dwarf. "Better that she should be food for the rats, than lose her immortal soul under that man's vile practices. Open the door! We are going out there together."

My flesh shrank sickly, but I knew it would not take long, for they were many which waited without. Carry's eyes sought mine; upon her white face rested a curiously contented smile that gave peace to my heart.

"It won't take long, Jack, will it?" came her whisper faintly.

I could feel her trembling against me. Inwardly I was groaning at the horrid thoughts that assailed me. Her tender flesh at the mercy of those sharp, slashing teeth; the swarming vermin pulling her down while she shrieked in involuntary agony. And then I could not bear it.

"I will go alone," I said roughly, twisting from her tight grasp upon my arm. "God will not let her soul be raped from Him. That, at least, He will save from the wreckage you would make of her delicate body. I am going. Take her into such safety as you can offer," I shouted at Dwight Harkness, and my hand flew to the door latch.

"Unusual. Most unusual," murmured the high, penetrating voice of the dwarf from his mantle, almost with approval. His greenly glittering eyes rested upon me in keen appraisal. "But my children are hungry. They are very hungry. And this young man is too athletic to be plump and tasty."

Across the room Harkness pounded in triumph, his eyes under their beetling brows bent upon poor Carry, who had lifted her small face heavenward in God knows what agony of desperate invocation. He laughed sardonically as he seized upon my little love's frail wrist, and jerked her toward him.

"Let that fool out to feed the children," he commanded in brutal merriment. "I cannot go through them carrying this girl, unless they have their—occupation," he finished ironically.

"You have forgotten your spells? Ho, ho, ho, chief master of magicians!"

There was a something subtle in the dwarf's voice that gave me pause even while my nerveless but determined fingers were lifting the latch that would let me out to my doom. I turned slowly, met something in those piercing eyes that was neither venomous nor vindictive, and hesitated.

Dwight Harkness, upon whose left arm hung the now limp body of my poor little sweetheart, turned also, with something of dark wonder and amazement on his heavily lined countenance.

"Am I not master?" he demanded heavily.

"Have you not staked your soul upon the acquisition of your occult secrets?" countered the dwarf.

"Then send that fool yonder to feed the little ones without, so that I can pass without more loss of time and without being obliged to resort to spells. I brought none for this wench."

I lifted the latch with intentional rattle, but without removing my gaze from our host's guarded visage.

"I cannot send him. You should know that. He must go of his own free will, driven by fear, or hate—or love. He is ready, old master of threadbare magic." An insulting titter.

"You are insolent!" hissed old Harkness, in a rage.

"I? Insolent? *I*? Ho, ho, ho!"

With a flash of fiery and resentful anger, the old magician turned and struck at the dwarfish figure. Whereupon, as if that act had been sensed, if not actually witnessed, by the horrid myriads, without, a deafening clamour of squeaks and shrill squeals set up about the hovel, that was only silenced by the uplifted hand of the dwarf, who had not stirred when the other struck at him, but who had somehow evaded that blow without visible effort.

"It needed only this, oh, foolish magician! You were sworn to serve me loyally if I in turn gave you my aid and let you call my children at your will. But you have forgotten that when they come, they are hungry and expectant. Ho, ho, ho! Open the door, young lover, and stand aside. Open it wide!"

God knows how I sensed that it meant good, not ill but something in his voice, in the sparkle of his shrouded eyes upon me, the glitter of them upon that evil old mage, made me obey. I opened the door with a sweeping gesture, and then turned my back upon the inevitable rush, for it seemed to me that none of us would be able to survive the assault of those thousands of greedy beasts without.

How it came to pass I do not know, but there was I standing with Carry in my arms, and about us was draped the shrouding mantle of that strange being into whose domicile we had wandered. He stood off, a bent and horrid creature, whose uncovered face showed him to be but a travesty upon the human form divine. God, it was of such a horror, so bestial, that I thanked my Maker Carry was unconscious.

If ever a human being resembled a beast, it was that one which leaped and laughed, and waved short pudgy arms as it danced its dance of ghastly death about the shrieking, fear-possessed magician, shorn now of his former power. An enormous, unshapely rat it seemed, erect upon hind legs, wreaking vindictive vengeance upon that hapless and miserable man whose pride in his magical arts had led him into overt rebellion against a being which must inevitably have been superior to him in evil power.

Through the open door poured a living torrent of squealing, squeaking rats, teeth bared as they fought and tumbled against their prey, piling in, wave upon wave.

"Save me! Spare me! I meant no harm!" screeched old Harkness, quailing in panic.

I could do nothing, for the beasts had hemmed me into the corner, and I could only strive to maintain my footing, shrouded as Carry and I were in the ratlike dwarf's grey mantle, at which those wild, squealing vermin sniffed, only to leave us entirely untouched. Incredible, nevertheless, they surged and battled about our corner, leaving it as clear as they left the space about that dwarfish being who had ordered me to give them entry.

"I've waited, like my children, you fool! I've waited," snarled the horridly unveiled creature, and danced and pranced in ugly glee. "I knew you would over-reach yourself one day, my master of forgotten secrets. At him, my little ones! At him, my children! He will not call you again, to send you away unfed. He has forgotten his spells. He cannot hurt you. At him, my children, at him!"

"But—I am master—master of the rats!" gasped Harkness, the devastating knowledge of approaching doom settling upon his agonized features as he brushed down first one, then another, of the rats that began to spring upon him and climb upon him from the tumbling torrent still pouring in at the doorway.

"You? Master of the rats! Ho, ho, ho! You commanded only because I permitted you, thrice-besotted fool! I—I—*I* am the Rat Master!"

God be thanked, Carry remained limp against my breast, and I gritted my teeth in the vain effort to control my jumping and agonized nerves, lest I begin to shriek like a futile echo the shrill screams that were issuing from the reddening lips of that doomed magician of evil spells. I closed my eyes, but imagination created such horrid reconstructions of that dreadful scene that my quivering nerves gave me no relief, even when all ceased as suddenly as it had begun. Silence reigned, where but a moment before had been the most utterly horrible sounds.

Then, only then, did I dare open my eyes. Upon the ground lay clean picked bones, white and glistening. Torn scraps of what had once been seemly garments lay scattered over the rough wooden flooring. No sign of rats or Rat Master. Nothing but we, ourselves, just as we had entered that hut. It might have been a dream, but for those white souvenirs of an evil man's fitting end. The grey mantle with its nauseating wild animal odour had been stripped from us. Carry hung on my arm, against my breast, her eyelids flickering, and I knew returning consciousness must not find us within that place, where her eyes would seek and find confirmation of the dread reality.

I strode without the doorway.

The sun had risen. The woods that had seemed thick about us that previous night had now shrunken to a sparse growth that barely hid the vista of highway, but a few hundred feet ahead of me. On the edge of the highway stood a car that I knew. It had been the property of the late Dwight Harkness, of unlamented memory.

Holding my little sweetheart safely to my heart, I went down the trail briskly to light and freedom and peace.

1939

THE WITHERED HEART

G. G. Pendarves

The third most prolific female contributor to *Weird Tales* was the British writer Gladys Gordon Trenery (1885–1938) who wrote as G. G. Pendarves. She was born in Liverpool but of a Cornish family and spent much time in Cornwall, the setting for several of her stories. She had been a music teacher but turned to journalism and began writing fiction in 1923 with "The Kabbalist" in the recently launched *Hutchinson's Mystery-Story Magazine*. She had ten stories in that magazine, the sixth of which, "The Devil's Graveyard" (December 1924) was also her first in *Weird Tales* (August 1926). The sale was probably made directly by Hutchinson's as there was a frequent trade between magazines in the UK and US, but it could be that Trenery made the sale herself. She visited the United States in the late 1920s and probably sought out markets because, though she returned to the UK, most of her subsequent sales were to American magazines.

Of her nineteen stories in *Weird Tales*, four were reprinted in the magazine and two of those were reprinted again, "The Eighth Green Man" (March 1928) and "The Sin Eater" (December 1938). "The Eighth Green Man" involves a secret society, the Sons of Enoch, and the fate of those who do not follow its rules. "The Sin-Eater" relates to an actual role in England at one time in which a man or woman performed a ritual meal just before someone's death to take on their sins, allowing them to die purified. Several of her stories were about possession, but she rang enough changes to make each original and interesting. "The Withered Heart" from the November 1939 issue, is one such variant. It was her last appearance in *Weird Tales* as Gladys had died in August 1938 aged only 53.

DEAR JOHN,

If a fifteen years' friendship means anything to you, come at once. Sorry to hustle you like this, good old slow-worm that you are, but we've simply got to go into session about this thing before the month's out. The Ides of March are on Tuesday next, May 31st, this year.

My whole future is at stake and you've got to come and help. It's a very very queer thing, and Jonquil and I don't agree at all about it. I wish to heaven we'd found the box earlier and had more time to argue it all out. I see Jonquil's point of view, of course, and feel in a way bound to carry on for her sake, but—well, you know my views about playing round with anything like magic and necromancy. Jonquil says I'm morbid, still—Oh, well! come and see us through it.

RAFE.

MAY 27TH, 1938.

I tried to pretend to myself that I couldn't go, that I wouldn't go! But even as I made these protestations inwardly, I was giving instructions to the boy, Joe, who daily and conscientiously thwarts my best efforts to grow flowers, fruit and vegetables. For a quarter of an hour or so my foredoomed struggle went on.

"—and Joe! that gallon of weed-killer is for the whole lawn, don't pour it over one dandelion root.

"*It's merely one of his latest ideas, he gets them like measles. I won't be fooled into rushing off and leaving my garden just now.*

"Joe! if you let that dog bury his bones in the new seedling-bed, I'll kill you when I get back and bury you with them.

"*All rubbish about his future! Another few weeks would make all the difference here! Why next Tuesday?*

"Don't forget the quassia for the gooseberries, Joe!

"*—and what the devil has magic to do with his future? No! I won't go! I won't waste—*"

By this time I was in the potting-shed, kicking off my heavy shoes and scrambling hastily into another and cleaner pair. Like iron to a magnet, I was drawn to the house where my mind continued to carry on acrimonious debates while my body intelligently took no notice of my mental disturbance and obeyed my will.

I packed a bag, interviewed my old housekeeper who expressed her disapproval of my plans by serving up watery coffee and an India-rubber omelette for my lunch, and set off within the hour with parting instructions to expect me back in God's good time.

It would have been more fitting to have said in the devil's own time. So far, however, no tinge of the saturnine malice which had, after a lapse of two centuries, begun to manifest itself, darkened the joyful anticipation of seeing my friend, Rafe Dewle.

I clambered into my old Austin-twelve and set her battered bonnet northwards. Those last hours on the open road when life was still free and untainted! Never, never again shall I experience anything like them. Knowledge has crippled imagination since then—evil polluted every spring of happiness.

On Shap Fells I stopped to cool my engine. Around me, yellow gorse breathed out its honey perfume; bumble-bees fussed to and fro as I lay stretched out on the heath and watched white cloud-feathers drift in the blue above. I slept for a brief spell on the warm breathing earth with the thin lonely call of curlews in my ears and the sense of hoary guardian hills all about me.

In sleep, the first faint brush of evil touched me. I dreamed that I journeyed on—on into a dark valley where, amidst mist and darkness and confusion, I felt the approach of invisible and threatening hosts. Yet I must go on swiftly—swiftly! Someone was waiting. Someone was in danger. I must hurry, hurry, hurry!

I woke to find my sunlit hemisphere all dark and angry. The great hills reared up threateningly into thunderous cloudbanks. Gusts of wind scattered the golden gorsebloom and whistled the coming storm along over shivering grass and heather.

With a sense of urgent fear left by my dream I started my car and dropped by long winding loops of road down to the valley, and, as I tore along leafy green lanes toward Keswick this fear persisted. Once past the town, I drove even more quickly, cutting across the head of Borrow-dale under dark Helvellyn's shadow and along the unfrequented road which led to *Braunfel*.

The rambling old manor house lay some twelve miles from town. I'd known it well when Rafe and I were boys together. His people had been wealthy landowners before 1914. The war took their men. The lean following years took their money and lands. *Braunfel* was on its last legs, financially, and I wondered why Rafe hadn't sold up before his marriage. I couldn't reconcile what little I knew of Jonquil French with the austere bare life that Rafe's inheritance offered. Their meeting and the marriage that so swiftly followed had been romantic and impassioned, a sort of Lochinvar affair; for Rafe had snatched her from another and very wealthy suitor almost at the church doors.

So characteristic of him and that hot Magyar blood of his! Even the lovely spoiled Jonquil French had succumbed to it. But for how long?

His letter indicated the thin end of a wedge to my mind. I'd met his bride in London and had not particularly liked her—not the wife for Rafe at all. I'd no idea what was the mysterious "thing" the pair disagreed about, of course, and I wished he'd been more explicit. Planning a good sensational story for me, no doubt. He loved being melodramatic.

At last I could see the bulk of *Braunfel* ahead, grey in shafts of pale clear light piercing a curtain of rain. About it, wide untended meadows stretched. Behind, the bare face of the fell, where only stumps remained of the great fir forest that had been so beautiful a background to the ancient house. War victims, those sheltering lovely trees! And no plantations showed their young green promise for the future. How gaunt *Braunfel* appeared! Not only that—it was positively sinister. I tried in vain to put the thought away. There was a look of boding grimness hanging over the massive pile that even neglected lands and bare scarred hillside could not wholly explain.

My old car splashed along the last mile of muddy lane between high ragged hedges. The road turned and twisted like a sea-serpent. Preoccupied and depressed, I took a sharp angle and put on my brakes with a curse. A tall and very agile figure seemed to leap from right under the Austin's bonnet.

"Rafe! What the deuce—"

"Hello! Hello! you old mud-turtle! I forgive you—don't apologize!"

He opened the car-door, slid his long legs under the dashboard, put an arm about my shoulders and grinned in the old familiar way.

"You're a marvel, John. I didn't really count on your coming until tomorrow, but I got so restless thinking you might turn up that I've been hanging round for the last hour here. Never been so glad to see your solemn old mug in my life!"

My heart grew light at sight and sound of him. Marriage had not altered him as far as his friendship and affection were concerned;

they were mine still, perfectly unchanged, the warmest, strongest tie I had in the world.

I grunted and glowered up at his face, dark as a gipsy's, lighted up with the inner fire that burned so strongly in him. I never knew man, woman, or child with so glowing, so intense a quality.

"Same old mad March hare!" I grumbled. "I'd hoped marriage might have given you a grain or two of sense. I suppose you realize you've practically ruined my garden for the next six months by dragging me up here?"

"Splendid! I have made a hero of you!"

He burst out into a wild barbaric song and yelled and yodelled until I drowned him with my car's horn. The noise was insane. We broke down and laughed like hyenas at last and I drove on feeling younger than I'd ever expected to feel again—my twenty-eight years had weighed heavily since Rafe's marriage.

Saturday, May 28th. Once under the steep gabled roofs of *Braunfel*, my bubble of delight was pricked. The sight of Jonquil French—Jonquil Dewle I should say—brought back the formless fear of my queer dream on Shap Fell. Why the sight of a girl like a princess in a fairy-tale should depress a man, I didn't know. Jealousy? No, neither of Rafe nor of his exquisite bride.

I had been jealous, afraid she'd come between us: I knew now most emphatically that she had not. Nor did I envy him. A woman has never yet roused the passionate thrill of joy I feel at sight of a perfect flower. It's no use arguing with me, I can't help it; that's the way I'm made.

"Mr. Fowler—John, I mean! How *perfect* that you've come! What a relief! You simply can't imagine what a time I've had lately. How lovely and large and shy you look! Isn't he too perfect, Rafe?"

"Certainly not. I refuse to live with two perfect beings. John's a mere man like myself."

She blew him a kiss, pirouetted round the dark panelled room like a little red flame blown on the wind, dropped on one knee before me and raised her hands in an attitude of prayer.

"Dear, dear John! You *are* perfect! Oh, if you could only see yourself. Just like a lovely solemn pine tree planted in the middle of our library. Please, please may I kiss you—I really must."

In a flash she was on her light dancing feet, her arms about me, her pleading face upraised. I bent a stiff reluctant head, received a moth-like touch on my lips and watched her and Rafe clasp each other in ecstatic amusement.

"I take it back, darling." Rafe wiped his eyes. "He certainly is—perfect."

"Well, now you've settled that, perhaps you'll start explaining things. You haven't brought me here to point out the singular beauty of my character?"

"No," chuckled Jonquil. "But you wouldn't be of any use to us unless you were such a perfect wise old owl."

Her smile glanced like the sun on running water.

"Not time to explain before dinner. It's a long, sad tale. Rafe will take you up to your nice large draughty room, and when you hear a sound like a bull being massacred—come down for dinner. Rafe's invented a patent bugle-thing he uses when I'm late for meals; he's too lazy to walk the half-mile upstairs."

Left to myself in a bedroom whose size and dignity made me feel something like a small dry ham-sandwich on a platter designed for the traditional boar's head, I pushed open a diamond-paned lattice window, slumped down on the broad uncushioned seat beneath it and glared out at the cobbled garth below. Pigeons kept up a low bubbling complaint from roofs of stables and outbuildings—ruinous affairs, minus doors and windows, their slates and stones stained with centuries of rain, their woodwork grey and cracked, weeds, moss and lichen a green-gold signal of defeat.

It wasn't the garth, or the many evidences of poverty elsewhere that worried me, however, as I sat listening to the *broo! broo broo* of the pigeons. It was the thought of Jonquil.

It was impossible to do more than put into mere words her remarkable beauty, and what are words when it comes to a young, living, exquisitely made creature like her? She had crisp red-gold curls, eyes of changing deep warm brown that reminded me of wallflowers in sunlight, a milk-white skin, and body so light and quick in movement, so sure in poise, so extraordinarily expressive of her every mood that she seemed winged—a brilliant tropic bird darting and flashing to and fro.

But it was the will behind her laughing eyes that frightened me. Her will—blind, ignorant, unyielding, a terrible weapon in her reckless hands!

Abruptly, my dream possessed me again... I was hurrying along that dark valley into mists and darkness and confusion—someone needed my help—I must hurry, hurry, hurry. And now Jonquil was beside me, her hand on my arm, her voice laughing, persuading, telling me to come back, come back, come back—she hindered me—I could not shake off her detaining hand. Her clear laugh prevented my hearing what my ears were straining for. I only knew I must hurry, hurry, hurry—in the gathering darkness ahead someone needed me...

It wasn't until after leaving the dinner-table, graced no longer by Queen Anne silver and Waterford glass, that I realized the significance of Jonquil's inclusion in my disturbing and recurring dream.

Rain and wind turned the May night to chill discomfort. Rafe lighted the big library fire, piled up fir-cones and logs until a heartening blaze warmed a respectable area of the lofty room with its mouldering books, threadbare rugs and worm-eaten oak.

Stimulated by tobacco, whisky, and Rafe's company I began to discount my boding fears again—but not for long. Jonquil was as eager as Rafe seemed reluctant to enlighten me. He yielded to her importunity at last, lifted down an iron casket from a high bookshelf and set it on a heavy table near the fire.

"There you are, lady and gentleman!" he made an exaggerated showman's gesture. "This is the Luck of *Braunfel* and guaranteed to supply your heart's desire. To make its magic work you need a nice round full moon, a strong belief in ghosts and devils, and a bottle of my best whisky inside you. These will qualify you to commune with a Benevolent Gent who died two hundred years ago in the hope of an extraordinary Resurrection from the Dead."

His nonsense wasn't well received. The sight of that twelve-by-eight inch box filled me with a nasty crawling sensation of horror. I set down my glass and stared at it in silence.

Jonquil ran up to the table, tried to pull the box from beneath Rafe's long brown fingers.

"It's not fair—it's not fair to tell him like that! You're trying to prejudice him. Let *me* show him! Let *me* tell him!"

Instantly he became the bland infuriating nurse with a spoiled child, patted her shining coppery curls with one hand and imprisoned her impatient fingers with his other.

"Now! Now! Now! Remember there's a little visitor here, darling! Don't forget your pretty manners!"

He kissed and put her back in a chair with another admonitory pat on the head.

"This is my Ancestor! My Benevolent Gent—hereafter known as B.G., and I will not be intimidated by a woman with red hair!"

I knew Rafe well. He was stalling now. It was a very old habit of his to approach anything he deeply disliked with idiotic badinage. Well, he might deceive Jonquil, but not me. So I sat tight and waited. My hands and feet grew cold in spite of the hot cheerful fire. I was most acutely awake, my eyes on Rafe's face, when that cursed dream of mine recurred... a dark long valley stretched between us... he faded, dissolved into distance and smoky dark confusion...

"John! What is it?"

I found myself on my feet, blinking stupidly down into Jonquil's alarmed face. Rafe was staring at me across the table, his mouth open in surprise.

"Cramp?" he inquired. "Must have been a bad twinge. I never heard you yell like that before."

"Cramp!" I echoed feebly, then pulled myself together. "No—it's a tooth—going to have it out."

I mumbled apologies, filled my glass, drank and felt considerably better. My mind cleared.

"Let's get down to business." I waved my pipe toward the box on the table. "I want to know where *I* come in. Let's have the story straight, mind!"

"John, you *are* such a darling! When you look at me like that through those enormous specs I feel just like a criminal before a judge."

Jonquil sat very stiffly and raised a hand as if to take an oath:

"I promise not to interrupt—unless I *have* to."

She tucked her little green slippers under her, curled up in the corner of a settee, and assumed an air of child-like innocent patience. I watched her with a pang. She was so sure of herself. She knew so exactly what she wanted—and intended to get it at all costs.

"Well?" my voice was brusque with anxiety as I turned to Rafe. "Bring out the skeleton in the cupboard."

His lips twisted in a rather doubtful smile.

"Queer you should say that. It's not exactly a skeleton, but it is part of a dead body."

"What? Your Ancestor, did you say—was he embalmed?"

"His heart was."

He lifted the casket's heavy lid as he spoke. A breath of thin cold air blew across my face and neck as I leaned forward to watch. I hated to see him standing over that beastly box; there was something so repulsive and ominous about it that my flesh crept when his fingers touched its rusty lid. Intuition told me that he did more than open a lid—he opened a door to something deadlier than plague.

It was a relief to my taut nerves to see him take out two tangible objects and set them on the table. One was a fat little book, fastened with broad brass clasps and bound in solid leather. The other—I got to my feet and went to examine it more closely.

My gorge rose at sight of the dark dried thing. I've seen mummies, and some were hideous enough. I've prowled about laboratories and examined scientific specimens preserved in fluids, and many were fairly revolting to a mind and imagination like mine. But this little horror, black and withered, with a strange metallic sheen! In amazement I drew still closer, unable to credit my sight. Then I straightened up with a jerk and glanced at Rafe.

"It's living! It beats—the thing beats!"

He nodded—"Since 1738, according to his tombstone date."

I saw he shared my revulsion. I forced myself to touch the heart, and drew back in horror at finding the dark withered bit of muscle was warm.

Jonquil clapped her hands. "You see! You see! Now perhaps you'll persuade Rafe to do it. Oh, he must—he must!"

She could contain herself no longer and flashed across to us. There wasn't a vestige of fear in her eager face as she put out a delicate exploring hand and touched the withered heart. Her faith in it, her strong will to test it, lent the dreadful thing power, and I saw it swell under her fingers—saw the throbbing pulse beat stronger, fuller.

"No! Don't!"

Rafe's voice sharply admonished her. His hand snatched back her own. She looked from him to me and laughed, but the red-brown eyes were bright with impatient anger.

"How exasperating men are! You look like two old hens with a duckling! I didn't think you'd be afraid to, John."

She gave me a stormy scornful glance. Next moment she was curled up in her corner again, sudden as a puff of wind.

"John, darling!" her voice was honeysweet now; "that's a heart of gold. Quite literally a heart of gold for Rafe and me—if he chooses! Oh, I see what you're thinking. You're a sentimentalist like Rafe. I'm not. *His* heart won't reduce the Bank's overdraft, you know. *That*,"— she flicked an airy hand toward the table—"that heart will."

I caught Rafe's glance at her and sharply realized his carefully concealed unhappiness. His shining tower of romance was fast changing to an old house in need of repair. The solitary countryside where he and she would walk in dreams was being reduced to an estate whose every hedge and gate and meadow clamoured for money—money— money! I'd never felt the pinch of my own straitened circumstances before, but now I hated myself—I'd have given anything to put things right for Rafe. And I hated Jonquil too—unreasonably, fiercely, for making him unhappy.

I didn't answer her. I was watching Rafe as, with swift distasteful touch, he took up the repulsive little heart, restored it to its metal box and dropped the lid with a clang.

Then he picked up the squat leather book and I followed him to the fireside.

I was convinced he was as much relieved as I to have that beastly heart out of sight.

"Don't tremble in your shoes, old man! I'm not going to read this tome right through. It's full of queer stories and experiments that don't concern our problem directly. This is the really juicy bit that does."

He drew a stiff yellowed crackling sheet from a pocket of the book's cover and unfolded it with a flourish.

"This is the apple of discord in the house of Dewle! This is the bee in Jonquil's bonnet! This is what's muting the family lute! *A scrap of paper*—a thing capable of starting anything in the world—wars, duels, murders—all the trouble that is, or ever will be."

"A cheque for £1,000,000 is a scrap of paper I'd love to see—with your name on it, dearest!"

"It was only £100,000 this morning," he reminded her. "Even a B.G. has limits, you must remember."

"And those that don't ask, don't get," she retorted with a flirt of her red curls.

"Well, we'll see what John thinks of my ancestor, Count Dul's *billet-doux*." He gave me a swift glance. "There's a preliminary but I'll spare you about his grave. It's been lost for generations, but Jonquil discovered it after reading this."

I could see the black thick lettering through the semi-transparent paper as Rafe held it up. He seemed to know it pretty well by heart, to judge by the way he galloped through the closely written lines:

> *This document concerns only those in whose veins my blood doth run, and who bear the ancient name of Dul. Let any such read these words with faith to believe and courage to obey, and to them will I grant the wish that lies most closely to their heart, be it for life beyond mortal span, for riches, for fame, or for the sweet delights of love. Let him who would seek my aid ask in the full knowledge that I, Count Dul, have power to give him his desire.*
>
> *For his part, he must most strictly observe such instructions as are writ hereafter, failing not in any particular. Let him take careful heed therefore to obey.*

THE DEED MUST BE DONE UPON A CERTAIN NIGHT and that the first night of a month of June when the moon is at the full between its second and third quarters.

I MUST BE SUMMONED BY ONE WHO STANDS BESIDE MY GRAVE and in such words as are graven upon the inner side of the Box in which this document shall be discovered, together with the Book and my Heart.

AT THE FIRST LINE OF THE CONJURATION MY KINSMAN SHALL LIGHT A FLAME and it shall be of oil poured out in a black bowl and set at the foot of the grave.

AT THE SECOND LINE HE SHALL SPRINKLE EARTH UPON THE GRAVE and it shall be earth which fire has made bitter, and rain has washed, and the four winds blown upon.

AT THE THIRD LINE HE SHALL SET MY HEART AT THE HEAD OF THE GRAVE; then, kneeling beside it, he shall cut his left hand until his blood drops from it upon the heart.

LASTLY HE SHALL SUMMON ME IN A LOUD VOICE AND PRONOUNCE HIS WISH. And I shall hear him. And I will come to him. And whatsoever boon he asks, it shall be his.

Rafe stopped reading as abruptly as he'd begun, and held out the paper.

"You can read the Conjuration yourself. It's a bit melodramatic to declaim aloud just now."

I read in silence, then sat staring into the fire. The touch of the paper, its crabbed evil lettering and the hateful words themselves filled me with loathing.

"Well?" Rafe continued. "How's that for an ancestor? Jonquil's convinced that if I do my little song and dance he'll come rushing back from—well, this Book leaves no doubt from *where*—with a Present for a Good Boy under his ghostly arm."

"Yes, I'm convinced he would."

"Oh, John! You dear! You absolute darling!" cried Jonquil. "You *do* think there's something in it? You really and truly do! Oh, I'm thrilled. Rafe's been so exasperating about it. Now he'll simply *have* to give in."

"I didn't say that I agreed with you," I interrupted.

She sat up with a jerk, scattering cigarette ash over the satin iridescence of her dress. Black cold rage possessed me, brain and body. I knew I'd never make her understand—spoiled lovely little materialist that she was. Superstition urged her to snatch at this promised wealth. Ignorance blinded her to the hideous risk.

"You don't agree with me? You've just said you believed the Count could and would return!"

"Yes. I believe that?"

"Well?" Her face grew radiant again. "Then you're just teasing! You *are* on my side, after all."

"No. Once and for all, I'm utterly against you. The man that wrote that promise and left behind him that foul thing"—I pointed to the box on the table—"must have been the devil's own brother."

"Oh-h-h!" wailed Jonquil. "You're not going to talk about demons and dangers and unholy powers, too! Rafe's been croaking like a raven for three whole days—and now you!"

"Go to it, old man!" urged Rafe. "She won't take it from me, but perhaps you can make her see it's not just money for jam."

I knew I couldn't move her, but I tried—explained, reasoned, argued, all to no purpose.

"It's no use trying to frighten me. You believe Count Dul can be brought back," she repeated for the twentieth time, "and that he could make Rafe a rich man. That's enough for me. He's only a ghost, poor thing! Perhaps he was just a harmless eccentric old man. Wouldn't make a will. Wanted to give it himself to his descendants."

"Harmless! What about that heart of his—beating two hundred years after his death? D'you think unaided human knowledge could leave *that* behind? Count Dul will surely return if the door is opened to him. But it's forbidden. The dead may not—*must* not return."

"I can't see why not. You don't actually know any more than I do myself. You've read a lot of stuffy books and believe everything in them. I haven't. I'm unprejudiced. I'm willing to take risks."

"You mean to let Rafe take them."

Rafe, who'd sat listening with a queer twisted smile, laughed out at this.

"Hear! Hear! Exactly. Is *she* to do a pantomime scene at midnight by the grave of a disreputable old nobleman? No! Is *she* to chat with a two-hundred year old devil-worshipper in the moonlight? No! Is *she* asked to shed her good red blood on a thing that looks like a bit of cat's meat? No!"

"Well, Rafe, darling! It probably *is* all nonsense and I'm tired of arguing about it. Still—"

She jumped up from the settee and stood before the fire, facing the two of us.

"John has helped me, after all." She dropped me a mocking curtsy. "Yes, you dear old Solomon! You've helped enormously. Now I feel absolutely certain there *is* something in it, or you wouldn't be so worried.

"You know, darling," she turned to Rafe, "you promised to be guided by John's opinion. He's given it. He completely believes in your ancestor. And so do I—now! I'll never forgive you if you don't take a chance and try this thing out."

"Jonquil!" I was on my feet now, almost incoherent with fury. "What I believe in is the risk—the damnable risk of trying such a thing. You only believe in the money you want and shut your eyes to anything else. D'you suppose for a moment that dead Thing has waited two centuries to give you a fortune?"

She burst out laughing. "John, if you could only see yourself! You look like one of the Minor Prophets in action! There's a picture in the National Gallery that exactly—"

"Rafe!" I was almost shouting now. "*You* know enough, if she doesn't, to realize the wicked insanity of doing such a thing. D'you remember Harland and the sticky end he came to? And Browning who's gibbering away in an asylum? They happen to be men we know personally, but think of the hundreds of others who've been fools enough to think necromancy's a mere parlour game—who've deliberately walked into hell! It's hushed up—such cases always are. People are called mad, or reputed dead of heart attacks, etc. The truth is too beastly to publish."

"There's a good deal in what you say." Rafe had assumed a poise of amused detachment now. "I've not delved into occult lore as you have, old man. I dislike what I know, however. Still, Jonquil's attitude of 'nothing venture, nothing win' has a lot to recommend it."

She flew to him, took his hand in both her own.

"Oh! I knew, I *knew* you'd be an angel! You really mean to try it out?"

His answering look at her eager lovely face, his gesture as he rumpled her flaming aureole of hair, was sufficient for me. She'd won. My hot angry opposition had decided him, had pushed him into doing so. And I cursed myself for a pompous muddle-headed fool. I'd tilted the balance down—down to hell. If I'd kept calm and laughed at Count Dul, made light of the whole affair, Jonquil's belief might have faded. I'd lost my temper with her—lost my best chance by forcing Rafe to take her part...

My dream enveloped me in its swirling vapour... I was driving furiously down that long desolate valley—in the cloudy smothering darkness I heard a voice—Count Dul! Count Dul! Count Dul! The piercing cry was echoed by howls of laughter from the swirling mists—I drove on—on—someone needed me—someone I loved, needed me...

Sunday, May 29th. I spent a night of wretched anger and self-reproach and misery, interspersed with lapses into the haunting terror of my dream.

Rafe found me at eight a.m., empty pipe between my teeth, sitting on the stone parapet of a bridge, my thoughts dark and cold as the water I watched so gloomily.

"Not worth the usual penny, I can see!"

Rafe came to perch beside me.

"Still, there's some excuse for you. Enough to make anyone broody—my estate! Reminds me of the hymn, 'Change and decay in all around I see'."

He patted me on the back.

"Cheer up, Jacko! And don't worry about the way things have turned out. This way—or another! What odds? I'm tremendously bucked up to have you here, and I'm bent on enjoying myself while I can. Forget Tuesday night—forget it! After all, you never know."

His look, his voice, his friendly touch cheered me. After all, as he said, one never *did* know! It was a relief to let myself be bluffed by his absurdly high spirits. Depression slipped off like a wet cloak as we tramped home for breakfast as carefree as if the pair of us had nothing more on our minds than a boat-race, or a thesis to be finished.

Jonquil appeared in high feather at the breakfast table—adorable with Rafe, mockingly sweet with me. And, of course, she scarcely talked of anything but Count Dul—how and when and where and what was going to happen about the wealth with which the family fortune was to be restored.

Rafe refused to be serious for even a moment about the B.G., as he called the Count. He was in the unreasoning fey mood that always seized him before any special test in our college days.

"I think the date's a mistake," he remarked. "The old boy meant April 1st."

I didn't remind him that the last night of May, this year, was peculiarly fitted for Count Dul's return. He knew considerably more than he acknowledged of ceremonial magic. It was unlikely that the significance of next Tuesday's date had escaped him. Together, as students, we'd read the Fourth Book of *Philosophia Occulta*, and the works of Pirus de Mirandola, and the *Grimoire* of Pope Honorius.

Above all, he'd read the book which Count Dul had left behind him. I'd borrowed and read it too, from cover to cover, and it was plain that Rafe's ancestor had, after many experimental essays, followed the teachings and practises of the infamous Lord of Corasse. These entailed observance of astronomy and, according to them, such a purpose as the return of the dead could only be accomplished at certain rare conjunctions of the stars and moon and planets. Rafe must be aware of these facts.

"Perhaps," Jonquil's face sparkled with excitement, "perhaps it will be priceless old jewellery he brought from Hungary. Count Dul was the first of your family to settle in England, wasn't he, Rafe?"

"He came because he was pushed," he replied. "They found he'd smuggled emeralds mined in the High Tatra Alps. He escaped from a particularly spectacular death connected with rope and four horses by a miracle—and, tradition records, by the aid of the devils he served."

"Emeralds!" breathed Jonquil, her eyes two deep pools of ecstasy. "How I adore emeralds! I shall keep the very most beautiful for myself, Rafe. You can sell the rest if I have just one perfect stone to wear."

"Certainly, Madam!"

He whipped out a notebook and pencil and assumed a business-like air.

"Let me see, now! What size and colour does Madam prefer? I would not like to order something unsuitable. Oval, round, or square? Green or rose-red?"

"Rose-red," she took him up promptly. "A very very large square-cut stone set as a pendant with diamonds."

He licked his pencil and printed her order laboriously.

"You can take off that superior smirk, my child," he assured her. "There are such things as rose-red emeralds."

Their discussion went on to the end of the meal. Then she announced that we were all going to climb Hawes Fell.

"I've found a black bowl for the oil. All we need now is the earth."

"Earth! Climb up five hundred feet on a good Sabbath day of rest! Your breakfast has flown to your head, child. Think again—what about my untilled acres?"

"Doesn't it say the earth must be bitter with fire, and washed with rain, and blown on by the four winds? Very well, then. Wasn't there a heath-fire on Hawes Fell last month? It's as black as soot now and soaked in rain, and every wind in the world blows up there."

She'd made up her mind. It was to be earth from Hawes Fell, and the remainder of the day was spent in getting it.

Tuesday Night, May 31st. Tuesday morning—afternoon—night. At last, Tuesday night.

Rafe and I stood waiting for Jonquil in the library. It was after eleven p.m. In a few minutes we should set out across the fields to where Count Dul's grave lay. From the Book he'd left it was clear that in England, as in his own native country, the Count had been excommunicated by the Church and his body buried therefore in unconsecrated ground. It was Jonquil's indefatigable curiosity that had discovered the grave with its broken headstone in one of Rafe's outlying meadows. It was this initial discovery that had first determined her to carry out the remainder of the Book's instructions.

"Who actually found the metal box?" I asked now.

The constraint between Rafe and myself on this last day had made me desperate. He'd steadily avoided being alone with me until now, although I'd persistently sought such opportunity, for today Jonquil had, for the first time, weakened in her project.

Too obstinately proud to say outright she was afraid, she'd endeavoured in roundabout ways to get Rafe to change his mind. He'd refused to rise to her bait, brushed aside her every tentative move toward cancelling the date he'd determined to keep with his B.G.

But her wavering had given me a gleam of hope. Perhaps I might persuade him out of his insanely dangerous rendezvous even now. I felt sure Jonquil had given me this last chance to do so.

"Was it you who found the box?" I repeated.

He gave me a queer slanting look, half speculative, half sad.

"It found me," he laughed. "Slipped from the top of a bookshelf. I haven't the slightest recollection of seeing it in the house before. Never heard my father mention it. Must have been pushed out of sight somehow—it fell with a crash right at my feet and the Book and the B.G.'s heart rolled on the floor."

"Rafe! Don't go on with this. Even Jonquil doesn't want it now. You know—you surely know the risk. Why will you—"

He caught my eye, and changed colour. I saw he was trying to bring himself to answer me, and waited. He began to speak in quick, almost stammering words.

"Yes, I know the risk. I know, old man, but—I must go on now. It's been heaven—these last six months with Jonquil—heaven! But it can't last. We married in haste, but I'm damned if I'll let her 'repent at leisure.' It's a million to one I'll come through—with money, or without it, tonight, but—she'll remember I've tried."

"Rafe! You can't... you won't—"

"I will. It's easier to die than to lose her. I can face any hell but that."

"But she's going to—to lose you. And she's afraid of that now. She'd be glad—thankful if you gave up."

He smiled, as he'd smiled a thousand times when I'd missed some obvious point.

"Dear old chap! You don't know Jonquil. She's temperamental—just working up to the proper gooseflesh mood for tonight's orgy. No use, John! I'd never live it down if I failed her now. She's a child, an adorable child. I've had more than most men—and I'm choosing the easiest way out."

Jonquil's light step sounded on the uncarpeted old stairway.

"Ready?" her shining curls appeared round the door. "It's after eleven o'clock. We ought to start."

We went out to the great, echoing hall; our feet, on the old-fashioned red tiles, clanked dismally.

"This the picnic basket?" Rafe took up Count Dul's box from an oak chest. "Got the champagne and oysters, dear? Right! Let's start."

The night was cool, almost cold. Wind stirred in the treetops. Tall solemn elms on either side of the avenue whispered uneasily as we passed between their double ranks. Overhead a brilliant sky of stars, and a proud moon sailing in full majesty.

I wondered if any remote world up there was like the one I trod; if any other beings knew such bitterness and horror and evil as we did on our earth. I wondered if I could go on living here—alone, when Rafe—when Rafe—

Suddenly my dream blotted out moon, stars, and earth... I had reached the end of that awful valley—breathless, spent from long pursuit—before me a broken pathway descended to the lip of a yawning chasm. And along that path, walking with steady purposeful tread, a man's tall figure loomed. Rafe—it was Rafe! In agony I stumbled after him...

My dream blew like mist from across my vision. I was back in a country lane with Rafe and Jonquil, under the full moon's menace, the moon that would presently light Count Dul from hell.

"Here's our field-path." Jonquil turned aside to an old stile of flat stones laid with gaps between to keep cattle from crossing.

We followed her, cut across a field to another stile and across it to the desolate overgrown rocky bit of wasteland that was our objective. In another minute Jonquil stopped and pointed.

"There! There it is!"

The white merciless moon showed up every grass-blade and flower and stone of the hummock before us. Nature had flung a poisonous pall over the dead, and even the moon's glare could not blanch the blotched evil of henbane, viper's bugloss and deadly nightshade, or the scarlet-spotted fungus on Count Dul's grave. A cracked and sunken headstone leaned awry at the head of it. The worn lettering showed only a few words of whatever inscription had been cut two hundred years ago—COUNT DUL... DIED 1738... A WARNING TO ALL WHO READ...

Rafe looked at his watch, glanced up at the moon as it climbed to its fateful meridian. He'd doffed his armour once more. With mocking brilliant smile he looked down on the horrible grave and airily kissed his hand.

"Rafe!" Jonquil's brows went up in anxiety. "You *must* be serious."

"Darling! I'm sure the B.G. wouldn't like it. Think what a gay old dog he was in his time. Think how much he must have enjoyed himself to have tried for two centuries to get back again. Must make his little trip enjoyable, you know! About time I got to the front door to meet him. I suppose it's no use arguing any more—you won't go home?"

"For the hundredth time—no, dearest! You might take my rose-red emerald and run off with some other pretty lady."

She was looking up into his face and, even to my jaundiced eyes, was a sight to stir the blood of any man. For a second, Rafe's devil-may-care mask dropped, his dark burning eyes and drawn features showed such anguish that I started forward with a cry. This was my dream... his tall figure—so dear, so obstinate, so tragic—moving steadily onward to the edge of an abyss...

At once he recovered himself. Behind the brilliant smile he turned to me I read entreaty. He wanted me to take Jonquil away. He was in terror of what she would see and hear, in terror that she might be endangered too. But I knew also, and it was the only poor comfort I had left, that he wanted me—needed me as he and I always needed each other in a tight corner.

No one on earth—nor from hell—should move me from that graveside, and I confess I was glad that Jonquil should be there also. I wanted to spare her nothing.

I hoped if Rafe did not survive that she too would be destroyed.

I don't know how much of my thoughts he read, but in any case she wouldn't have left with me. He turned away, opened the metal casket, lifted out of it the withered pulsing heart and set it down at the head of the grave under the deeply sunken headstone.

My fascinated gaze was held by the horrible little thing. I saw it throb and quiver to the beat—beat—beat of whatever infernal power quickened life in it. I saw its dark withered walls gleam in the moonlight like tarnished copper.

At the other end of the grave, Rafe uprooted a clump of spotted henbane, set down a small black bowl and poured oil into it.

Jonquil's small hands clasped in excitement. She watched with dancing eyes, her curls ruffled about her eager flowerlike face.

Rafe glanced at his watch again, smiled once more at Jonquil. He didn't look toward me—I was thankful for it.

"Now for my old B.G. Stand back! Stand back, there!" he waved an imperious hand. "Make way for the Count Dul—make way—"

He took from his pocket the crackling parchment on which the conjuration was written, its black lettering very plain in the moonlight, ran his eye over it for the last time, although I was certain every word of it was stamped deep in his memory.

His voice rang out as I'd heard it ring on the playing-fields when we were boys together:

For your sightless eyes—this Flame!

He stooped to set alight the oil in the black bowl.

For your fleshless bones—this Earth!

He scattered dry dark soil from the basket.

For your withered heart—this Blood!

He knelt, held out his left hand and slashed it with a knife until blood dripped upon the heart. Then he got swiftly to his feet. His loud voice challenged the dead:

Wake from your sleep, Count Dul!
Rise from your grave, Count Dul!
Return from the dead, Count Dul!
Give me wealth—wealth for my boon!

My body was turned to ice, my feet rooted to the ground, my whole being concentrated on Rafe's tall rigid figure standing at the graveside—at the mouth of hell.

His last word echoed and reverberated like an organ-note; louder—louder it swelled and boomed, until the quiet night hummed and quivered, and the poisonous grave-weeds slowly withered, blackened, lay in dust, until the earth beneath them cracked widely open and the burning oil shot up into a red roaring fire that was cold as wind off an ice-field and seemed to lick the stars.

It froze the tears on my cheek. It chilled even the unbearable anguish in my heart.

The heart—in the red name's brilliance—shone, incandescent, fiercely alive, then vanished.

In that moment the flame sank to earth again, the noise of its burning ceased—silence far more ominous fell, while overhead the great moon looked down in passionless survey.

The grave yawned widely open; from its void rose a wisp of dark smoke that turned and wreathed and twisted and coiled in ever denser volume as it swelled and blew and eddied to and fro above the gaping grave, blind, purposeless, uncertain. Then a nucleus formed in the vaporous evil, a dull purplish-red heart-shaped glowing core about which the dark mist swiftly formed and re-formed to a tall swaying pillar—an imperceptibly growing outline—a recognizable human body whose white face of damnation stared into Rafe's, whose awful rotted hands reached out to touch, to hold, to bind him fast.

And now I could not distinguish Rafe from the smothering infernal Thing itself. It swirled about him. It covered head and hands and feet from sight. When he moved, he moved within the enveloping darkness. When his face turned to me I saw only the dreadful livid face of the dead.

Still I was frozen there, unable to speak, to move, to do more than see and hear the Thing that now moved forward with fixed pale staring eyes and loose dark lips that mouthed and laughed and whispered as it came.

I could not turn to look at Jonquil. I felt her arms about me, clutching—I felt her warm soft body pressed to mine, her face against my cold and empty heart. I heard her long shrieks echoing above the thin dry whisper of the Thing that steadily advanced—nearer—nearer.

It halted beside us. Now I could see Rafe's tortured eyes, his face and form behind the clouded horror that enfolded him—he was shut up inside it like a chrysalis in a dark cocoon. He was Count Dul—Count Dul was Rafe!

Next moment Jonquil was plucked from my side. Her body was flung down on the dew-wet earth, her curls gleamed as two hands met about her throat, choking a last thin cry...

The Thing that killed her rose and moved back to the grave. Now I could see Rafe more distinctly beneath the wavering cloud of evil. His dreadful garment grew thin, and patchy, drifted from him, lost density and outline as it hovered over the open grave.

And the grave's darkness sucked it down out of sight, back to the hell from which it came.

The yawning hole closed up. The ugly weeds grew rank again upon the hummock. A sunken headstone leaned awry at its end.

In the same moment, I was released and ran stumbling over the long grass to where Rafe lay huddled.

A month later. Rafe was not dead. But he would have died—he *would* have died if that devil hadn't barred his way out!

By some infernal miracle, and after lying unconscious for a week, Rafe woke to full possession of his faculties. No memory was spared him of that fatal resurrection, or of Jonquil's unthinkable end.

He lives to remember it hour after hour, day after day, week after week.

For another two months his torture will endure. Then he will be hanged. That much is certain. He confessed to the murder of his wife and stands trial next week. He'll plead guilty and there'll be practically no defence. Neither he nor I mean to confess a word of the actual truth. It would condemn him to years and years of life as a criminal maniac—remembering—remembering...

A murderer—and a millionaire! Oh, yes! Count Dul kept his promise. A will turned up when the Chief Inspector of Police was going through Rafe's papers in the library—the thing toppled off a bookcase at the inspector's feet. It stated that the count had left a legacy buried in the cellars of *Braunfel*.

The police dug it up. Emeralds! An astounding collection which was photographed and written up in every rag in the country.

The finest gem was a great rose-red emerald, cut square and set with diamonds as a pendant.

I burned the Book and the Conjuration. I threw the metal box into Lake Derwent water. But I couldn't find the heart—I went over every inch of the grave and all round it.

Rafe takes this as a sign Count Dul's power is expended. I'm thankful that he doesn't understand.

I know that devil will return somehow—somewhere! Jonquil's death means life for him. Her will to live is added to his own.

When Rafe dies, he will look for her—and never find her. Never. She is one with the Count now, part of his thought, his will, his enduring evil.

Whether I can learn his secret, earn enough to meet him—and destroy him—I don't yet know.

When I am left alone, it will be all that remains worth doing in a world of fear and shadows.

1927

LEONORA

Everil Worrell

Everil Worrell (1893–1969) contributed nineteen stories to *Weird Tales* spanning one of the longest lasting careers in the magazine, from "The Bird of Space" (September 1926) to "Call Not Their Names" (March 1954). Probably her best-known story—certainly the most reprinted—is the vampire story "The Canal" (December 1927) which was adapted for Rod Serling's *Night Gallery* series in 1973, directed by no less than Leonard Nimoy. She was particularly proud of "The Hollow Moon" (May 1939) which seems a fairly unlikely story of vampires that live within the moon and visit Earth for their prey, but which is full of memorable imagery that led to a striking illustration by Harold DeLay. She was proud to tell *Weird Tales* readers that the story was used as a recommended text for science students by a couple of high schools in Washington D.C. and Norfolk, Virginia. "Leonora" was one of her earliest stories from the January 1927 issue and drew its inspiration from a German legend of a soldier who returns from the dead to be with his fiancée. The legend was the inspiration for Gottfried Burger's poem "Lenore" (1774). Worrell's version is a profound warning against going out alone at night!

I am writing this because I shall not long be able to write it. Why does one long for the understanding and sympathy of his fellow beings—long to have that, even after the worst has befallen and he has gone from this life to that which awaits him? How many bottles laden with last messages float on lonely, unknown ocean surges, or sink to the bottom of the sea?

It will be so with this, my last message. That is, it will go uncredited, unbelieved, uncomprehended, although it will doubtless be read. But I have told my story many times, and heard them say that I am mad. I know they will say that, after I am gone—gone from behind these bars into the horrors of the fate that will overtake my spirit somewhere out in the open spaces and the blackness of night into which it will go. *He* will be there, one of the shadows that lurk in old cemeteries and sweep across lonely roads where the winds moan and wander homeless and hopeless across the waste spaces of the earth from dusk till dawn. Dawn!

But I will tell my story for the last time.

Even now, my years are those of a young girl. I am only seventeen, and they say I have been mad more than a year. When I was sixteen, my eyes were bright and my cheeks red with a colour that did not come off when I washed my face. I lived in the country, and I was an old-fashioned girl in many ways. I roamed freely over the countryside, and my wanderings were shared by my only close friend, or else were lonely. The name of my friend was Margaret. Mine was Leonora.

The two of us lived only a quarter of a mile apart, and between us ran a lonely little road crossed by another like it. Our parents believed that it was safe for us, or for any child, to traverse this road between our houses alone at any hour. We had done it from our youngest days. It should have been safe, for we were far from cities, and malefactors of any sort were utterly unknown in our secluded part of the country. There were disadvantages attendant on living in such isolation, but there were advantages, too. Margaret's family were simple farmer folk of sterling worth. My father was a student of some means, who could afford to let the world go by.

On dark or stormy nights, sundown generally found me safe indoors for the night, spending the evening by the open fire. Moonlight nights I loved, and on nights when the moon was bright I often stayed at Margaret's house, taking advantage of my freedom to wander home alone as late as midnight. Sometimes Margaret did this, too, staying late with me and going home without thought of fear; but I was the venturesome one, the one who loved to be abroad in the moonlight—

Do horrors such as came to me march toward one from the hour of birth, so that every trait, every characteristic is inclined to meet them?

Up to my sixteenth birthday, my life had been like a placid stream. It had been without excitement, and almost without incident. Perhaps its very calm had made me ready for adventure.

On my sixteenth birthday, Margaret dined at my house and I supped with her. It was our idea of a celebration. It was October, and the night of the full moon. Afterward, we went outside to walk and talk away from the ears of my father.

I did not start home until nearly midnight. I would not reach home until a little after that, but that would not matter, because my father would be asleep in bed, and, in any case, not worried about me or interested in the hour of my arrival. The bright colours of autumn leaves, strangely softened and dimmed in the moonlight, rose all around me. Single leaves drifted through the still air and fell at my feet. The moon had reached mid-heaven, and the sky was like purple velvet.

I was happy. It was too beautiful a night to go home. It was a night to enjoy to the fullest—to wander through, going over strange roads, going farther than I had ever gone. I threw out my arms in the moonlight, posing like a picture of a dancing girl which my father had—I had never seen a dancer!—and flitted down the road. As I reached the crossroad, the sound of our clock chiming midnight drifted to my ears, and I stopped.

A beautiful high-powered car stood just at the entrance to our road, its headlights off, its parking lights hardly noticeable in the brilliant moonlight.

I knew it was a fine car, because my father had one, and on rare occasions the fit took him to drive it. When he drove it I went with him, and I noticed cars, for I loved them. I loved their strength and speed, and their fine lines. I loved to rush through the air in my father's car, and was never happier than when I could coax him to drive the twenty miles to the state road, and go fast on the perfect paving. But aside from my father's car, I had never seen a good one on these little back country roads.

I stopped, although I knew I ought to go on. And as I stopped just short of the crossroad, the big car glided softly forward a few feet until it stopped, blocking the road to my father's house. My father's motor was a silent one; but this car actually moved without the slightest sound.

Until now I had not seen the driver. Now I looked at him.

His face was shadowy in the moonlight. Perhaps it did not catch the direct light. There was a suggestion of strong, very sharply cut features, of a smile and a deep-set gaze—

My pen shakes until I can hardly write the words. But I heard the doctor say today that I had nearly reached the end of my strength, and any night with its horrors may be the end. I must control myself and think of the things I am writing down as they seemed to me at the time.

I was just turned sixteen, and this was romance. And so I stopped and talked to him, although we exchanged few words. That night he did not ask me to ride with him, and so I was less afraid. For with the romance was fear—but I answered his questions.

"What is your name?" he asked; and I answered, "Leonora."

"It is music in my ears," he said softly; and again, I felt that this was romance. I felt it again, when he added: "I have been looking for you for a long time."

Of course, I did not dream—I did not think that he meant that. I had read novels, and love stories. I knew how to take a compliment.

"Do you often pass this way as late as this?"

Something made me hesitate. But something about him, something about our meeting alone in the moonlight, fascinated me. If I said "no," perhaps I would never see him again.

"Very often, when the moon is full," I said, and moved to go around the car. In a moment the gloved hand that rested on the wheel had touched the broad brim of his hat; another movement, and the car shot silently ahead and was gone.

I ran home with a beating heart. My last words had almost made a rendezvous of the night of the next full moon. If I desired, there might be another encounter.

Yet it was two months later when we met again. The very next full moon had been clear, cloudless, frostily cold—a lovely November night. But that night I was afraid. I was so afraid that I even avoided the full light of the moon when I crossed our yard in the early evening to bring in a book I had left lying outside. At the thought of traversing the road that led to Margaret's house, every instinct within me rebelled. At midnight, I was lying in my bed, with the covers drawn close around me, and my wide-open eyes turned resolutely away from the patch of moonlight that lay, deathly white, beneath my open window. I was like a person in a nervous fit—I, who had never known the meaning of nerves.

But the second month, it was different.

After all, it was a fine thing to have mystery and romance, for the taking, mine. Or were they mine for the taking? Perhaps the man in the long, low car had never come again, would never come again. But his voice had promised something different. Would he be there tonight? Had he been there a month ago? Curiosity began to drive me before it. After all, he had made no move to harm me. And there had been something about him, something that drew and drew me. Surely my childish fears were the height of folly—the product of my loneliness.

I went to Margaret's, and stayed late—almost, as on that other night, until the clock struck 12. At last, with a self-consciousness that was noticeable only to me, I wrapped my heavy coat around me and went out into the night.

The night had changed. It was bitterly cold, and there was a heavy, freezing mist in the air which lay thickly in the hollows. The shadows of the bare trees struck through the dismal vapours like dangling limbs of skeletons—

What am I writing, thinking of? The scream that pierced the night, I could not suppress. I must control myself, or they will come and silence me. And I must finish this tonight. I must finish it before the hour of dawn. That is the hour I fear, worse than the hour of midnight. It is the hour when Those outside must seek their dreadful homes, the hour when striking fleshless fingers against my window-pane is not enough, but They would take me with Them where They go—where I, but not another living soul, have been before! And whence I never shall escape again.

I walked down, slowly, toward the crossroad. I would not have lingered. I would have been glad to find the crossroad empty. It was not.

There stood the car, black—I had not noticed its colour before—low-hung, spectral fingers of white light from its cowl lights piercing the mist. The crossroad was in the hollow, and the mist lay heavily there—so heavily that I could hardly breathe.

He was there in the car, his face more indistinct in the shadow of his broad-brimmed hat than it had been before, I thought, his gloved hand resting as before upon the wheel. And again, with a thrill of fear, there went a thrill of fascination through me. He was different!—different from everyone else, I felt. Strangeness, romance—and his manner was that of a lover. In my inexperience, I knew it.

"Will you ride tonight, Leonora?"

It had come—the next advance—the invitation!

But I was not going with him. I had got the thrill I had come for. He had asked me, and that was enough. It was enough, now, if I never saw him again. This was a better stopping point. (Remember that I was only sixteen.)

A stranger had come out of the night, had been mysteriously attracted to me, and I to him. He had asked me to ride with him.

I do not know what I said. Somehow, I must have communicated to him what I felt—my pleasure in being asked, my refusal.

His gloved hand touched his hat in the farewell gesture I remembered.

"Another night, Leonora. Leonora!"

The car glided forward and was gone. But the echo of his voice was in my ears. His voice—deep, strange, *different*—but the voice of a lover. My inexperience was sure. And already I doubted if, after all, this would be enough for me if I never saw him again. Another time, he would be as punctilious, as little urgent. But he might say—What would he say?

*

The January moon we hardly saw, so bitter were the storms of that winter, so unbreaking the heavy clouds that shut us from the sky.

The February full moon was crystal-clear in a sky of icy light. The snow-covered ground sparkled, and the branches of the trees were ice-coated, and burned with white fire. But I clung to the fireside, and again crept early within my blankets, drawing them over my head. I was in the grip of the fear that had visited me before. I was like a person in the grip of a phobia, such as they say that I have now, shunning the moonlight and the open air.

It was March.

Next month would bring the spring, and then would follow summer. The world would be a soft and gentle world again, in which fear would have no place. Yet I began to long for a repetition of the meetings at the crossroad, a repetition that should have the same setting—the rigours of winter, rather than the entirely different surroundings of the season of new buds and new life. My last attack of unreasoning terror had passed away again, and again it seemed as though it left behind it a reaction that urged me more strongly than ever toward adventure.

Had *he* been at the crossroad in the bitter storms of January, and on the sparkling white night which I spent close indoors? Would he be there on the night of the next full moon, the March moon?

There was still no breath of spring in the air on that night. The winter's snow lay in the hollows, no longer whitely sparkling, but spoiled by the cold rains that had come since it had fallen. The night sky was wild with wind-torn clouds, and the moonlight was now clear and brilliant, now weirdly dim, and again swept away by great, black, sweeping shadows. The air was full of the smell of damp earth and rotted leaves.

I did not go to Margaret's. I sat by the fire, dreaming strange dreams, while the clock ticked the hours slowly by, and the fire sank low. At 11, my father yawned and went up to his room. At a quarter before 12, I took my heavy cloak, and wrapped it around me. A little later, I went out.

I knew that I would find him waiting. There was no doubt of that tonight. It was not curiosity that drove me, but some deeper urge, some urge I know no name for. I was like a swimmer in a dangerous current, caught at last by the undertow.

The car stood in the crossroad, low and dark. Although it was a finely made machine, I was sure, it seemed to me for the first time to be in some way *very* peculiar. But at that moment a cloud swept across the face of the moon, and I lost interest in the matter, with a last vague thought that it must be of foreign make.

Then, suddenly, I was aware that for the first time the stranger had opened the door of the car before me. Indeed, this was the first time I had approached on the side of the vacant seat beside the driver.

"We ride tonight, Leonora. Why not? Why not? And what else did you come out for?"

That was true. For the first time I now met him, not on my way home, not on my way anywhere. I had met him, only to meet him. And he expected me to ride. He had never forced, or tried to urge me, but tonight he expected me to ride. Wouldn't it seem silly to have come out only to exchange two or three words and go back, and wouldn't it be better to go with him? A less inexperienced girl might take the trouble to leave her house on a stormy March night for the sake of a real adventure—only a very green country girl would have come out at all for less. I would go.

I had entered the car. I sat beside him, and when the moon shone out brightly I tried to study his face as he started the car down the narrow road. I met with no success. I had become conscious of a burning anxiety to see more clearly what was the manner of this man who had been the subject of so much speculation, the reason of so many dreams. But here beside him I could see him no more clearly than I had seen him from the road. The side of his face which was turned toward me, and which was partly exposed between the deep-brimmed hat and the turned-up collar of his cloak, was still deeply shaded by the car itself; so that I had the same elusive impression as before, of strong, sharp features, a deep-set gaze, a smiling expression—

We drove fast, over strange roads. So closely was my attention centred upon my companion, that I did not concern myself with the way we went. Later, I was to become uneasy over the distance we had traversed; but when I did, he reassured me, and I believed that we were then on our way home, and nearly there. I thought he meant by home, my father's house; and had I not thought that, my wildest nightmare could not have whispered to me what it was that *he* called "home"!

He was very silent. I spoke little, and he seldom answered me. That did not alarm me as it might have done, because of my ever-present conviction of my childishness, my crudeness. I blamed myself because my remarks were so stupid that they were not worth a reply, and the taciturnity that so embarrassed me yet added to the fascination that made me sit motionless hour after hour, longing more than anything else in the world to get a good look at the face beside me, to arouse more interest in my companion.

Once only, he spoke of his own accord. He asked me why I was called Leonora.

I asked him if he did not think it was a pretty name, remembering how he had said at our first meeting that it was "music in his ears." But I was disappointed, for he did not compliment my name again.

"Some would say it was an ill-starred name. But, luckily, people are not superstitious as they used to be."

"If that is lucky, you cannot call it ill-starred."

I wanted to provoke him into talking more to me. I wanted his attention. But he did not answer me.

I cannot go on. I cannot finish my story as I intended to do, telling things as they happened, in their right order. There are things I must explain, things that people have said about me that I must deny. And the night is growing late, and the rapping I hear all night long upon my window-pane, between the bars that shut me in but that will soon protect me no longer, is growing louder—as the dawn approaches. The pain in my heart, of which the doctor has said I would die soon, is growing unendurable. And when I come to the end of my story—*to the end, which I will set down*—I do not know what will happen then. But that which I am to write of is so dreadful that I have never dared to think of it. Not of that itself, but of the horrible ending to the story I am telling.

I must finish before the dawn, for it is at the dawn that They must go, and it is then that They would take me—where *he* waits for me, always at dawn.

But to explain first—people say I am mad. You who will read this will doubtless believe them. But tell me this:

Where was I, from the time I disappeared from my father's house until I was found, "mad," as they say, and clutching in my frenzied grasp—the finger of a skeleton? In what dread struggle did I tear that finger loose, and from what dreadful hand? And although I, a living woman, could not remain in the abode of death, if I have not been touched by the very finger of death, then tell me this:

Why is my flesh like the flesh of the dead, so that the doctors say it is like leprous flesh, although it is not leprous? Would God it were!

Now, let me go on.

*

Our silent drive continued through the flying hours. Flying hours, for I was unconscious of the lapse of time, excepting for the once when I vaguely became uneasy at our long journey, and was reassured. Had he who sat behind the wheel refused to answer my questioning then, perhaps I would then have become frantic with terror. But his deep, soothing voice worked a spell on me once more; and in his reply I thought I could detect a real solicitude which comforted me. I was assured that we would shortly reach my father's house; I would slip in before my father could possibly have waked, and avoid questioning.

As the night grew older, it became more dismal. The moon which had swung high overhead sent long shadows scurrying from every tree and shrub, every hill and hummock, as we dashed by. The wind had fallen, but yet blew hard enough to make a moaning, wailing sound which seemed to follow us through the night. The clouds that had swept in great masses across the sky had changed their shapes, and trailed in long, sombre, broken streamers like torn black banners. The smell of dank, soggy earth and rotting leaves, of mould and decay, was heavier since the wind had sunk a little. Suddenly, I had a great need for reassurance and comfort. My heart seemed breaking with loneliness, and with a strange, unreasoning despair.

I turned to the silent figure at my side. And it seemed that *he* smelled of the stagnant odour of decay that filled the night—that the smell, and the oppression, were heavier because I had leaned nearer to him!

I looked—with a more intense gaze than I had yet turned on him—not at the face that bent above me now, the face that still eluded and baffled me—but down at the arm next to me, at the sleeve of his cloak of heavy, black cloth. For something had caught my eye—something moved—Oh, what was this horror, and why was it so horrible?—A slowly moving *worm* upon his sleeve?

I shuddered so that I clashed my teeth together. I must control myself.

And then, as though my deep alarm were the cue for the hidden event to advance from the future upon me, the car was gliding to a stop. I tore my horrified gaze from the black-clad arm and looked out of the car. We were gliding *into a cemetery*!

"Not here! Oh, don't stop here!"

I gasped the words, as one gasps in a nightmare.

"Yes. Here."

The deep voice was deeper. It was deep and hollow. There was no comfort in it.

The mask was off my fear, at least. I was face to face with that, though I had not yet seen that other face—

I leaped from the car, and fell fainting beside it. Black, low-hung, and long and narrow—I had been to but one funeral in my life, but I knew it, now. It was the shape of a coffin!

After that, I had no hope. I was with a madman, or—

He dragged me—in gloved hands through which the hard, long fingers bruised my flesh—past graves, past tombstones and marble statues, and I was numb. I saw among the graves, or seemed to see— oh, let me say I saw strange things, for I have seen them since; and I was numb.

He dragged me toward an old, old, sunken grave headed by a time-stained stone that settled to one side, so long it had marked that spot. And suddenly the nightmare dreaminess that had dulled my senses gave way to some keener realization of the truth. I struggled, I fought back with all my little strength, till I tore the glove from his right hand, and the finger of his right hand snapped in my grasp— snapped, and—gave way!

I struggled in the first faint rays of dawn, struggled as I felt the old, old, sunken earth give way beneath my feet. And the sun rose over the edge of the earth, and flamed red into my desperate eyes. I turned for a last time to the inscrutable face, and in those blood-red rays of the dawn I saw at last revealed—the grinning, fleshless jaws, the empty eye-sockets of...

STATEMENT BY THE SUPERINTENDENT OF ST. MARGARET'S INSANE ASYLUM

This document was found in the room of Leonora ———, who was pronounced dead of heart-failure by the resident physician. Attendants who rushed to the room on hearing wild cries, and who found her dead, believe the fatal attack to have been caused by the excitement of writing down her extraordinary narration.

The doctor who had attended her considered her the victim of a strange form of auto-hypnosis. She undoubtedly disappeared from her home on the night of the eighteenth of March, and was found two days later in an old cemetery, three hundred miles away. When found, she was incoherent and hysterical, and *was holding in her hand the finger of a skeleton*. How and where she might have come by this, it was and is impossible to surmise.

It seems, however, that she must have been lured from her home by some stranger, and have escaped or been abandoned near the cemetery; that she must have read of the legend of Leonora, and that it must have made a morbid impression on her mind which later, following the shock which caused her to lose her reason, dictated the form her insanity was to take.

It is true that her skin, from the time of her discovery in the graveyard, had a peculiar appearance suggestive of the skin of a leprous person, or even more of that of a corpse; and (which she does not mention) it also exuded a peculiar odour. These phenomena were among those attributed by the doctor to the effects of auto-hypnosis;

his theory being that, just as a hypnotized person may be made to develop a burn on the arm by the mere suggestion without the application of heat, Leonora had suggested to herself that she had been contaminated by the touch of death, and that her physical nature had been affected by the strength of the suggestion.

1926

ODE TO PEGASUS

Maria Moravsky

Maria Moravsky (1890–1947), or to revel in her full name Maria Magdalena Frederica Ludvigovna Moravskaya, was born in Warsaw, Poland, in 1890—though at the time Poland was part of the Russian Empire and Russia had yet to adopt the Gregorian calendar, so it was still 1889 for her! She developed as a promising poet and had three collections of verse published in Russia before the Revolution in 1917. Fleeing persecution, she escaped to the United States which she saw as a place of freedom, though she soon found it a cultural desert compared to her native land. Although she taught herself English, she found it difficult writing poetry in another language and turned to journalism. One of her earliest essays, "The Greenhorn in America" in the November 1918 *Atlantic Monthly*, reveals her initial frustration with life in America where everyone is in a hurry and not taking time to appreciate life. But she began to sell to several of the major magazines, including *Harper's*, and was soon earning money whilst, as she recalled, her friends and relatives back in Russia were starving. In 1920 she married Ted Coughlan, at the time a poultry dealer, but later became a writer of detective fiction with whom she sometimes collaborated.

Her first appearance in *Weird Tales* was with the following story, in the November 1926 issue. It still reveals her lyrical style even when writing in another language. It also seems to me to be an allegory of her memories of fleeing Russia. She had only five stories in *Weird Tales*, spanning twenty years, the last "The Green Brothers Take Over" in the January 1948 issue appeared six months after her death. She had a further six stories in the short-lived rival, *Strange Stories*, in 1939–40, so there is ample material for a representative collection.

She also contributed a brief poem to *Weird Tales* in the November 1942 issue and I cannot help but wonder if this reflected her state of mind at the time. Entitled "Into Fantasy" it ran:

> Midnight strikes. An owl hoots,
> I am sick of hope and delays.
> I will brew mandragora roots.
> To drug my humdrum days.

It has been suggested that Moravsky did not die in 1947 but moved to Chile, married a local postman, and died there in 1958 or so. But there is ample evidence that she died in a Miami hospital in June 1947 of a stroke and was cremated. Unless, perhaps, she sought to emulate Ambrose Bierce!

E ric could not sleep. There were mosquitoes in his room, and they sang in low monotonous voices the praise of sleeplessness. The pallid moon shone straight into his eyes, and in its waning light the boy saw the weathervane on the garage roof spinning round and round in the changing wind.

The weathervane represented a horse with wings, because, before the advent of automobiles, the garage used to be a stable. A famous family of horse-lovers kept their race-horses there. It had been long ago, Eric was told, maybe fifty years, maybe more... Eric was still of the age when fifty years and eternity are of practically the same length. The old weathervane silvered by the moon looked ancient to him, as ancient as the horse Pegasus of which he had recently learned in school. A wonderful horse!

The wind grew stronger, its direction still undefined. Eric felt sleepy now, his head dizzier and dizzier as the silver horse spun faster. Soon the buzzing of the mosquitoes grew faint, but another disturbing sound startled him: it was the whinnying of a horse.

Nobody kept horses on that modern street, in the up-to-date suburb where Eric's foster-parents owned their ultra-modern house. Even the milkman would come shattering the early hours of the morning with the rattling automobile truck. Eric looked curiously down the deserted street, milky-white in the misty dawn. It seemed empty. Then some irresistible feeling of ill-directed curiosity made him look upward.

The moon was so pale now that it resembled a thin piece of melting ice. The grey roof of the distant ex-stable could not be discerned in the milky mists. Only the weathervane shone brightly, the top of its metallic wings reflecting the unseen sunrise.

The rounds it made now seemed wider and wider. It was as if the horse detached itself from its tether of steel wire. It was growing larger and larger, it flew more and more slowly around the roof's peak. Eric rubbed his eyes and jumped from the bed. Strange things began to happen.

The great horse flew lower. It reached Eric's window. It alighted on the broad roof of the veranda above which the small dormer window peeped at the world. Then, before Eric could formulate the sudden and beautiful desire, he saw it fulfilled. He was on the silvery back of the great horse, between the powerful wings beating the air with harmonious low swish.

Rosy clouds formed an oval track over which the great horse galloped. The unspeakable rapture which was Eric's began to fade as rapidly as it came; he heard his foster-mother's voice calling: "Eric, it's 7 o'clock! Are you up?"

She did not know how high up he was, thought Eric. He would not answer, for fear of disturbing her. She might worry about this new sport he had discovered. She was always extremely solicitous, caring for his safety till it hurt. No, he would not call back from his brilliant place in the clouds; but she might hear the swish of the great wings and look up, and then all the fun would end. He must prevent that. Gently he slapped the horse's shining side and whispered into its trembling ear: "Higher! Take me higher!"

The horse whinnied so that the buildings below trembled with awe. Its wings shot upward with uncanny speed. Never in his life had Eric ridden so fast, not even on that memorable day when his foster-father took him to the stadium and let him fly in an airplane.

"Eric!"

He heard his mother's voice growing weaker yet more penetrating than before. There was anxiety in it, and Eric could not bear that. Through his great exhilaration it sounded, persistent, appealing... He looked with a sigh toward the distant stars he had hoped to reach, then put his mouth against Pegasus' ear once more: "I must go down, to earth."

He closed his eyes, not to see the hateful descent. Heights often made him dizzy, and he was afraid to fall during the rapid downward flight. He opened his eyes only when his feet touched the window-sill of his room.

"The boy is very nervous; too much day-dreaming. The other day when his teacher asked him what he would like to be when he grows up, he answered: 'A flyer in the sky.'"

Mr. Torrence smiled tolerantly at the anxiety sounding in his wife's voice.

"Well, it isn't such an impractical dream, after all. Many level-headed men become pilots nowadays. In fact, one has to be very level-headed to make a success of it. I would not object if Eric—"

"Edwin Torrence! Such a dangerous occupation! You would hardly allow him to choose it if the boy were your own child."

She instantly felt that the reproach was undeserved by her husband, who had been so fond of the boy, and amended her words with an affectionate pat on his shoulder. She admitted that she was too anxious about the boy. Feminine nonsense, all that! Yes, she would try to cure herself of it. It would be selfish to stand in the boy's way should he choose to become a pilot. Secretly she hoped he would not.

"As to his nervousness, we must consult a specialist," Mr. Torrence concluded hopefully. "It is natural at his age. The dangerous period between adolescence and youth, you know."

Mr. Torrence thought he knew all about what he called human mechanism.

As the years went by, several nerve specialists went over Eric's consciousness and subconsciousness with a fine-toothed comb. Nothing seemed neglected there, in the inner circle of his soul. He apparently overcame his habit of day-dreaming, and embraced willingly the risky but sane career of a pilot, which Mr. Torrence suggested to him, thinking that was what the boy wanted himself.

Eric no longer rode the great white horse. Instead, he mastered many ugly synthetic horses with dead motionless wings which depended on the noisy motors to lift them up to the sky. Once there, he seemed to regain the illusions of which the nerve specialists had robbed him. The rosy clouds at sunrise were almost as beautiful and exciting as during that first ride in the sky when he saw them from Pegasus' back.

Yet the airplane rides never gave him as much thrill as that first dazzling ride. Outwardly he was a careful, persevering, level-headed driver, always minding weather forecasts, never accepting insane bets. He would not loop the loop or engage in the neck-breaking pastime of the tailspin. He would test most minutely every new plane entrusted to him, before he ever mounted it. It was because of these qualities that he was chosen to take a part in the great airplane race, the unseen track of which lay between New York and San Francisco.

His aged foster-mother was dead by now, so her kindly fretting and worry could not stop him from accepting the honour of racing. His father, even more level-headed than his foster-son, saw no obstacles to it. He was rather proud of this boy whom he had made over, he thought, from a highly strung dreamer into a practical first-rate pilot. He would be dismayed, perhaps, and his pride would waver if he knew that, just on the day of the race, his level-headed foster-son was occupied with a thing which was anything but practical. In the midst of the last preparations and fixings of his plane, he laid down his grease-proof gloves, took out the thin penknife given to him by his foster-mother when he was a boy, and for the better half of an hour scratched something on the upper part of the left wing of the plane. When he finished his eyes held a distant and dreamy look like that which would steal into them in the days of his earliest childhood.

It was the last hour of the race. The great expanse of the Pacific widened before Eric's eyes, tired from incessant wind from which even his glasses could not wholly protect him. His face was hollow and smeared with perspiration. His head ached dully. It seemed to him that he had flown for days. He was so tired that he did not care any longer about the winning of the race. Although he was far ahead of all his competitors, the thought of it gave him no thrill. All his weary brain craved was unconsciousness. Unconsciousness of sleep or even death.

The numerous shocks of the changeable wind currents, the falling into air pockets, being beaten by the rain and sudden unexpected crop of hail never predicted by the weather report, and above all these physical trials the supreme trial of ambition urging him on and on at top speed, ambition imposed upon him by his father's pride—all this was breaking his inner endurance. While his body still struggled on, the real Eric was almost unconscious of its efforts. He was so deathly tired, it seemed that nothing more could shock him.

But as his tired eyes glimpsed the greenish blue expanse of the misty ocean, with the large, queerly shaped clouds hung low over it, and the seagulls' wings catching the glimpses of the unseen sunshine hidden somewhere behind these low clouds, he experienced a shock similar to that of his first ride... Had it been his first ride in an airplane or a car, or—something else? He was so tired he could not recall it.

Yet all his being strained like a hound on a leash, toward some great experience which was about to be his. The great clouds above sailed lower, became pregnant with some unseen presence... Strange things began to happen.

A great white horse emerged from the farthest cloud. It grew nearer and nearer the rattling plane, drowning the unharmonious voice of the querulous motor with the musical swish of its wings.

"Pegasus!" cried Eric.

"Something is wrong with that motor," warned the first layer of his consciousness.

"Pegasus!" cried the real Eric.

The great horse was now near, within the reach of his hand. But his hands clung to the despised synthetic thing which he was driving. His eyes were looking upward, while his ears tried to detect the ominous missings in the beats of the motor. He was like a house divided against itself, when he felt strange waves of powerful thought coming toward him.

The luminous eyes of the great horse were now quite near. It was from them that the thoughts radiated. These orbs of concentrated moonlight flashed into his awed soul the message: "You have forgotten me! You have forgotten Pegasus, for this thing of metal and gas."

"I never forgot you!" shouted Eric. "Look on the outside of the left wing! I have written an ode in your honour. It is scratched on the aluminium so clearly a seagull could read it."

"Then leave this machine and mount me," came the luring command.

His mortally tired hands ceased to cling to the guide-stick. Overwhelming dizziness came over him. He lurched forward, then leapt. Next moment he was on the back of the great horse heading into eternity.

*

The mangled thing they found among the steaming wreck of the winning airplane was not Eric. It was only his body worn to death by the tiresome realities of life.

1939

MOMMY

Mary Elizabeth Counselman

Mary Elizabeth Counselman (1911–1995) appeared regularly in *Weird Tales* for twenty years with thirty stories from "The House of Shadows" (April 1933) to "Way Station" (November 1953), though she also contributed several poems, one as early as April 1932. "The House of Shadows" is a simple ghost story about a house whose former inhabitants refuse to go. She went almost full circle with her last piece, "Way Station", an amusing story about a house which serves as a stopover for ghosts of the recently deceased. Counselman continued to contribute to *Weird Tales* when it was revived with stories in the first two paperback issues edited by Lin Carter in 1980/81, so you could say she contributed to the magazine for almost fifty years. Her work appeared in many other magazines, including several poems in the *Saturday Evening Post*, but it is her stories for *Weird Tales* that have sustained her reputation.

She made her mark with one of the magazine's most popular stories, "The Three Marked Pennies" (August 1934) which she wrote when she was fifteen. The story can be found in the Tales of the Weird volume *Doorway to Dilemma*. Another popular story was "Parasite Mansion" (January 1942) where, after a car accident, a woman finds herself in a house full of weird people. It became one of her better-known stories after it was adapted for the TV series *Boris Karloff's Thriller* in 1961.

Counselman had married in 1941 and lived with her increasingly abusive husband and baby son on a houseboat—in fact a converted paddle-steamer—on the Coosa River in Gadsden, Alabama. Many of her stories are set in Alabama or other southern states. Several were collected as *Half in Shadow* which exists in two variant editions, the British paperback in 1964 and the American hardcover from Arkham House in 1978.

Several of her stories deal with children and motherhood. I reprinted "The Unwanted" (January 1951) in the Tales of the Weird collection *Queens of the Abyss*. Here's another, equally moving and atmospheric, from the April 1939 issue.

"I want to adopt a child about seven years old," Mrs. Ellison had explained to the matron a few hours before.

Now, standing in the big bare yard of the Acipco County Orphanage, she studied each of the smaller girls who scampered past her. There was a chubby dark-curled mite seesawing near the tall iron gate, Mrs. Ellison noted. A lovely cherub, she thought, who would make a wonderful little daughter for a childless widow like herself. Pumping madly in one of the swings was another, brown-eyed and laughing as she herself had been at that age.

So many motherless children, herded together like livestock and perforce treated almost as such—how was one to make the great decision that would change one's own life as well as the child's for ever after today?

"Good Heavens! I'm shopping for a daughter," the tall gentle-eyed woman mused guiltily. "How inhuman! It... it should be the other way 'round, if only a child had vision enough to select..."

Her thought snapped off like a twig. Something was tugging at her skirt with timid insistence, and she peered down, startled to find a thin homely little girl looking up at her. The penetrating blue eyes were much too large for that sallow sensitive face. Two mouse-coloured braids hung over narrow shoulders against the starched collar of her orphanage uniform, and the arm that reached up at Mrs. Ellison was match-thin and peppered with freckles like the face and neck.

I don't believe I've ever seen a more unattractive child, was the woman's first thought. But then the little girl smiled, and her face lighted slowly as a candle in a dark room. It was a sweet strange smile, full of wistfulness and yet the paradox of a quiet *knowledge*.

"Are you the lady my mommy sent for me?" her small voice piped. It was a timid voice, rather vague like the blue eyes, but oddly compelling for all that.

Mrs. Ellison knelt down, smiling. Her hands moved, smoothing the ratty braids. The child wouldn't look so homely with careful attention, her thoughts veered, while she murmured aloud:

"I don't know, sweetheart. Has your mommy gone to Heaven?"

The child regarded her gravely for a moment. Then she shook her head.

"No, ma'am. My mommy comes to see me any time I want her to. She talks to me every night, an'—"

At that instant the matron bustled up, starched and puffing, a tiny frown of annoyance creasing her smooth forehead at sight of the little girl with the kneeling woman.

"Mrs. Ellison, I'm so sorry I was delayed... Run along to your play, Martha dear," she commanded briskly. "Matron wants to talk to the nice lady. Run away; that's a good girl."

The visitor rose, puzzled at her tone of impatience. But the thin-faced child hesitated only a second, during which her deep blue eyes searched for something in Mrs. Ellison's expression with a solemn intensity. Then she wheeled without a word and walked slowly away toward a group of children near by. At her approach, however, they promptly turned and left her standing there, leaning against the trunk of a giant white oak that dwarfed her small body.

Mrs. Ellison watched the by-play with a queer pang. "Who is that child?" she murmured. "There's... there's something different about her."

"Martha?" The matron's laugh of exasperation knifed into her mood. "I'm sure you wouldn't care to take on *that* responsibility! She's really our problem child. Doesn't get on with the other children and constantly breaks our petty rules here. Oh, I don't mean she's deliberately bad, but—"

"Just a misfit?" The tall brown-haired visitor nodded her sympathy. "Perhaps it's the mother's interference. I understand from little Martha that she visits her quite often, and that's always hard on a child's morale. A pity she couldn't just take her away from here and support her the best way she—"

Mrs. Ellison broke off, conscious that the matron was smiling at her quizzically.

"My dear," the orphanage head spread her hands, "that child has no mother—she died over a year ago. Tuberculosis, I'm told, aggravated by night work in a cotton mill. I see I must explain our little Martha to you...

"The poor baby had such a shock, she's never been able to adjust herself. Some minds, tortured beyond endurance, fall into amnesia as an escape. Others—like poor little Martha's—simply build up a dream-world in which they need not face the cruel truth. She has a positive fixation that her mother is beside her at all times. 'Why, I can see her in the night, can't you?' she'll say, time and again. Carries on long imaginary conversations in the ward after lights-out, so that the other children complain of her keeping them awake. They don't dislike her, but I think they're a bit afraid of her."

"Afraid?" Mrs. Ellison quirked an eyebrow at the absurdity. "Why on earth should anyone be afraid of that pitiful little mite?"

The matron fidgeted, then gave a nervous laugh. "Well"—she averted her gaze sheepishly—"well, it *is* odd. Some unexplainable things have happened since the child has been here at the Home with us.

"I must tell you first that Martha's mother was a remarkable woman. Physically a wreck, and morally... There was no father, you understand. A drunken sailor, most probably, as the woman seems to have been a cheap dance-hall hostess before her child was born in a charity hospital.

"But little Martha's birth seemed to bring out the best in her—a fierce maternal instinct. It happens often—rather proving, I think, the divinity in all mankind. Anyway, the mother changed her mode of living at once, got a job in the mill, and literally killed herself working for her child.

"She fought death with a stubborn will that prolonged her life by months, they tell me. But in the end her frail body gave way.

"At the last she called little Martha to her bedside and made the child some sort of crazy promise that she would *never leave her*, no matter what anyone said about death and the like. Her sick body was only a worn-out coat, she told the child, that her *real* 'mommy' was throwing away so that it could not hinder her any longer in taking care of her baby.

"A natural thing to say, of course, but disastrous in its effect on a child's impressionable mind. It developed a complex in Martha... so weirdly borne out by coincidence, however, that I... I sometimes catch myself wondering! Really, it's... it's uncanny!"

Mrs. Ellison laughed softly. She was a matter-of-fact woman, little given to fantasy. But, nettled by her scepticism, the matron gave details.

"You think I'm imagining things?" she bridled. "Listen! There was the time a certain actress wanted to adopt the child. I can't think why she chose homely little Martha—unless as a foil for her own beauty. But all was in order and Martha was being sent for, although she behaved badly and screamed all night that her 'mommy' hadn't sent this lady for her.

"With the woman's secretary waiting in our very antechamber for Martha to be dressed, we received a call from the actress's press agent saying the deal was off. It appears she was simply adopting Martha as a publicity stunt, to swing public opinion her way when a nasty scandal broke in which her name would be involved. *But that very morning she had fallen downstairs and fractured her nose!* In case the plastic surgery wasn't successful, her agent informed me, the dear lady's contract might not be renewed and 'she couldn't support a child.' We read between the lines, of course, as the actress had millions salted away...

"But there it stands. Martha was saved from such an adoption because *something* tripped that cold-blooded woman and temporarily marred her looks!"

Mrs. Ellison gave another soft laugh. "A timely coincidence," she murmured. "Poor little Martha!"

"Yes," the matron nodded wryly. "But it strengthened her belief that her 'mommy' was watching over her interests night and days! As for the other children here, they're as convinced as she is... especially since the time that circus came to town, and our amusement fund didn't stretch over the last ten of our enrolment.

"Martha was one of those who drew lots and lost. She was heartbroken, like the other nine losers. Then suddenly, as I was lining up those who could go, little Martha ran forward and tugged at my arm.

"'Matron! Matron!' she cried, her eyes shining with excitement. 'Mommy says I can go! Mommy says to take all the others, and she'll pay their way somehow, so I can go!'

"Of course, that outburst upset the other children and raised their hopes so, I hadn't the heart to leave them behind. I decided to borrow the difference from our food bill and juggle accounts later. A foolhardy impulse, but you'll understand how I felt.

"So off they went to the circus, every one of them. They were fairly dancing with anticipation waiting outside the big tent while I bought the tickets; but my conscience was beginning to prickle. Those ten extra tickets meant a scantier diet for all of them well into the next month's budget, and I was sure the board would discover it and give me a severe reprimand.

"I stopped short right there, thinking it over and wishing heartily that I could spank little Martha. But at that moment I... I happened to glance down at the sawdust.

"There just under my foot was a small wad of paper money neatly folded around some silver change. My heart almost stopped, let me tell you, when I counted it—*the exact amount, to a penny, for those ten tickets!* I had the local paper advertise later for its loser, but no one claimed it. I've... I've often speculated on the many ways it could have got there."

Mrs. Ellison's smile had faded a trifle, but now it came back, full of gentle tolerance. "Perhaps some drunken person dropped it," she suggested. "Surely, my dear matron, there's nothing supernatural about losing money on a circus ground!"

"Humph! Oh. Well... maybe not." The plump orphanage head looked disgruntled but unconvinced. "There were other times," she pursued stoutly. "That time, for instance, when little Martha swallowed an open safety pin, the way children will do if you don't watch them every minute!

"It was a terrible day last fall, when we had that ice storm, you remember. Wires were down, and we couldn't locate a doctor, with the poor little thing choking and crying, and that open pin jabbing into her throat with every move she'd make! I was frantic, and Miss Peebles, our resident nurse, was at her wit's end... when all of a sudden this interstate bus broke down, spang in front of the Home gate..."

Mrs. Ellison's eyes twinkled faintly. "And I suppose," she put in, teasingly, "there was a doctor for little Martha on the bus?"

The matron did not return her smile, but surreptitiously mopped off a dew of moisture that sprang to her upper lip at the memory.

"A doctor?" she replied grimly. "*There were eight*—coming home from the state medical convention! One was an ear, eye, nose and throat specialist. Of course, he had that safety-pin out in a jiffy.

"What was so queer, the bus driver said it was battery trouble, with his new battery and wiring just checked carefully at the last station! Oh, it *could* happen, yes. I grant you, it *could* happen."

Mrs. Ellison chuckled. The chuckle seemed to annoy the matron, and she burst out afresh.

"There are dozens of minor incidents like that," she declared. "Martha is eternally finding things the other children will pass a hundred times. Pennies in the grass. A half-package of gum. A broken toy fire-engine, once, that some child must have thrown over the Home fence in a temper. Ask Martha where she gets them, and she'll invariably answer: 'Mommy gave it to me,' with those big eyes of hers as innocent as a lamb's. If I scold her and tell her to say she found it, she'll just say: 'Oh, yes—but Mommy told me where it was.'

"All that has made a vast impression on the other children. That's why they're a bit in awe of her—because they believe she's hourly guarded and pampered by a... by a—"

The matron floundered, reddening. Mrs. Ellison lifted one eyebrow humorously at the plump house-mother; saw the flush deepen in her round cheeks.

"By a ghost?" she finished, gently derisive. "My dear matron, I'm astonished that a sensible woman like yourself would permit such a silly notion to survive! Why, it's medieval!"

The orphanage head folded her lips primly. "Well," she said in a tone that defied argument, "I only say it's queer, and that's what it is! The children are afraid of Martha, and she's a problem I'm at a loss to solve. If only somebody would take her off my hands—somebody I wouldn't mind her going to, with the child's good at heart. But, there! Nobody wants the poor homely little thing, though she asks everybody who comes here if she's 'the lady her mommy sent' to adopt her. It's a crying shame—but who'd want a crazy child when there are so many normal ones to be had?"

She followed the visitor's gaze with a look of perplexity, and regarded the little girl sitting cross-legged on the ground, playing by herself while others scampered past in noisy groups.

But Mrs. Ellison was folding her gloves and putting them in her purse with the gesture of a knight drawing on his gauntlets of chain-mail. Then she faced the matron and announced:

"Who'd want her? *I* do! And just as soon as it can be arranged! That fixation has been nourished too long in the child's mind. But a home, some new toys and a little affection will make her forget that nonsense. So... if you'll just rush the formalities, I'd be ever so grateful."

The matron blinked at her, surprised for a moment, a tiny flicker of doubt burning behind her spectacles. Then she shrugged and sighed deeply.

"That I will!" was her promise. "I only hope you won't regret it, Mrs. Ellison. Frankly, I haven't been able to cope with the situation. It's... it's a strange case, and needs a lot of understanding. Don't be too impatient with the child."

"Nonsense!" The visitor squared her shoulders firmly. "Martha simply needs a mother." And she strode across the grounds toward the small figure playing alone under the oak tree with a handful of acorn cups.

The matron, watching her, shook her head doubtfully as Mrs. Ellison knelt beside the child. Then, with reluctance, she turned away, for there were some two hundred other orphans who demanded her daily attention.

Little Martha looked up shyly, gravely questioning. Mrs. Ellison studied the vague sweet smile accorded her and gathered the child impulsively into her arms. But she was chagrined at the lack of response. Little Martha, not quite cold to her advance, was like a small bony doll in her embrace, neither affectionate nor defiant. One hand clutched an acorn cup with a tiny grass handle, but the other hung limp and did not steal about her neck as Mrs. Ellison had half expected. It was almost a challenge, she thought, and smiled at the absurdity.

"Martha dear," she whispered, "you are going home with me and be my little girl. I'll give you a pony and cart, and lots of dollies, and have your hair curled like that little girl over there. Would you like that?"

The blue eyes lighted, giving Martha's sallow face a certain quaint beauty for all its freckles and angularity.

"Oh, yes'm!" she breathed. "I... I would! But I'll have to ask Mommy first," she added shyly. "Tonight I guess maybe she'll tell me if you're the one."

"Now, now!" Mrs. Ellison laughed with an effort. "You must call *me* your mommy, dear, because you'll be my own little girl tomorrow!"

"Yes'm," the grave child nodded obediently, "I'll call you Mother, if Mommy says it's all right. Oh, I... I do hope you're the one!"

And Mrs. Ellison left, feeling baffled and entirely unsure whether or not she had won that first match.

The ponderous amount of red tape was snipped through, true to the matron's promise. A few days later, with a late autumn sun gilding the yellow leaves a brighter gold, Mrs. Ellison again drove to the Acipco County Orphanage.

She had dismissed her chauffeur, bought a woolly Sealyham pup at a pet shop en route, as well as a lovely little blue silk dress, and set forth rather grimly. These, she thought, are my weapons. With these I will slay forever the ghost of Martha's "mommy," and she'll haunt that lonely child no longer!

An hour later, they were whirling out of the orphanage driveway—a tall gentle-eyed woman at the steering-wheel and, close beside her, a little girl in a blue dress, ecstatically hugging her new puppy.

Threading her way through the afternoon traffic, Mrs. Ellison smiled and chatted merrily, but her heart seethed. Confound that selfish hysterical woman, dying on her hospital cot! She had left a mark on this wistful credulous baby that time could not erase!

For a moment, glancing sidewise at her adopted daughter, Martha's second mother hated that first one who stood between them like an invisible wall, in spite of everything she could do.

Or, did she? Eerily Mrs. Ellison felt an alien presence in that wide car seat—but not between her and the child. Rather, it seemed that *someone... something...* was seated on the other side of little Martha, allied with her new mother, guarding the child on one side while she herself guarded the other.

The tall woman shook herself angrily. What utter rot! Was she, too, succumbing to the child's hallucination? She must exorcize that spirit now, or admit defeat by something that did not exist.

"Do you love your new mommy?" she coaxed, bending sidewise to hug little Martha with one arm.

The child snuggled closer. Wide blue eyes blazed up at her, aglow with happiness. "Oh, yes, Mother! You are really and truly my mother now, aren't you? So I'll tell you a secret," as the woman's face lighted with triumph. "Mommy told me last night that she picked you out for me a long, long time ago! An' she said—"

"Martha!" Mrs. Ellison drew back sharply as from an unexpected blow. "Stop talking like that!" she commanded shortly. "I want you to forget all that nonsense about your mother. Remember and love her always, of course. But your mommy went to Heaven over a year ago, and you must stop pretending that—"

A scream from the child cut her short. Mrs. Ellison broke off, jerked her head around, and was transfixed with horror to see a huge and driverless gasoline truck hurtling down upon them from the long narrow hill they were slowly ascending.

The great red juggernaut was picking up speed. It careened from kerb to kerb like a drunken monster, making for their car with a blood-chilling accuracy, blunt-nosed and heavy as a locomotive.

Panic swept over Mrs. Ellison, freezing her hands to the steering-wheel. A few more yards, and disaster would strike them head-on with a grinding crash. It seemed to the woman that she could hear that sickening sound already... and there was not an alley, not a convenient driveway for them to dart into. Only a low rock wall on one side, a sloping terrace on the other. And, as though realizing the futility of further motion, the car stalled dead in the path of the runaway truck.

"Oh, darling—*jump!*" Mrs. Ellison screamed. "Jump out and run! I... I can't—"

But the child at her side had not even heard her. For one who faced death, she seemed strangely calm. Her sallow face had gone so pale that the freckles stood out darkly, and her grip on the new puppy tightened. But her lips moved softly in a half-prayer that was almost inaudible to the woman beside her.

"Mommy! Mom-my!" the whisper fairly screamed. "Make it stop, Mommy! *Please make it stop!*"

Mrs. Ellison tugged at the child, intent on pulling her out of the doomed car in a last wild chance at safety. But before she could wrench open the car door... there was a metallic squeal of stripped gears.

Looking up, wild-eyed, she saw the onrushing truck hop sidewise awkwardly and come to a scraping halt against the kerb—a scant five feet above them.

People came running then—frightened residents, and a policeman, and the white-faced truck-driver. They crowded about the truck, then rushed to the stalled car where Mrs. Ellison was slumped weakly at the wheel. Beside her sat a homely little girl whose strange quiet smile caused them to look at her and look again intently.

"Jeez, lady!" the truck-driver babbled an incoherent apology. "I sure thought I had her braked steady! Jeepers, if that packing-case on the seat hadn't a-fell against the gear-shift and knocked her into reverse, you... you might a-been—"

Mrs. Ellison merely nodded in answer. She could not trust her voice. She could only stare in a dazed way at the truck, then shift her gaze queerly to the little girl seated beside her.

"Are... you quite all right, Martha dear?" she whispered after a moment. "Then, let's you and I and... and Mommy go along home."

1946

DAEMON

C. L. Moore

If there is any one female writer who might be considered the Queen of *Weird Tales* in its heyday, that must surely be C. L. Moore (1911–1987), or Catherine Lucille Moore to state her full maiden name. She felt she was a born storyteller and placed two stories in her college magazine before her first professional sale with the instant classic "Shambleau" in the November 1933 *Weird Tales*. It introduced the character of Northwest Smith, a rather world-weary planetary equivalent of a wild-west outlaw. Set on Mars, Smith rescues a young alien girl from a mob and sees her safely home, at which point she seduces him with her alien allure. Ten of the stories appeared in *Weird Tales* alongside Moore's other series character Jirel of Joiry, who first appeared in "The Black God's Kiss" (October 1934). She is a swordswoman who fights supernatural evil in a mythical medieval France. There were only six Jirel stories, including a collaboration with her future husband, Henry Kuttner, which also included Northwest Smith, and both series left a profound impression on readers. The letters published in the reader column "The Eyrie" were full of praise. Farnsworth Wright kept a tally of reader's favourite stories and Moore came out top in the whole year for both 1933 and 1934. The total tally for the tenure of Wright's editorship from 1924 to 1939 had "Shambleau" as the second most popular story, beaten only by A. Merritt's "The Woman of the Wood". Moore featured again in tenth place, with the second Northwest Smith story, "Black Thirst" (April 1934).

Moore did not contribute to *Weird Tales* again after 1939. She married Henry Kuttner in June 1940 and thereafter most of their work was in collaboration and shifted more to the science-fiction magazines. The Moore-Kuttner partnership produced some of the very best science fiction of the 1940s and 1950s mostly under various pseudonyms including Lewis Padgett, C. H. Liddell and Lawrence O'Donnell.

The Jirel and Northwest Smith stories are both included in the SF Gateway omnibus volume *C. L. Moore* (2014) and rather than reprint a part-series story here I looked for another of her solo weird tales and chose "Daemon" from the October 1946 issue of another much-cherished pulp magazine *Famous Fantastic Mysteries*. This story would have been well at home in *Weird Tales* and shows Moore's full imaginative power.

Padre, the words came slowly. It is a long time now since I have spoken in the Portuguese tongue. For more than a year, my companions here were those who do not speak with the tongues of men. And you must remember, *padre*, that in Rio, where I was born, I was named Luiz *o Bobo*, which is to say, Luiz the Simple. There was something wrong with my head, so that my hands were always clumsy and my feet stumbled over each other. I could not remember very much. But I could see things. Yes, *padre*, I could see things such as other men do not know.

I can see things now. Do you know who stands beside you, *padre*, listening while I talk? Never mind that. I am Luiz *o Bobo* still, though here on this island there were great powers of healing, and I can remember now the things that happened to me years ago. More easily than I remember what happened last week or the week before that. The year has been like a single day, for time on this island is not like time outside. When a man lives with *them*, there is no time.

The *ninfas*, I mean. And the others...

I am not lying. Why should I? I am going to die, quite soon now. You were right to tell me that, *padre*. But I knew. I knew already. Your crucifix is very pretty, *padre*. I like the way it shines in the sun. But that is not for me. You see, I have always known the things that walk beside men—other men. Not me. Perhaps they are souls, and I have no soul, being simple. Or perhaps they are daemons such as only clever men have. Or perhaps they are both these things. I do not know. But I know that I am dying. After the *ninfas* go away, I would not care to live.

Since you ask how I came to this place, I will tell you if the time remains to me. You will not believe. This is the one place on earth, I think, where they lingered still—those things you do not believe.

But before I speak of them, I must go back to an earlier day, when I was young beside the blue bay of Rio, under Sugar Loaf. I remember the docks of Rio, and the children who mocked me. I was big and strong, but I was *o Bobo* with a mind that knew no yesterday or tomorrow.

Minha avó, my grandmother, was kind to me. She was from Ceará where the yearly droughts kill hope, and she was half blind, with pain in her back always. She worked so that we could eat, and she did not scold me too much. I know that she was good. It was something I could see; I have always had that power.

One morning my grandmother did not waken. She was cold when I touched her hand. That did not frighten me for the—good thing—about her lingered for a while. I closed her eyes and kissed her, and then I went away. I was hungry, and because I was *o Bobo*, I thought that someone might give me food, out of kindness...

In the end, I foraged from the rubbish heaps.

I did not starve. But I was lost and alone. Have you ever felt that, *padre*? It is like a bitter wind from the mountains and no sheepskin cloak can shut it out. One night I wandered into a sailors' saloon, and I remember that there were many dark shapes with eyes that shone, hovering beside the men who drank there. The men had red, windburned faces and tarry hands. They made me drink *'guardiente* until the room whirled around and went dark.

I woke in a dirty bunk. I heard planks groaning and the floor rocked under me.

Yes, *padre*, I had been shanghaied. I stumbled on deck, half blind in the dazzling sunlight, and there I found a man who had a strange and shining daemon. He was the captain of the ship, though I did not know it then. I scarcely saw the man at all. I was looking at the daemon.

Now, most men have shapes that walk behind them, *padre*. Perhaps you know that, too. Some of them are dark, like the shapes I saw in the saloon. Some of them are bright, like that which followed my grandmother. Some of them are coloured, pale colours like ashes or rainbows. But this man had a scarlet daemon. And it was a scarlet beside which blood itself is ashen. The colour blinded me. And yet it drew me, too. I could not take my eyes away, nor could I look at it long without pain. I never saw a colour more beautiful, nor more frightening. It made my heart shrink within me, and quiver like a dog that fears the whip. If I have a soul, perhaps it was my soul that quivered. And I feared the beauty of the colour as much as I feared the terror it awoke in me. It is not good to see beauty in that which is evil.

Other men upon the deck had daemons too. Dark shapes and pale shapes that followed them like their shadows. But I saw all the daemons waver away from the red, beautiful thing that hung above the captain of the ship.

The other daemons watched out of burning eyes. The red daemon had no eyes. Its beautiful, blind face was turned always toward the captain, as if it saw only through his vision. I could see the lines of its closed lids. And my terror of its beauty, and my terror of its evil, were nothing to my terror of the moment when the red daemon might lift those lids and look out upon the world.

The captain's name was Jonah Stryker. He was a cruel man, dangerous to be near. The men hated him. They were at his mercy while we were at sea, and the captain was at the mercy of his daemon. That was why I could not hate him as the others did. Perhaps it was pity

I felt for Jonah Stryker. And you, who know men better than I, will understand that the pity I had for him made the captain hate me more bitterly than even his crew hated him.

When I came on deck that first morning, because I was blinded by the sun and by the redness of the scarlet daemon, and because I was ignorant and bewildered, I broke a shipboard rule. What it was, I do not know. There were so many, and I never could remember very clearly in those days. Perhaps I walked between him and the wind. Would that be wrong on a clipper ship, *padre*? I never understood.

The captain shouted at me, in the Yankee tongue, evil words whose meaning I did not know, but the daemon glowed redder when he spoke them. And he struck me with his fist, so that I fell. There was a look of secret bliss on the blind crimson face hovering above his, because of the anger that rose in him. I thought that through the captain's eyes the closed eyes of the daemon were watching me.

I wept. In that moment, for the first time, I knew how truly alone a man like me must be. For I had no daemon. It was not the simple loneliness for my grandmother or for human companionship that brought the tears to my eyes. That I could endure. But I saw the look of joy upon the blind daemon-face because of the captain's evil, and I remembered the look of joy that a bright shape sometimes wears who follows a good man. And I knew that no deed of mine would ever bring joy or sorrow to that which moves behind a man with a soul.

I lay upon the bright, hot deck and wept, not because of the blow, but because I knew suddenly, for the first time, that I was alone. No daemon for good or evil would ever follow me. Perhaps because I have no soul. *That* loneliness, father, is something not even you could understand.

The captain seized my arm and pulled me roughly to my feet. I did not understand, then, the words he spoke in his Yankee tongue, though later I picked up enough of that speech to know what men were saying around me. You may think it strange that *o Bobo* could learn a foreign tongue. It was easy for me. Easier, perhaps, than for a wiser man. Much I read upon the faces of their daemons, and there were many words whose real sounds I did not know, but whose meaning I found in the hum of thoughts about a man's head.

The captain shouted for a man named Barton, and the first mate hurried up, looking frightened. The captain pushed me back against the rail so that I staggered, seeing him and the deck and the watching daemons through the rainbows that tears cast before one's eyes.

There was loud talk, and many gestures toward me and the other two men who had been shanghaied from the port of Rio. The first mate tapped his head when he pointed to me, and the captain cursed again in the tongue of the foreigners, so that his daemon smiled very sweetly at his shoulder.

I think that was the first time I let the captain see pity on my face when I looked at him.

That was the one thing he could not bear. He snatched a belaying pin from the rail and struck me in the face with it, so that I felt the teeth break in my mouth. The blood I spat upon the deck was a beautiful colour, but it looked paler than water beside the colour of the captain's daemon. I remember all the daemons but the red one leaned a little forward when they saw blood running, snuffing up the smell and the brightness of it like incense. The red one did not even turn his blind face.

The captain struck me again because I had soiled his deck. My first task aboard the *Dancing Martha* was to scrub up my own blood from the planking.

Afterward they dragged me to the galley and threw me into the narrow alley at the cook's feet. I burned my hands on the stove. The captain laughed to see me jump back from it. It is a terrible thing that, though I heard his laughter many times a day, I never heard mirth in it. But there was mirth on his daemon's face.

Pain was with me for many days thereafter, because of the beating and the burns, but I was glad in a way. Pain kept my mind from the loneliness I had just discovered in myself. Those were bad days, *padre*. The worst days of my life. Afterward, when I was no longer lonely, I looked back upon them as a soul in paradise might look back on purgatory.

No, I am still alone. Nothing follows me as things follow other men. But here on the island I found the *ninfas*, and I was content.

I found them because of the Shaughnessy. I can understand him today in a way I could not do just then. He was a wise man and I am *o Bobo*, but I think I know some of his thoughts now, because today I, too, know I am going to die.

The Shaughnessy lived many days with death. I do not know how long. It was weeks and months in coming to him, though it lived in his lungs and his heart as a child lives within its mother, biding its time to be born. The Shaughnessy was a passenger. He had much money, so that he could do what he willed with his last days of living. Also he came of a great family in a foreign land called Ireland. The captain hated him for many reasons. He scorned him because of his weakness, and he feared him because he was ill. Perhaps he envied him too, because his people had once been kings and because the Shaughnessy was not afraid to die. The captain, I know, feared death. He feared it most terribly. He was right to fear it. He could not know that a daemon rode upon his shoulder, smiling its sweet, secret smile, but some instinct must have warned him that it was there, biding its time like the death in the Shaughnessy's lungs.

I saw the captain die. I know he was right to fear the hour of his daemon...

Those were bad days on the ship. They were worse because of the great beauty all around us. I had never been at sea before, and the motion of the ship was a wonder to me, the clouds of straining sail above us and the sea all about, streaked with the colours of the currents and dazzling where the sun-track lay. White gulls followed us with their yellow feet tucked up as they soared over the deck, and porpoises followed too, playing in great arcs about the ship and dripping diamonds in the sun.

I worked hard, for no more wages than freedom from blows when I did well, and the scraps that were left from the table after the cook had eaten his fill. The cook was not a bad man like the captain, but he was not a good man, either. He did not care. His daemon was smoky, asleep, indifferent to the cook and the world.

It was the Shaughnessy who made my life worth the trouble of living. If it had not been for him, I might have surrendered life and gone into the breathing sea some night when no one was looking. It would not have been a sin for me, as it would be for a man with a soul.

But because of the Shaughnessy I did not. He had a strange sort of daemon himself, mother-of-pearl in the light, with gleams of darker colours when the shadows of night came on. He may have been a bad man in his day. I do not know. The presence of death in him opened his eyes, perhaps. I know only that to me he was very kind. His daemon grew brighter as the man himself grew weak with the oncoming of death.

He told me many tales. I have never seen the foreign country of Ireland, but I walked there often in my dreams because of the tales he told. The foreign isles called Greece grew clear to me too, because the Shaughnessy had dwelt there and loved them.

And he told me of things which he said were not really true, but I thought he said that with only half his mind, because I saw them so clearly while he talked. Great Odysseus was a man of flesh and blood to me, with a shining daemon on his shoulder, and the voyage that took so many enchanted years was a voyage I almost remembered, as if I myself had toiled among the crew.

He told me of burning Sappho, and I knew why the poet used that word for her, and I think the Shaughnessy knew too, though we did not speak of it. I knew how dazzling the thing must have been that followed her through the white streets of Lesbos and leaned upon her shoulder while she sang.

He told me of the nereids and the oceanids, and once I think I saw, far away in the sun-track that blinded my eyes, a mighty head rise dripping from the water, and heard the music of a wreathed horn as Triton called to his fishtailed girls.

The *Dancing Martha* stopped at Jamaica for a cargo of sugar and rum. Then we struck out across the blue water toward a country called England. But our luck was bad. Nothing was right about the ship on that voyage. Our water-casks had not been cleaned as they should be, and the drinking water became foul. A man can pick the maggots out of his salt pork if he must, but bad water is a thing he cannot mend.

So the captain ordered our course changed for a little island he knew in these waters. It was too tiny to be inhabited, a rock rising out of the great blue deeps with a fresh spring bubbling high up in a cup of the forested crags.

I saw it rising in the dawn like a green cloud on the horizon. Then it was a jewel of green as we drew nearer, floating on the blue water. And my heart was a bubble in my chest, shining with rainbow colours, lighter than the air around me. Part of my mind thought that the island was an isle in Rio Bay, and somehow I felt that I had come home again and would find my grandmother waiting on the shore. I forgot so much in those days. I forgot that she was dead. I thought we would circle the island and come in across the dancing Bay to the foot of the Rua d'Oporto, with the lovely city rising on its hills above the water.

I felt so sure of all this that I ran to tell the Shaughnessy of my delight in homecoming. And because I was hurrying, and blind to all on deck with the vision of Rio in my eyes, I blundered into the captain himself. He staggered and caught my arm to save his footing, and we were so close together that for a moment the crimson daemon swayed above my own head, its eyeless face turned down to mine.

I looked up at that beautiful, smiling face, so near that I could touch it and yet, I knew, farther away than the farthest star. I looked at it and screamed in terror. I had never been so near a daemon before, and I could feel its breath on my face, sweet-smelling, burning my skin with its scorching cold.

The captain was white with his anger and his—his envy? Perhaps it was envy he felt even of me, o Bobo, for a man with a daemon like that one hanging on his shoulder may well envy the man without a soul. He hated me bitterly, because he knew I pitied him, and to receive the pity of o Bobo must be a very humbling thing. Also he knew that I could not look at him for more than a moment or two, because of the blinding colour of his daemon. I think he did not know why I blinked and looked away, shuddering inside whenever he crossed my path. But he knew it was not the angry fear which other men felt for him which made me avert my eyes. I think he sensed that because he was damned I could not gaze upon him long, and that too made him hate and fear and envy the lowliest man in his crew.

All the colour went out of his face as he looked at me, and the daemon above him flushed a deeper and lovelier scarlet, and the captain reached for a belaying pin with a hand that trembled. That which looked out of his eyes was not a man at all, but a daemon, and a daemon that quivered with joy as I was quivering with terror.

I heard the bone crack when the club came down upon my skull. I saw lightning dazzle across my eyes and my head was filled with brightness. I remember almost nothing more of that bad time. A little night closed around me and I saw through it only when the lightning of the captain's blows illumined the dark. I heard his daemon laughing.

When the day came back to me, I was lying on the deck with the Shaughnessy kneeling beside me bathing my face with something that stung. His daemon watched me over his shoulder, bright mother-of-pearl colours, its face compassionate. I did not look at it. The loneliness in me was sharper than the pain of my body, because no daemon of my own hung shining over my hurts, and no daemon ever would.

The Shaughnessy spoke in the soft, hushing Portuguese of Lisboa, that always sounded so strange to me.

"Lie still, Luiz," he was saying. "Don't cry. I'll see that he never touches you again."

I did not know until then that I was weeping. It was not for pain. It was for the look on his daemon's face, and for loneliness.

The Shaughnessy said, "When he comes back from the island, I'll have it out with him." He said more than that, but I was not listening. I was struggling with a thought, and thoughts came hard through the sleepiness that always clouded my brain.

The Shaughnessy meant kindly, but I knew the captain was master upon the ship. And it still seemed to me that we were anchored in the Bay of Rio and my grandmother awaited me on the shore.

I sat up. Beyond the rail the high green island was bright, sunshine winking from the water all around it, and from the leaves that clothed its slopes. I knew what I was going to do.

When the Shaughnessy went away for more water, I got to my feet. There was much pain in my head, and all my body ached from the captain's blows, and the deck was reeling underfoot with a motion the waves could not give it. When I got to the rail, I fell across it before I could jump, and slid into the sea very quietly.

I remember only flashes after that. Salt water burning me, and great waves lifting and falling all around me, and the breath hot in my lungs when the water did not burn even hotter there. Then there was sand under my knees, and I crawled up a little beach and I think I fell asleep in the shelter of a clump of palms.

Then I dreamed that it was dark, with stars hanging overhead almost near enough to touch, and so bright they burned my eyes. I dreamed I heard men calling me through the trees, and I did not answer. I dreamed I heard voices quarrelling, the captain's voice loud and angry, the Shaughnessy's tight and thin. I dreamed of oarlocks creaking and water splashing from dipping blades, and the sound of it receding into the warmth and darkness.

I put up a hand to touch a star cluster that hung above my head, and the cluster was bright and tingling to feel. Then I saw that it was the Shaughnessy's face.

I said, "Oh, *s'nhor*," in a whisper because I remembered that the captain had spoken from very close by.

The Shaughnessy smiled at me in the starlight. "Don't whisper, Luiz. We're alone now."

I was happy on the island. The Shaughnessy was kind to me, and the days were long and bright, and the island itself was friendly. One knows that of a place. And I thought, in those days, that I would never see the captain again or his beautiful scarlet daemon smiling its blind, secret smile above his shoulder. He had left us to die upon the island, and one of us did die.

The Shaughnessy said that another man might have perished of the blows the captain gave me. But I think because my brain is such a simple thing it mended easily, and perhaps the blow that made my skull crack let in a little more of wit than I had owned before. Or perhaps happiness did it, plenty of food to eat, and the Shaughnessy's tales of the things that—that you do not believe, *meu padre*.

The Shaughnessy grew weak as I grew strong. He lay all day in the shade of a broad tree by the shore, and as his strength failed him, his daemon grew brighter and more remote, as if it were already halfway through the veil of another world.

When I was well again, the Shaughnessy showed me how to build a thatched lean-to that would withstand the rain.

"There may be hurricanes, Luiz," he said to me. "This *barraca* will be blown down. Will you remember how to build another?"

"*Sim*," I said. "I shall remember. You will show me."

"No, Luiz. I shall not be here. You must remember."

He told me many things, over and over again, very patiently. How to find the shellfish on the rocks when the tide was out, how to trap fish in the stream, what fruit I might eat and what I must never touch. It was not easy for me. When I tried to remember too much it made my head hurt.

I explored the island, coming back to tell him all I had found. At first I was sure that when I had crossed the high hills and stood upon their peaks I would see the beautiful slopes of Rio shining across the water. My heart sank when I stood for the first time upon the heights and saw only more ocean, empty, heaving between me and the horizon.

But I soon forgot again, and Rio and the past faded from my mind. I found the pool cupped high in a hollow of the crags, where clear sweet water bubbled up in the shadow of the trees and the streamlet dropped away in a series of pools and falls toward the levels far below. I found groves of pale trees with leaves like streaming hair, rustling with the noise of the waterfall. I found no people here, and yet I felt always that there were watchers among the leaves, and it seemed to me that laughter sounded sometimes behind me, smothered when I turned my head.

When I told the Shaughnessy this he smiled at me.

"I've told you too many tales," he said. "But if anyone could see them, I think it would be you, Luiz."

"*Sim, s'nhor*," I said. "Tell me again of the forest-women. Could they be here, do you think, *s'nhor*?"

He let sand trickle through his fingers, watching it as if the fall of sand had some meaning to his mind that I could not fathom.

"Ah, well," he said, "they might be. They like the olive groves of Greece best, and the tall trees on Olympus. But every mountain has its oread. Here, too, perhaps. The Little People left Ireland years ago and for all I know the oreads have fled from civilization too, and found such places as this to put them in mind of home...

"There was one who turned into a fountain once, long ago. I saw that fountain in Greece. I drank from it. There must have been a sort of magic in the waters, for I always went back to Greece after that. I'd leave, but I couldn't stay long away." He smiled at me. "Maybe now, because I can't go back again, the oreads have come to me here."

I looked hard at him to see if he meant what he said, but he shook his head and smiled again. "I think they haven't come for me. Maybe for you, Luiz. Belief is what they want. If you believe, perhaps you'll really see them. I'd be the last man to deny a thing like that. You'll need something like them to keep you company, my friend—afterward." And he trickled sand through his fingers again, watching it fall with a look upon his face I did not understand.

The night came swiftly on that island. It was a lovely place. The Shaughnessy said islands have a magic all their own, for they are the place where earth and ocean meet. We used to lie on the shore watching the fire that burned upon the edges of the waves lap up the beach and breathe away again, and the Shaughnessy told me many tales. His voice was growing weaker, and he did not trouble so much any more to test my memory for the lessons he had taught. But he spoke of ancient magic, and more and more in these last days, his mind turned back to the wonders of the country called Ireland.

He told me of the little green people with their lanterns low down among the ferns. He told me of the *unicórnio*, swift as the swiftest bird, a magical stag with one horn upon its forehead as long as the shaft of a spear and as sharp as whatever is sharpest. And he told me of Pan, goat-footed, moving through the woodland with laughter running before him and panic behind, the same panic terror which my language and the Shaughnessy's get from his name. *Pânico*, we Brazilians call it.

One evening he called to me and held up a wooden cross. "Luiz, look at this," he said. I saw that upon the arms of the cross he had made deep carvings with his knife. "This is my name," he told me. "If anyone ever comes here asking for me, you must show them this cross."

I looked at it closely. I knew what he meant about the name—it is that sort of enchantment in which markings can speak with a voice too tiny for the ears to hear. I am *o Bobo* and I never learned to read, so that I do not understand how this may be done.

"Some day," the Shaughnessy went on, "I think someone will come. My people at home may not be satisfied with whatever story Captain Stryker invents for them. Or a drunken sailor may talk. If they do find this island, Luiz, I want this cross above my grave to tell them who I was. And for another reason," he said thoughtfully. "For another reason too. But that need not worry you, *meu amigo*."

He told me where to dig the bed for him. He did not tell me to put in the leaves and the flowers. I thought of that myself, three days later, when the time came...

Because he had wished it, I put him in the earth. I did not like doing it. But in a way I feared not to carry out his commands, for the daemon of the Shaughnessy still hovered above him, very bright, very bright—so bright I could not look it in the face. I thought there was music coming from it, but I could not be sure.

I put the flowers over him and then the earth. There was more to go back in the grave than I had taken out, so I made a mound above him, as long as the Shaughnessy was long, and I drove in the stake of the wooden cross, above where his head was, as he had told me. Then for a moment I laid my ear to the markings to see if I could hear what they were saying, for it seemed to me that the sound of his name, whispered to me by the marks his hands had made, would lighten my loneliness a little. But I heard nothing.

When I looked up, I saw his daemon glow like the sun at noon, a light so bright I could not bear it upon my eyes. I put my hands before them. When I took them down again, there was no daemon.

You will not believe me when I tell you this, *padre*, but in that moment the—the feel of the island changed. All the leaves, I think, turned the other way on the trees, once, with a rustle like one vast syllable whispered for that time only, and never again.

I think I know what the syllable was. Perhaps I will tell you, later—if you let me.

And the island breathed. It was like a man who has held his breath for a long while, in fear or pain, and let it run out deeply when the fear or the pain departed.

I did not know, then, what it was. But I thought it would go up the steep rocks to the pool, because I wanted a place that would not remind me of the Shaughnessy. So I climbed the crags among the hanging trees. And it seemed to me that I heard laughter when the wind rustled among them. Once I saw what I thought must be a *ninfa*, brown and green in the forest. But she was too shy. I turned my head, and the brown and green stilled into the bark and foliage of the tree.

When I came to the pool, the unicorn was drinking. He was very beautiful, whiter than foam, whiter than cloud, and his mane lay upon his great shoulders like spray upon the shoulder of a wave. The tip of his long, spiralled horn just touched the water as he drank, so that the ripples ran outward in circles all around it. He tossed his head when he scented me, and I saw the glittering diamonds of the water sparkling from his velvet muzzle. He had eyes as green as a pool with leaves reflecting in it, and a spot of bright gold in the centre of each eye.

Very slowly, with the greatest stateliness, he turned from the water and moved away into the forest. I know I heard a singing where he disappeared.

I was still *o Bobo* then. I drank where he had drunk, thinking there was a strange, sweet taste to the water now, and then I went down to the *barraca* on the beach, for I had forgotten already and thought perhaps the Shaughnessy might be there...

Night came, and I slept. Dawn came, and I woke again. I bathed in the ocean. I gathered shellfish and fruit, and drank of the little stream that fell from the mountain pool. And as I leaned to drink, two white dripping arms rose up to clasp my neck, and a mouth as wet and cold as the water pressed mine. It was the kiss of acceptance.

After that the *ninfas* of the island no longer hid their faces from me.

My hair and beard grew long. My garments tore upon the bushes and became the rags you see now. I did not care. It did not matter. It was not my face they saw. They saw my simpleness. And I was one with the *ninfas* and the others.

The oread of the mountain came out to me often, beside the pool where the unicorn came to drink. She was wise and strange, being immortal. The eyes slanted upward in her head, and her hair was a shower of green leaves blowing always backward in a wind that moved about her when no other breezes blew. She used to sit beside the pool in the hot, still afternoons, the unicorn lying beside her and her brown fingers combing out his silver mane. Her wise slanting eyes, the colour of shadows in the forest, and his round green eyes the colour of the pool, with the flecks of gold in each, used to watch me as we talked.

The oread told me many things. Many things I could never tell you, *padre*. But it was as the Shaughnessy had guessed. Because I believed, they were glad of my presence there. While the Shaughnessy lived, they could not come out into the plane of being, but they watched from the other side... They had been afraid. But they were afraid no longer.

For many years they have been homeless now, blowing about the world in search of some spot of land where no disbelief dwells, and where one other thing has not taken footing... They told me of the isles of Greece, with love and longing upon their tongues, and it seemed to me that I heard the Shaughnessy speak again in their words.

They told me of the One I had not yet seen, or more than glimpsed. That happened when I chanced to pass near the Shaughnessy's grave in the dimness of the evening, and I saw the cross that bore his name had fallen. I took it up and held it to my ear again, hoping the tiny voices of the markings would whisper. But that is a mystery which has never been given me.

I saw the—the One—loitering by that grave. But when I put up the cross, he went away, slowly, sauntering into the dark woods, and a thin piping floated back to me from the spot where he had vanished.

Perhaps the One did not care for my presence there. The others welcomed me. It was not often any more, they said, that men like me were free to move among them. Since the hour of their banishment, they told me, and wept when they spoke of that hour, there had been too few among mankind who really knew them.

I asked about the banishment, and they said that it had happened long ago, very long ago. A great star had stood still in the sky over a stable in a town whose name I do not know. Once I knew it. I do not remember now. It was a town with a beautiful name.

The skies opened and there was singing in the heavens, and after that the gods of Greece had to flee. They have been fleeing ever since.

They were glad I had come to join them. And I was doubly glad. For the first time since my grandmother died, I knew I was not alone. Even the Shaughnessy had not been as close to me as these *ninfas* were. For the Shaughnessy had a daemon. The *ninfas* are immortal, but they have no souls. That, I think, is why they welcomed me so warmly. We without souls are glad of companionship among others of our kind. There is a loneliness among our kind that can only be assuaged by huddling together. The *ninfas* knew it, who must live forever, and I shared it with them, who may die before this night is over.

Well, it was good to live upon the island. The days and the months went by beautifully, full of clear colours and the smell of the sea and the stars at night as bright as lanterns just above us. I even grew less *Bobo*, because the *ninfas* spoke wisdom of a kind I never heard among men. They were good months.

And then, one day, Jonah Stryker came back to the island.

You know, *padre*, why he came. The Shaughnessy in his wisdom had guessed that in Ireland men of the Shaughnessy's family might ask questions of Captain Stryker—questions the captain could not answer. But it had not been guessed that the captain might return to the island, swiftly, before the Shaughnessy's people could discover the truth, with the thought in his evil mind of wiping out all traces of the two he had left to die.

I was sitting on the shore that day, listening to the songs of two *ninfas* of the nereid kind as they lay in the edge of the surf, with the waves breaking over them when the water lapped up the slopes of sand. They were swaying their beautiful rainbow coloured fish-bodies as they sang, and I heard the whisper of the surf in their voices, and the long rhythms of the undersea.

But suddenly there came a break in their song, and I saw upon one face before me, and then the other, a look of terror come. The green blood in their veins sank back with fear, and they looked at me, white with pallor and strangely transparent, as if they had halfway ceased to be. With one motion they turned their heads and stared out to sea.

I stared too. I think the first thing I saw was that flash of burning crimson, far out over the waves. And my heart quivered within me like a dog that fears the whip. I knew that beautiful, terrible colour too well.

It was only then that I saw the *Dancing Martha*, lying at anchor beyond a ridge of rock. Between the ship and the shore a small boat rocked upon the waves, light flashing from oar-blades as the one man in the boat bent and rose and bent to his work. Above him, hanging like a crimson cloud, the terrible scarlet glowed.

When I looked back, the *ninfas* had vanished. Whether they slid back into the sea, or whether they melted away into nothingness before me I shall never know now. I did not see them again.

I went back a little way into the forest, and watched from among the trees. No dryads spoke to me, but I could hear their quick breathing and the leaves trembled all about me I could not look at the scarlet daemon coming nearer and nearer over the blue water, but I could not look away long, either. It was so beautiful and so evil.

The captain was alone in the boat. I was not quite so *Bobo* then and I understood why. He beached the boat and climbed up the slope of sand, the daemon swaying behind him like a crimson shadow. I could see its blind eyes and the beautiful, quiet face shut up with bliss because of the thing the captain had come to do. He was carrying in his hand a long shining pistol, and he walked carefully, looking to left and right. His face was anxious, and his mouth had grown more cruel in the months since I saw him last.

I was sorry for him, but I was very frightened, too. I knew he meant to kill whomever he found alive upon the island, so that no tongue could tell the Shaughnessy's people of his wicked deed.

He found my thatched *barraca* at the edge of the shore and kicked it to pieces with his heavy boots. Then he went on until he saw the long mound above the Shaughnessy's bed, with the cross standing where his head lay. He bent over the cross, and the markings upon it spoke to him as they would never speak to me. I heard nothing, but he heard and knew. He put out his hand and pulled up the cross from the Shaughnessy's grave.

Then he went to the ruins of my *barraca* and to the embers of the fire I kept smouldering there. He broke the cross upon his knee and fed the pieces into the hot coals. The wood was dry. I saw it catch flame and burn. I saw, too, the faint stirring of wind that sprang up with the flames, and I heard the sighing that ran through the trees around me. Now there was nothing here to tell the searchers who might come afterward that the Shaughnessy lay in the island earth. Nothing—except myself.

He saw my footprints around the ruined *barraca*. He stooped to look. When he rose again and peered around the shore and forest, I could see his eyes shine, and it was the daemon who looked out of them, not the man.

Following my tracks, he began to move slowly toward the forest where I was hiding.

Then I was very frightened. I rose and fled through the trees, and I heard the dryads whimpering about me as I ran. They drew back their boughs to let me pass and swept them back after me to bar the way. I ran and ran, upward among the rocks, until I came to the pool of the unicorn, and the oread of the mountain stood there waiting for me, her arm across the unicorn's neck.

There was a rising wind upon the island. The leaves threshed and talked among themselves, and the oread's leafy hair blew backward from her face with its wise slanting eyes. The unicorn's silver mane tossed in that wind and the water ruffled in the pool.

"There is trouble coming, Luiz," the oread told me.

"The daemon. I know." I nodded to her, and then blinked, because it seemed to me that she and the unicorn, like the sea *ninfas*, were growing so pale I could see the trees behind them through their bodies. But perhaps that was because the scarlet of the daemon had hurt my eyes.

"There is a man with a soul again upon our island," the oread said. "A man who does not believe. Perhaps we will have to go, Luiz."

"The Shaughnessy had a daemon too," I told her. "Yet you were here before his daemon left him to the earth. Why must you go now?"

"His was a good daemon. Even so, we were not fully here while he lived. You must remember, Luiz, that hour I told you of when a star stood above a stable where a child lay, and all our power went from us. Where the souls of men dwell, we cannot stay. This new man has brought a very evil soul with him. It frightens us. Yet since he had burned the cross, perhaps the Master can fight..."

"The Master?" I asked.

"The One we serve. The One you serve, Luiz. The One I think the Shaughnessy served, though he did not know it. The Lord of the opened eyes and the far places. He could not come until the Sign was taken down. Once you had a glimpse of him, when the Sign fell by accident from the grave, but perhaps you have forgotten that."

"I have not forgotten. I am not so *Bobo* now."

She smiled at me, and I could see the tree behind her through the smile.

"Then perhaps you can help the Master when the time comes. We cannot help. We are too weak already, because of the presence of the unbeliever, the man with the daemon. See?" She touched my hand, and I felt not the firm, soft brush of fingers but only a coolness like mist blowing across my skin.

"Perhaps the Master can fight him," the oread said, and her voice was very faint, like a voice from far away, though she spoke from so near to me. "I do not know about that. We must go, Luiz. We may not meet again. Good-bye, *caro bobo*, while I can still say good-bye…" The last of it was faint as the hushing of the leaves, and the oread and the unicorn together looked like smoke blowing from a campfire across the glade.

The knowledge of my loneliness came over me then more painfully than I had felt it since that hour when I first looked upon the captain's daemon and knew at last what my own sorrow was. But I had no time to grieve, for there was a sudden frightened whispering among the leaves behind me, and then the crackle of feet in boots, and then a flicker of terrible crimson among the trees.

I ran. I did not know where I ran. I heard the dryads crying, so it must have been among trees. But at last I came out upon the shore again and I saw the Shaughnessy's long grave without a cross above it. And I stopped short, and a thrill of terror went through me. For there was a Something that crouched upon the grave.

The fear in me then was a new thing. A monstrous, dim fear that moves like a cloud about the Master. I knew he meant me no harm, but the fear was heavy upon me, making my head spin with panic. *Pânico…*

The Master rose upon the grave, and he stamped his goat-hoofed foot twice and set the pipes to his bearded lips. I heard a thin, strange wailing music that made the blood chill inside me. And at the first sound of it there came again what I had heard once before upon the island.

The leaves upon all the trees turned over once, with a great single whispering of one syllable. The syllable was the Master's name. I fled from it in the *pânico* all men have felt who hear that name pronounced. I fled to the edge of the beach, and I could flee no farther. So I crouched behind a hillock of rock on the wet sand, and watched what came after me from the trees.

It was the captain, with his daemon swaying like smoke above his head. He carried the long pistol ready, and his eyes moved from left to right along the beach, seeking like a wild beast for his quarry.

He saw the Master, standing upon the Shaughnessy's grave.

I saw how he stopped, rigid, like a man of stone. The daemon swayed forward above his head, he stopped so suddenly. I saw how he stared. And such was his disbelief, that for an instant I thought even the outlines of the Master grew hazy. There is great power in the men with souls.

I stood up behind my rock. I cried above the noises of the surf, "Master—Great Pan—I believe!"

He heard me. He tossed his horned head and his bulk was solid again. He set the pipes to his lips.

Captain Stryker whirled when he heard me. The long pistol swung up and there was a flash and a roar, and something went by me with a whine of anger. It did not touch me.

Then the music of the pipes began. A terrible music, thin and high, like the ringing in the ears that has no source. It seized the captain as if with thin, strong fingers, making him turn back to the sound. He stood rigid again, staring, straining. The daemon above him turned uneasily from side to side, like a snake swaying.

Then Captain Stryker ran. I saw the sand fly up from under his boots as he fled southward along the shore. His daemon went after him, a red shadow with its eyes still closed, and after them both went Pan, moving delicately on the goat-hoofs, the pipes to his lips and his horns shining golden in the sun.

And that midday terror I think was greater than any terror that can stalk a man by dark.

I waited beside my rock. The sea was empty behind me except for the *Dancing Martha* waiting the captain's orders at its anchor. But no *ninfas* came in on the foam to keep me company; no heads rose wreathed with seaweed out of the water. The sea was empty and the island was empty too, except for a man and a daemon and the Piper who followed at their heels.

Myself I do not count. I have no soul.

It was nearly dark when they came back along the beach. I think the Piper had hunted them clear around the island, going slowly on his delicate hoofs, never hurrying, never faltering, and that dreadful thin music always in the captain's ears.

I saw the captain's face when he came back in the twilight. It was an old man's face, haggard, white, with deep lines in it and eyes as wild as Pan's. His clothing was torn to ribbons and his hands bled, but he still held the pistol and the red daemon still hung swaying above him.

I think the captain did not know that he had come back to his starting place. By that time, all places must have looked alike to him. He came wavering toward me blindly. I rose up behind my rock.

When he saw me he lifted the pistol again and gasped some Yankee words. He was a strong man. Captain Stryker. With all he had endured in that long chase, he still had the power to remember he must kill me. I did not think he had reloaded the pistol, and I stood up facing him across the sand.

Behind him Pan's pipes shrilled a warning, but the Master did not draw nearer to come between us. The red daemon swayed at the captain's back, and I knew why Pan did not come to my aid. Those who lost their power when the Child was born can never lay hands upon men who possess a soul. Even a soul as evil as the captain's stood like a rock between him and the touch of Pan. Only the pipes could reach a human's ears, but there was that in the sound of the pipes which did all Pan needed to do.

It could not save me. I heard the captain laugh, without breath, a strange, hoarse sound, and I saw the lightning dazzle from the pistol's mouth. The crash it made was like a blow that struck me here, in the chest. I almost fell. That blow was heavy, but I scarcely noticed it then. There was too much to do.

The captain was laughing, and I thought of the Shaughnessy, and I stumbled forward and took the pistol by its hot muzzle with my hand. I am strong. I tore it from the captain's fist and he stood there gaping at me, not believing anything he saw. He breathed in dreadful, deep gasps, and I found I was gasping too, but I did not know why just then.

The captain's eyes met mine, and I think he saw that even now I had no hate for him—only pity. For the man behind the eyes vanished and the crimson daemon of his rage looked out, because I dared to feel sorrow for him. I looked into the eyes that were not his, but the eyes behind the closed lids of the beautiful, blind face above him. It I hated, not him. And it was it I struck. I lifted the pistol and smashed it into the captain's face.

I was not very clear in my head just then. I struck the daemon with my blow, but it was the captain who reeled backward three steps and then fell. I am very strong. One blow was all I needed.

For a moment there was no sound in all the island. Even the waves kept their peace. The captain shuddered and gave one sigh, like that of a man who comes back to living reluctantly. He got his hands beneath him and rose upon them, peering at me through the hair that had fallen across his forehead. He was snarling like an animal.

I do not know what he intended then. I think he would have fought me until one of us was dead. But above him just then I saw the daemon stir. It was the first time I had ever seen it move except in answer to the captain's motion. All his life it had followed him, blind, silent, a shadow that echoed his gait and gestures. Now for the first time it did not obey him.

Now it rose up to a great, shining height above his head, and its colour was suddenly very deep, very bright and deep, a blinding thing that hung above him too hot in colour to look at. Over the beautiful blind face a look of triumph came. I saw ecstasy dawn over that face in all its glory and its evil.

I knew that this was the hour of the daemon.

Some knowledge deeper than any wisdom warned me to cover my eyes. For I saw its lids flicker, and I knew it would not be good to watch when that terrible gaze looked out at last upon a world it had never seen except through the captain's eyes.

I fell to my knees and covered my face. And the captain, seeing that, must have known at long last what it was I saw behind him. I think now that in the hour of a man's death, he knows. I think in that last moment he knows, and turns, and for the first time and the last, looks his daemon in the face.

I did not see him do it. I did not see anything. But I heard a great, resonant cry, like the mighty music that beats through paradise, a cry full of triumph and thanksgiving, and joy at the end of a long, long, weary road. There was mirth in it, and beauty, and all the evil the mind can compass.

Then fire glowed through my fingers and through my eyelids and into my brain. I could not shut it out. I did not even need to lift my head to see, for that sight would have blazed through my very bones.

I saw the daemon fall upon its master.

The captain sprang to his feet with a howl like a beast's howl, no mind or soul in it. He threw back his head and his arms went up to beat that swooping, beautiful, crimson thing away.

No flesh could oppose it. This was its hour. What sets that hour I do not know, but the daemon knew, and nothing could stop it now.

I saw the flaming thing descend upon the captain like a falling star. Through his defending arms it swept, and through his flesh and his bones and into the hollows where the soul dwells.

He stood for an instant transfixed, motionless, glowing with that bath of crimson light. Then I saw the crimson begin to shine *through* him, so that the shadows of his bones stood out upon the skin. And then fire shot up, wreathing from his eyes and mouth and nostrils. He was a lantern of flesh for that fire of the burning spirit. But he was a lantern that is consumed by the flame it carries...

When the colour became too bright for the eyes to bear it, I tried to turn away. I could not. The pain in my chest was too great. I thought of the Shaughnessy in that moment, who knew, too, what pain in the chest was like. I think that was the first moment when it came to me that, like the Shaughnessy, I too was going to die.

Before my eyes, the captain burned in the fire of his daemon, burned and burned, his living eyes looking out at me through the crimson glory, and the laughter of the daemon very sweet above the sound of the whining flame. I could not watch and I could not turn away.

But at last the whine began to die. Then the laughter roared out in one great peal of triumph, and the beautiful crimson colour, so dreadfully more crimson than blood, flared in a great burst of light that turned to blackness against my eyeballs.

When I could see again, the captain's body lay flat upon the sand. I know death when I see it. He was not burned at all. He looked as any dead man looks, flat and silent. It was his soul I had watched burning, not his body.

The daemon had gone back again to its own place. I knew that, for I could feel my aloneness on the island.

The Others had gone too. The presence of that fiery daemon was more, in the end, than their power could endure. Perhaps they shun an evil soul more fearfully than a good one, knowing themselves nothing of good and evil, but fearing what they do not understand.

You know, *padre*, what came after. The men from the *Dancing Martha* took their captain away next morning. They were frightened of the island. They looked for that which had killed him, but they did not look far, and I hid in the empty forest until they went away.

I do not remember their going. There was a burning in my chest, and this blood I breathe out ran from time to time, as it does now. I do not like the sight of it. Blood is a beautiful colour, but it reminds me of too much that was beautiful also, and much redder...

Then you came, *padre*. I do not know how long thereafter. I know the Shaughnessy's people brought you with their ship, to find him or his grave. You know now. And I am glad you came. It is good to have a man like you beside me at this time. I wish I had a daemon of my own, to grow very bright and vanish when I die, but that is not for *o Bobo* and I am used to that kind of loneliness.

I would not live, you see, now that the *ninfas* are gone. To be with them was good, and we comforted one another in our loneliness but, *padre*, I will tell you this much. It was a chilly comfort we gave each other, at the best. I am a man, though *bobo*, and I know. They are *ninfas* and will never guess how warm and wonderful it must be to own a soul. I would not tell them if I could. I was sorry for the *ninfas*, *padre*. They are, you see, immortal.

As for me, I will forget loneliness in a little while. I will forget everything. I would not want to be a *ninfa* and live forever.

There is one behind you, *padre*. It is very bright. It watches me across your shoulder, and its eyes are wise and sad. No, daemon, this is no time for sadness. Be sorry for the *ninfas*, daemon, and for men like him who burned upon this beach. But not for me. I am well content.

I will go now.

1954

MORE THAN SHADOW

Dorothy Quick

Dorothy Quick (1896–1962) seems to be unfairly forgotten amongst authors in *Weird Tales* even though she was the most prolific female contributor if you also count poetry—25 poems and 15 stories. She had sold both stories and poetry to other magazines before her debut in *Weird Tales* in the January 1934 issue with the poem "Candles". She was already known to the editor Farnsworth Wright who had bought stories from her for the magazine's short-lived companion title *Oriental Stories*, starting with "Scented Gardens" (Spring 1932).

Quick's desire to write was encouraged by no less than the author Mark Twain whom she met on a steamship returning from England in 1907 when she was only ten. They became firm friends through correspondence though Twain died three years later. Towards the end of her life Quick wrote a tribute to Twain, *Enchantment: A Little Girl's Friendship with Mark Twain* (1961). She would go on to appear in many magazines and produce several mystery novels.

Her first story in *Weird Tales* was "The Horror in the Studio" (June 1935) which not only led the issue but was illustrated on the cover by Margaret Brundage. It is, alas, a rather mundane story of spirit possession on the set of an historical movie in Hollywood. Her interest in the Middle Ages re-emerged in "The Lost Door" (October 1936) a more atmospheric story in which a man inherits a French chateau where his presence invokes an ancient haunting. Quick returned to 17th-century France in "Blue and Silver Brocade" (October 1939), the start of a trilogy she wrote for John W. Campbell's new magazine, *Unknown*, about a quilt which can take people back in time. Under Campbell's guidance Quick developed her writing skills and shifted from stories written to order, to those where the poet within her took over. In "Edge of the Cliff" (March 1941) a girl who is the victim of domestic abuse is considering suicide and a stranger helps her decide. Throughout her stories she generates the belief that there is a pathway to another life if only you could find the key.

In selecting a story for this volume I was spoiled for choice but settled on this simple tale of how legends can impact upon the present.

The third time it happened she was aware of its strangeness. Up till then it hadn't mattered or seemed important, but the third time made her realize that something unusual was taking place and that there was cause for alarm.

She had just finished lunch and thought the philodendrons on either side of the mantelpiece needed watering. So, because she had gotten into the habit of saving water during the shortage, she took her glass, which was as full as when the maid had filled it, and started towards the fireplace. Halfway there the glass, for no reason which she could account, slipped from her hand.

The water spilled on the delft blue rug and rapidly began to coagulate into a shape as the glass rolled off towards the fireplace.

She watched the wet shape on the rug; "It *is* a little dog," she half whispered.

Almost as though an artist had painted it, there on the rug was the outline of a dog, a tiny dog with puffy, curly hair and, due to the way the water had absorbed and the wet and dry patches, it had a most beguiling expression. It was so real that she had to restrain herself from bending over to pick it up.

It looked exactly like a little dog waiting to be lifted into its mistress's arms. It had dimension and a definite personality. It seemed more than a shadow or a wet spot.

Just then Mona remembered that this had happened before—twice.

The first time had been at the table—here in the dining room. Her youngest daughter, aged three, had upset her glass of milk, purposely Mona suspected, knowing her offspring didn't like the bounty of the cow. She was just about to utter a reprimand when the child, Carol, had cried out, "Look, Mummy, it's a little dog."

The milk had run across the table as fluids do and settled in front of Mona's place. The shape of the damp place on the linen tablecloth was definitely that of a little dog.

The same little dog at which she was looking now, Mona thought and shuddered.

That day at the table she had laughed. It had seemed funny. Because the spilled milk had settled in the form of a little dog Carol had escaped the scolding and Mona had mopped up the milk reluctantly because the little dog shape was so cunning.

But she forgot about it almost immediately.

Three days later, a rainy Sunday afternoon it was, she was sitting in the living room with her husband, Hal; the three children, Carol, Meg and Harry, Jr. were playing nearby. Ellen, the maid, brought the tea. Mona gave the two older children a very weak version and Carol had milk in her cup. Then she handed Hal his stronger share. He started with it towards his favourite chair. The cup, which had seemed firm on its saucer, could not have been, for it bounced off, spilling the tea on the beige carpet.

For an instant there was silence. Then Carol came running over from the other side of the room. "Little dog, little dog," she exclaimed, pointing to the wet spot.

Mona stared. It was true. There was the outline of a little dog, curly-haired, with an uplifted paw.

Her husband laughed, "You're right, Carol. It *is* a little dog, and it's cute too. I'd like a little dog like that around the house."

Carol clapped her hands, "Daddy, get one for Carol."

"Maybe," Hal nodded, "if we could find an attractive one like that."

The other two children were there by then, exclaiming, saying they'd like a dog too.

Hal got another cup of tea and reached his favourite chair with it safely before he delivered the pronouncement, "You can't all have dogs. If you'll just settle for a community animal—"

By the time the argument was over the carpet had dried and Mona forgot the whole business as quickly as the children did. But now here was the dog again, and more real than ever.

Tiny, curly-haired, with a front paw elevated appealingly, a sharp, pointed nose, utterly beguiling. "It must be a poodle," Mona thought, "a very small poodle. But why does it keep happening? Is it an omen, does it mean we ought to have a dog?"

It was probably a trick of wind ruffling the rug, but it seemed as though the paw was further outthrust and the outline of the little creature quivered with eagerness.

Ellen came into the dining room. Mona called her, pointed to the spot. "What does that look like?" she asked.

The girl giggled, "Why, for all the world like a little dog, the kind the leprechauns keep. 'Tis said in Ireland the little people ride them on moonlight nights."

"Where do they go?" Mona was surprised at herself for putting the question.

"Now that we do not be asking." Ellen lapsed into the brogue she'd brought with her two years ago when she came over to visit her Aunt Mary who cooked for Mr. and Mrs. Hal Devitt. "But," she dropped her voice as though afraid of being overheard, "some say the little dogs take them over the mountain to the land of youth."

A quotation from Yeats leaped into Mona's mind.

Where nobody gets old and godly and grave
Where nobody gets old and crafty and wise
Where nobody gets old and bitter of tongue
And she is still there, busied with a dance,
Deep in the dewy shadow of a wood
Or where stars walk upon the mountainside.

The words had always appealed to Mona, ever since she had played the girl in the play the graduating class had done at school, "The Land of Heart's Desire." The lines had stuck in her mind and now they were echoing over and over, "Deep in the dewy shadows of a wood, or where stars walk upon a mountaintop."

And the little dog could take you there—over the mountaintop to the land of heart's desire where—what was it the child in the play had said? "Could make you ride upon the winds, run on the top of the dishevelled tide, and dance upon the mountains like a flame." Her mind went back to the play. There had been more. She remembered the child's speech:

You shall go with me, newly married bride
And gaze upon a merrier multitude.

Then there had been Irish names, Nuala, Ardoe the wise, Feacra and Finvarra,

And their land of Heart's Desire
Where beauty has no ebb, decay, no flood,
But joy is wisdom. Time an endless-song.

The little dog could take you to that!

Mona caught herself up sharply. The coincidence of the dog's outline happening three times and Ellen's old-world leprechauns with their dogs to ride had woven a spell over her—that and Yeats' magic poetry. But she mustn't be a dreamer as she had been in the part of Maire which she had acted in the play—and never forgotten. She could remember now how when she had sunk to the floor, playing dead, the child having stolen her soul away. She had felt that it would have been worth it to find that land where people were forever young, never to grow old, "to dance upon the mountains like a flame". It would have been worth losing your soul, she had thought.

Then the curtain had fallen and the child was her schoolmate, Meg, again, and she was Mona, alive and hoping Hal had liked her performance.

He had; that very night he had proposed. "I shouldn't yet. I've got three more years of college, but, after seeing you so ethereal, so beautiful, and so far away, I had to be sure of you. Will you marry me, Mona, when I can support you?"

She would, and they had been married before he had taken his place in his father's law office. They had been very happy. Their life had been full. They loved each other, had three wonderful children, she had wanted nothing. Yet why did the outline, something more than a shadow, of a dog, make her remember and long for the Land of Heart's Desire? This was nonsense. She mustn't even think of it any more. She turned to Ellen. "Get a cloth," she commanded and was ashamed at the edgy tone in her voice, "and mop it up."

"Yes ma'm," said Ellen, and then in a sharp tone of surprise, "But it's all dry—the little dog has gone."

A week after that the dog came. It was a poodle and Carol found it down by the garden gate. She and Meg came running to Mona, the little bunch of black fluff clasped tightly in Meg's arms.

Out of the chorus of exclamations and requests of "Can we keep him?" Mona gathered that the dog had been sitting by the gate, that it had greeted the children like a long-lost friend, that they already adored it. There was no sign of a collar or licence tag. It hadn't been clipped, and it was adorable. The minute they put it down it capered up to Mona, turned several circles in front of her and then put up one paw, "Like the dog on the rug" Mona thought. She felt strange about the dog, but she had to admit it was captivating. When it jumped up in her arms and cuddled its head against her neck she was completely won over.

"Yes. You can keep it if no one claims it," she said, absurdly conscious of the appeal of the little creature. She was as desirous as the children to have the little dog, but common sense warned her not to let them count too much on having it. "But I'm sure that it has an owner. It's such a beautiful dog," she caressed the little head, "that it must belong to someone. It's probably lost—run away maybe. They might advertise for it in the paper—"

"We don't have to read the papers," Meg suggested with practicality.

"That wouldn't be honest," Mona told them. "We will watch out. In the meantime you can play with him. Suppose you get him some milk, Harry."

Harry obliged. Mona reluctantly put the little dog down. It drank a little, then cavorted about, jumping up on the children, licking their hands. When it came to Carol it leaped into her lap and, putting its paws on her shoulders, seemed to be whispering into her ear.

"Did you ever see anything so cute?" Meg asked.

Mona was conscious of a twinge of jealousy. She had loved the feeling of the tiny head nestling close to her face. She shoved her feeling into the back of her consciousness and agreed that the little dog was cute.

So did Hal and Ellen. They all hoped that no one would claim the tiny poodle. It was so gay, such good company. It seemed to know just what their mood was and fit into it.

"I've always heard poodles were smart," Hal said after it had been with them two days, "but I swear this one is almost human."

With that the little dog climbed up his leg and licked the man's big hand as though it were saying "thank you". "See what I mean?" boomed Hal, patting the small head. "I certainly hope no one comes for it."

No one did.

After a week they felt safe; and as though "Jet," so called for his beady, black eyes and "because he was jettisoned" Hal added, and then had to explain to the children what the word meant.

They all, except Ellen, adored the poodle. Ellen kept insisting there was something strange about him. The poodle seemed to like them all equally well. To Mona there was something specially appealing about the little dog. She actually reached the point where she tried to get him off to herself, carrying him into her room to be with her while she napped—but, whether by design or not, he always barked, or made some noise that brought the children running.

Baby Carol would put up her three-year-old hands to the bed. "Yet" she would call, "Yet," her tongue not able to master the intricacies of the letter J.

Then Mona would have to lift the little thing down, and off he would go with the children scampering with all the abandon of youth—so oddly at variance with the wise look in his shoe-button eyes.

"It's that that makes me love him so," Mona thought, "that queer mixture of youth and wisdom. It's amazing what a difference a dog makes, in a house."

And it really was. The children never needed to be amused now. They had Jet. If they got restless he brought his ball, dropped it in Meg or Harry's lap for them to throw. He retrieved without being taught. Even Hal was forced into the game and Mona—no matter how busy the children were there was always some time during the day when the dog cuddled up into her neck as he had done the first day he came.

Mona found herself looking forward to it almost as a ritual. "It's ridiculous," she scolded herself, "but when he's there I seem to have visions of a never-never land, Yeats' Land of Heart's Desire. I suppose because I thought of the play with all that nonsense of Ellen's when he first came and its association of ideas. But it's uncanny, really."

Finally she told Hal about it. "I think I'm going mad. I keep wishing he'd grow life-size and I could ride away on his back. I see visions in which I—sober, sedate Mona—dance upon the mountains like a flame. Do you think I'm crazy?"

Hal looked at his pretty wife. "You're anything but sedate, Mona. You know you're lovely and you're not nuts either. There's something about that animal—you know, when he licks my hand it feels like water touching my skin. I think of the rushing waters of a bright brook with motes dancing in the sunlight, and I feel like chucking business and going fishing. Pretty silly the end of April."

"Well, you could go to Florida," Mona said seriously.

"Now don't you go encouraging me. I don't have a vacation till August! I just wanted to explain the dog's effect on me." He patted Mona's shoulder. "You see, dear, it's because the little dog is so young, so blithe and gay he releases our inhibitions. It's good for us."

Mona wasn't convinced. "The children are young, blithe and gay. They don't make me want to 'dance on the mountain like a flame.'"

Hal threw back his head and laughed. "That would be pretty difficult to do. Have you ever seen a flame dance on a mountain? These poetic imageries are all right until you break them down. Then what have you—nothing, nothing at all."

He was right of course. A flame could dance in a fireplace but on a mountain it would be, as Hal said, nothing, or a forest fire. She joined in her husband's laughter and forgot the whole business when he suggested they might go out dancing.

They hadn't done that for a long time. It would be fun indeed. "I'll go nap," she told him, "so I'll look my best."

"You always do." He kissed her as he had when they were engaged. Mona forgot everything but the moment.

The poodle was on her bed waiting for her—wagging its pom-pom tail in an utter abandon of ecstasy, cavorting up and down regardless of her blue satin bedspread. Mona wondered idly how he'd gotten up on the high bed. He was such a little thing. "Jet," she said in the manner proverbial to all dog lovers, "Good Jet" and patted the tiny head.

As she took off her dress the poodle watched her gravely. He was like a little old woman sitting on the end of the bed—or a gnome. She slipped into a wrapper, a filmy thing of lace and nylon and curled up on the bed. In two seconds flat he was beside her, nestled into the curve of her shoulder, his head close to her cheek.

For once the children didn't come and she lay there strangely content, her fingers caressing the soft wool of Jet's pompadour.

Presently she began to hear a weird music, soft and slow, unlike any she had ever heard before, a line from a song came to her—"Strange Music of the Spheres." Someone must be playing a radio, she thought, and yet no radio had ever produced music like this, yet in some odd way it seemed mixed up with the poodle's rhythmic breathing and the Yeats' play came back into her mind. *The Land of Heart's Desire, where nobody gets old.*

Then she must have fallen asleep for the poodle began to talk. "I can take you there—where everything is wondrous strange and beautiful, where running water makes music all day long, where there is no age, no pain, nothing but happiness. Will you come with me? Ride upon my back to eternal joy?"

And then incredibly the poodle was beside the bed, the size of a pony, small but big enough to carry her.

Mona knew instinctively that if she got on his back she would achieve the Land of Heart's Desire. Out of the large body the same poodle eyes looked into hers. In them was eternal youth and an age-old wisdom. But there was something else—something that filled her with horror—a cold, calculating look that was evil. She shivered and pulled her robe close.

In her ears the music swelled and the poodle's voice mingled with it. "Come, come with me to eternal joy. Just get on my back."

The music was louder. Suddenly she forgot the evil, forgot everything but the promise of eternal joy. She swung around on the bed, her legs dangling over the side. Then she was on her feet and the poodle threw back its coal black head and made a sound that was half human, half animal, but wholly triumphant, and it was the same evil she saw in the shining eyes. For the first time she was aware of the dog's sharply pointed white teeth. She had noticed the incisors when the poodle had been small, thought they were over-large. Now they looked exactly like the fangs they were. She visioned them dripping with blood—her blood—and she stopped advancing, standing, stock still. Her eyes met those of the dog's, those jet-like button eyes that had given him his name.

"No," she whispered, "no, I cannot come."

"Only one step." The voice came from the poodle's throat, mingling with the music. "Only one step and it is yours—eternal youth—with me." The poodle's eyes were veiled. It lifted one foot enticingly. "Come," it insisted, and moved nearer to her.

Again she began to move towards the dog who now seemed larger than ever. "You won't get out of the door with me on your back," she said.

"There will be no doors for us now, or ever again," the dog replied. It looked at her again.

*

This time she saw the evil in its eyes but she didn't care. The music had her in its spell. The poodle had charmed her, too. She no longer thought it evil or that it was strange it had enlarged itself. She knew that it would bear her through the door or the wall, if necessary, to another world—to eternal joy or eternal damnation. She didn't care which as long as the music lasted.

She took another step. The poodle cavorted like a prancing horse as it had done when it was a tiny dog showing off. "Hurry," its words rang in her ears. "Hurry, get on my back so we can ride."

She put her hand on its shining topknot, the black hair that was soft as cashmere.

The music enveloped her like a mantle of lovely vibrating sound.

She put her other hand on the poodle's back that was cleanshaven, smooth as Broadtail and as high as her shoulder.

Just as she was about to swing herself into place the door opened and the children tumbled in, Baby Carol, Meg and Harry Junior.

"Mother," Meg said reproachfully, "you've got Jet in here."

She was back on her bed, the poodle lying curled against her neck, tiny as always, but looking at her with deep unfathomable eyes.

Even as she looked at it she saw and felt the deep sigh that wracked its fragile little body.

In her ears was a whisper, "Too late." The music was gone.

"Yet, Yet," Baby Carol was pushing herself against the bed.

"I was asleep," Mona told herself, "and I dreamed, but what a dream!"

Almost in a daze she reached up for the poodle, cradled the tiny body in her two hands. "Run along little Jet," she said.

The poodle leaned towards her and licked her cheek.

For an instant she thought she heard the music again. But it was only wishful thinking. Except for the children the room was quiet.

"Yet, Yet," Baby Carol was calling.

Mona gave the poodle to Harry Junior.

"Run along, children," she admonished, "Mother has to dress."

They left her and she got off the bed. She felt enervated. "What a dream!" she said, half out aloud. "I'm actually exhausted—over a dream—no, I guess it was more than a dream. It was in the nightmare class."

She shook the memory of it off, bathing her face with cold water to get rid of it. She dressed quickly. When she reached the living room and Hal she wore her new Dior taffeta suit with the bell-like flaring skirt and the jewelled cap that perched jauntily on her golden curls.

"Mona," her husband exclaimed, "you're ravishing." He kissed her.

"What a fool I was," she thought, "to want to leave him for eternal joy—even in a dream! Why, I've got eternal joy with him! And the children. It took a nightmare to make me realize it, though."

She sighed as the poodle had sighed.

"Come along," Hal said.

"Shouldn't we tell the children good-bye?" she asked.

"I sent them off to the garden to play—and I've told Ellen we're going out. Come on dear, tonight is entirely our own."

"I must tell you about the silliest dream I had," she began as they hailed a taxi.

"Later," he said. "Right now I want to talk about you and how lovely you are."

She never did tell him about the dream.

It was late when they reached home. "It's been a perfect evening," Mona said as Hal put his key in the front door lock.

The door swung open before he turned the key. A white-faced Ellen stood inside peering out at them anxiously.

"Is anything wrong?" Mona asked, alarmed by the look on her maid's face.

Ellen kept staring. "Did you take the baby with you?" she asked. Her voice was unsteady.

"No," Hal replied tersely. "Why?"

Ellen's lips quivered. "I so hoped you'd taken her, even though I was sure you hadn't. She's gone. She wasn't there when I called the children for supper—neither she nor the little dog. I asked Meg and Harry where she was and they said the last time they'd seen her she was playing with Jet in the far corner of the garden."

"But surely—" Mona began over Hal's, "We'd better phone the police."

"Oh, no sir." Ellen wailed, "It's no use. It's May eve, the time when the 'little people' have power. They've spirited her away. The little dog was their emissary. He came ahead to get someone from this house. I never liked the little dog. I think I knew from the first—"

"Nonsense," Hal broke in, "there was nothing wrong with the dog. There are no little people. I'll phone the police and ask the neighbours—"

"I did that," Ellen cut in. "Two of them saw Carol. They said she was laughing happily, riding on the back of a poodle dog as large as a pony."

Mona remembered what she had thought was a dream—a nightmare. When the poodle had grown big—big enough to take her to the Land of Heart's Desire. She remembered the cold, calculating look—the evil.

It had been actuality, not a dream. In one sickening moment she glimpsed another world, another dimension and knew it was more than shadow and that she would never see her child again.

1935

THE HOUSE PARTY ON SMOKY ISLAND

L. M. Montgomery

It may seem a surprise to discover that the author of the perennially popular children's novel *Anne of Green Gables* (1908), Lucy Maud Montgomery (1874–1942), was a contributor to *Weird Tales*, even though it was only once with this story in the August 1935 issue, but Montgomery was nevertheless fascinated by the supernatural, though she was not a believer. She had an intense spiritual side which had been instilled from her childhood in Canada seeking out remote places where she felt an affinity with nature. Though an immensely successful writer, and extremely prolific, she had a difficult life with a fraught childhood after the early death of her mother, an emotionally disturbing marriage, and seemingly endless battles with her vindictive publisher over royalties on her works, so it is not too surprising that the despair and depression that developed over her life would lead to occasional stories that looked at the dark side of life. She enjoyed supernatural stories and turned to them now and then almost as a spiritual release. Montgomery had attended seances but remained sceptical.

Her earliest weird tale appears to have been "The Red Room" from 1898, more gothic than supernatural but full of atmosphere. One wonders whether Montgomery had read H. G. Wells's ghost story "The Red Room" which had appeared just two years earlier. A collection of her strange and dark stories was assembled by Rea Wilshurst as *Among the Shadows* (1990).

Of interest is her early tale "Davenport's Story" (1902) which is similar to the following in that both involve a group of people telling ghost stories. This story is deceptively simple as it unfolds with almost predictable inevitability but it is that very simplicity that makes it so effective and memorable.

When Madeline Stanwyck asked me to join her house party at Smoky Island I was not at first disposed to do so. It was too early in the season, and there would be mosquitoes. One mosquito can keep me more awake than a bad conscience: and there are millions of mosquitoes in Muskoka.

"No, no, the season for them is over," Madeline assured me. Madeline would say anything to get her way.

"The mosquito season is never over in Muskoka," I said, as grumpily as anyone could speak to Madeline. "They thrive up there at zero. And even if by some miracle there are no mosquitoes, I've no hankering to be chewed to pieces by black flies."

Even Madeline did not dare to say there would be no black flies, so she wisely fell back on her Madelinity.

"Please come, for my sake," she said wistfully. "It wouldn't be a real party for me if you weren't there, Jim darling."

I am Madeline's favourite cousin, twenty years her senior, and she calls everybody darling when she wants to get something out of him. Not but that Madeline... but this story is not about Madeline. It is about an occurrence which took place at Smoky Island. None of us pretends to understand it, except the Judge, who pretends to understand everything. But he really understands it no better than the rest of us. His latest explanation is that we were all hypnotized and in the state of hypnosis saw and remembered things we couldn't otherwise have seen or remembered. But even he cannot explain who or what hypnotized us.

I decided to yield, but not all at once.

"Has your Smoky Island housekeeper still got that detestable white parrot?" I asked.

"Yes, but it is much better-mannered than it used to be," assured Madeline. "And you know you have always liked her cat."

"Who'll be in your party? I'm rather finicky as to the company I keep."

Madeline grinned.

"You know I never invite anyone but interesting people to my parties"—I bowed to the implied compliment—"with a dull one or two to show off the sparkle of the rest of us"—I did not bow this time—"Consuelo Anderson... Aunt Alma... Professor Tennant and his wife... Dick Lane... Ted Newman... Senator Malcolm and Mrs. Senator... Old Nosey... Min Ingram... Judge Warden... Mary Harland... and a few Bright Young Things to amuse *me*."

I ran over the list in my mind, not disapprovingly. Consuelo was a very fat girl with a B.A. degree. I liked her because she could sit still for a longer time than any woman I know. Tennant was professor of something he called the New Pathology—an insignificant little man with a gigantic intellect. Dick Lane was one of those coming men who never seem to arrive, but a frank, friendly, charming fellow enough. Mary Harland was a comfortable spinster, Ted an amusing little fop, Aunt Alma a sweet, silvery-haired thing like a Whistler mother. Old Nosey—whose real name was Miss Alexander and who never let anyone forget that she had nearly sailed on the *Lusitania*—and the Malcolms had no terrors for me, although the Senator always called his wife "Kittens." And Judge Warden was an old crony of mine. I did not like Min Ingram, who had a rapier-like tongue, but she could be ignored, along with the Bright Young Things.

"Is that all?" I asked cautiously.

"Well... Doctor Armstrong and Brenda, of course," said Madeline, eyeing me as if it were not at all of course.

"Is that—wise?" I said slowly.

Madeline crumpled.

"Of course not," she said miserably. "It will likely spoil everything. But John insists on it... you know he and Anthony Armstrong have been pals all their lives. And Brenda and I have always been chummy. It would look so funny if we didn't have them. I don't know what has got into her. We all *know* Anthony never poisoned Susette."

"Brenda doesn't know it, apparently," I said.

"Well, she ought to!" snapped Madeline. "As if Anthony could have poisoned anyone! But that's one of the reasons I particularly want you to come."

"Ah, now we're getting at it. But why *me*?"

"Because you've more influence over Brenda than anyone else... oh, yes, you have. If you could get her to open up... talk to her... you might help her. Because... if something doesn't help her soon, she'll be beyond help. You know that."

I knew it well enough. The case of the Anthony Armstrongs was worrying us all. We saw a tragedy being enacted before our eyes and we could not lift a finger to help. For Brenda would not talk and Anthony had never talked.

The story, now five years old, was known to all of us, of course. Anthony's first wife had been Susette Wilder. Of the dead nothing but good; so I will say of Susette only that she was very beautiful and very rich. Luckily her fortune had come to her unexpectedly by the death of an aunt and cousin after she had married Anthony, so that he could not be accused of fortune-hunting. He had been wildly in love with Susette at first, but after they had been married a few years I don't think he had much affection left for her. None of the rest of us had ever had any to begin with. When word came back from California—where Anthony had taken her one winter for her nerves—that she was dead I don't suppose anyone felt any regret, nor any suspicion when we heard that she had died from an overdose of chloral; rather mysteriously, to be sure, for Susette was neither careless nor suicidally inclined. There were some ugly rumours, especially when it became known that Anthony had inherited her entire fortune under her will; but nobody ever dared say much openly. We, who knew and loved Anthony, never paid any heed to the hints. And when, two years later, he married Brenda Young, we were all glad. Anthony, we said, would have some real happiness now.

For a time, he did have it. Nobody could doubt that he and Brenda were ecstatically happy. Brenda was a sincere, spiritual creature, lovely after a fashion totally different from Susette. Susette had had golden hair and eyes as cool and green as fluorspar. Brenda had a slim, dark distinction, hair that blended with the dusk, and eyes so full of twilight that it was hard to say whether they were blue or grey. She loved Anthony so terribly that sometimes I thought she was tempting the gods.

Then—slowly, subtly, remorselessly—the change set in. We began to feel that there was something wrong—very wrong—between the Armstrongs. They were no longer quite so happy... they were not happy at all... they were wretched. Brenda's old delightful laugh was never heard, and Anthony went about his work with an air of abstraction that didn't please his patients. His practise had fallen off awhile before Susette's death, but it had picked up and grown wonderfully. Now it began dropping again. And the worst of it was that Anthony didn't seem to care. Of course he didn't need it from a financial point of view, but he had always been so keenly interested in his work.

I don't know whether it was merely surmise or whether Brenda had let a word slip, but we all knew or felt that a horrible suspicion possessed her. There was some whisper of an anonymous letter, full of vile innuendoes, that had started the trouble. I never knew the rights of that, but I did know that Brenda had become a haunted woman.

Had Anthony given Susette that overdose of chloral—given it purposely?

If she had been the kind of woman who talks things out, some of us might have saved her. But she wasn't. It's my belief that she never said one word to Anthony of the cold horror of distrust that was poisoning her life. But he must have felt she suspected him, and between them was the chill and shadow of a thing that must not be spoken of.

At the time of Madeline's house party the state of affairs between the Armstrongs was such that Brenda had almost reached the breaking-point. Anthony's nerves were tense, too, and his eyes were almost as tragic as hers. We were all ready to hear that Brenda had left him or done something more desperate still. And nobody could do a thing to help, not even I, in spite of Madeline's foolish hopes. I couldn't go to Brenda and say, "Look here, you know, Anthony never thought of such a thing as poisoning Susette." After all, in spite of our surmises, the trouble might be something else altogether. And if she did suspect him, what proof could I offer her that would root the obsession out of her mind?

I hardly thought the Armstrongs would go to Smoky Island, but they did. When Anthony turned on the wharf and held out his hand to assist Brenda from the motor-boat, she ignored it, stepping swiftly off without any assistance and running up through the rock garden and the pointed firs. I saw Anthony go very white. I felt a little sick myself. If matters had come to such a pass that she shrank from his mere touch, disaster was near.

Smoky Island was in a little blue Muskoka lake and the house was called the Wigwam... probably because nothing on earth could be less like a wigwam. The Stanwyck money had made a wonderful place of it, but even the Stanwyck money could not buy fine weather.

Madeline's party was a flop. It rained every day more or less for the week, and though we all tried heroically to make the best of things I don't think I ever spent a more unpleasant time. The parrot's manners were no better, in spite of Madeline's assurances. Min Ingram had brought an aloof, disdainful dog with her that everyone hated because he despised us all. Min herself kept passing out needle-like insults when she saw anyone in danger of being comfortable. I thought the Bright Young Things seemed to hold *me* responsible for the weather. All our nerves got edgy except Aunt Alma's. Nothing ever upset Aunt Alma. She prided herself a bit on that.

On Saturday the weather wound up with a regular downpour and a wind that rushed out of the black-green pines to lash the Wigwam and then rushed back like a maddened animal. The air was as full of torn, flying leaves as of rain, and the lake was a splutter of tossing waves. This charming day ended in a dank, streaming night.

And yet things had seemed a bit better than any day yet. Anthony was away. He had got some mysterious telegram just after breakfast, had taken the small motor-boat, and gone to the mainland. I was thankful, for I felt I could no longer endure seeing a man's soul tortured as his was. Brenda had kept her room all day on the good old plea of a headache. I won't say it wasn't a relief. We all felt the strain between her and Anthony like a tangible thing.

"Something—*something*—is going to happen," Madeline kept saying to me. She was really worse than the parrot.

After dinner we all gathered around the fireplace in the hall, where a cheerful fire of white birchwood was glowing; for although it was June the evening was cold. I settled back with a sigh of relief. After all, nothing lasted for ever, and this infernal house party would be over on Monday. Besides, it was really quite comfortable and cheerful here, despite rattling windows and wailing winds and rain-swept panes. Madeline turned out the electric lights, and the firelight was kind to the women, who all looked quite charming. Some of the Bright Young Things sat cross-legged on the floor with arms around one another quite indiscriminately as far as sex was concerned... except one languid, sophisticated creature in orange velvet and long amber ear-rings, who sat on a low stool with a lapful of silken housekeeper's cat, giving everyone an excellent view of the bones in her spine. Min's dog posed haughtily on the rug, and the parrot in his cage was quiet—for him—only telling us once in a while that he or someone else was devilish clever. Mrs. Howey, the housekeeper, insisted on keeping him in the hall, and Madeline had to wink at it because it was hard to get a housekeeper in Muskoka even for a Wigwam.

The Judge was looking like a chuckle because he had solved a jigsaw puzzle that had baffled everyone, and the Professor and Senator, who had been arguing stormily all day, were basking in each other's regard for a foeman worthy of his steel. Consuelo was sitting still, as usual. Mrs. Tennant and Aunt Alma were knitting pullovers. Kittens, her fat hands folded across her satin stomach, was surveying her Senator adoringly, and Miss Nosey was taking everything in. We were, for the time being, a contented, congenial bunch of people and I did not see why Madeline should have suddenly proposed that each of us tell a ghost story, but she did. It was an ideal night for ghost stories, she averred. She hadn't heard any for ages and she understood that everybody had had at least one supernatural occurrence in his or her life.

"I haven't," growled the Judge contemptuously.

"I suppose," said Professor Tennant a little belligerently, "that you would call anyone an ass who believed in ghosts?"

The Judge carefully fitted his fingertips together before he replied.

"Oh, dear, no. I would not so insult asses."

"Of course, if you don't *believe* in ghosts they can't happen," said Consuelo.

"Some people are able to see ghosts and some are not," announced Dick Lane. "It's simply a gift."

"A gift I was not dowered with," said Kittens complacently.

Mary Harland shuddered. "What a dreadful thing it would be if the dead really came back!"

"'From ghoulies and ghaisties and lang-legged beasties
And things that go bump in the night
Good Lord, deliver us,'" quoted Ted flippantly.

But Madeline was not to be sidetracked. Her little elfish face, under its crown of russet hair, was alive with determination.

"We're going to spook a bit," she said resolutely. "This is just the sort of night for ghosts to walk. Only of course they can't walk here because the Wigwam isn't haunted, I'm sorry to say. Wouldn't it be heavenly to live in a haunted house? Come now, everyone must tell a ghost story. Professor Tennant, you lead off. Something nice and creepy, please."

To my surprise, the Professor did lead off, although Mrs. Tennant's expression plainly informed us that she didn't approve of juggling with ghosts. He told a very good story, too—punctuated with snorts from the Judge—about a house he knew which had been haunted by the voice of a dead child who joined in every conversation bitterly and vindictively. The child had, of course, been ill-treated and murdered, and its body was eventually found under the hearthstone of the library. Then Dick told a tale about a dead dog that avenged its master, and Consuelo amazed me by spinning a really gruesome yarn of a ghost who came to the wedding of her lover with her rival... Consuelo said she knew the people. Ted knew a house in which you heard voices and footfalls where no voices or footfalls could be, and even Aunt Alma told of "a white lady with a cold hand" who asked you to dance with her. If you were reckless enough to accept the invitation you never lost the feeling of her cold hand in yours. This chilly apparition was always garbed in the costume of the Seventies.

"Fancy a ghost in a crinoline," giggled a Bright Young Thing.

Min Ingram, of all people, had seen a ghost and took it quite seriously.

"Well, show me a ghost and I'll believe in it," said the Judge, with another snort.

"Isn't he devilish clever?" croaked the parrot.

Just at this point Brenda drifted downstairs and sat down behind us all, her tragic eyes burning out of her white face. I had a feeling that there, in that calm, untroubled scene, full of good-humoured, tolerably amused, commonplace people, a human heart was burning at the stake in agony.

Something fell over us with Brenda's coming. Min Ingram's dog suddenly whined and flattened himself out on the rug. It occurred to me that it was the first time I had ever seen him looking like a real dog. I wondered idly what had frightened him. The housekeeper's cat sat up, its back bristling, slid from the orange velvet lap and slunk out of the hall. I had a queer sensation in the roots of what hair I had left, so I turned hastily to the slim, dark girl on the oak settle at my right.

"You haven't told us a ghost story yet, Christine. It's your turn."

Christine smiled. I saw the Judge looking admiringly at her ankles, sheathed in chiffon hose. The Judge always had an eye for a pretty ankle. As for me, I was wondering why I couldn't recall Christine's last name and why I felt as if I had been impelled in some odd way to make that commonplace remark to her.

"Do you remember how firmly Aunt Elizabeth believed in ghosts?" said Christine. "And how angry it used to make her when I laughed at the idea? I am... wiser now."

"I remember," said the Senator in a dreamy way.

"It was your Aunt Elizabeth's money that went to the first Mrs. Armstrong, wasn't it?" said one of the Bright Young Things, nicknamed Tweezers. It was an abominable thing for anyone to say, right there before Brenda. But nobody seemed horrified. I had another odd feeling that it *had* to be said and who but Tweezers would say it? I had another feeling... that ever since Brenda's entrance every trifle was important, every tone was of profound significance, every word had a hidden meaning. Was I developing nerves?

"Yes," said Christine evenly.

"Do you suppose Susette Armstrong really took that overdose of chloral on purpose?" went on Tweezers unbelievably.

Not being near enough to Tweezers to assassinate her, I looked at Brenda. But Brenda gave no sign of having heard. She was staring fixedly at Christine.

"No," said Christine. I wondered how she knew, but there was no question whatsoever in my mind that she did know it. She spoke as one having authority. "Susette had no intention of dying. And yet she was doomed, although she never suspected it. She had an incurable disease which would have killed her in a few months. Nobody knew that except Anthony and me. And she had come to hate Anthony so. She was going to change her will the very next day—leave everything away from him. She told me so. I was furious. Anthony, who had spent his life doing good to suffering creatures, was to be left poor and struggling again, after his practice had been all shot to pieces by Susette's goings-on. I had loved Anthony ever since I had known him. He didn't know it—but Susette did. Trust her for that. She used to twit me with it. Not that it mattered... I knew he would never care for me. But I saw my chance to do something for him and I took it. *I gave Susette that overdose of chloral. I loved him enough for that...* and for *this*."

Somebody screamed. I have never known whether it was Brenda or not. Aunt Alma—who was never upset over anything—was huddled in her chair in hysterics. Kittens, her fat figure shaking, was clinging to her Senator, whose foolish, amiable face was grey—absolutely grey. Min Ingram was on her knees and the Judge was trying to keep his hands from shaking by clenching them together. His lips were moving and I know I caught the word, "God." As for Tweezers and all the rest of her gang, they were no longer Bright Young Things but simply shivering, terrified children.

I felt sick—very, very sick. *Because there was no one on the oak settle and none of us had ever known or heard of the girl I had called Christine.*

At that moment the hall door opened and a dripping Anthony entered. Brenda flung herself hungrily against him, wet as he was.

"Anthony... Anthony, forgive me," she sobbed.

Something good to see came into Anthony's worn face.

"Have you been frightened, darling?" he said tenderly. "I'm sorry I was so late. There was really no danger. I waited to get an answer to my wire to Los Angeles. You see I got word this morning that Christine Latham had been killed in a motor accident yesterday evening. She was Susette's second cousin and nurse... a dear, loyal little thing. I was very fond of her. I'm sorry you've had such an anxious evening, sweetheart."

1940

FORBIDDEN CUPBOARD

Frances Garfield

Frances Garfield (1908–2000) was the writing alias of Francis Marita Obrist, a native of Kansas, who became Mrs. Manly Wade Wellman in June 1930. They would remain happily married for nearly fifty-six years until his death in 1986. She studied music and singing and her first career was in teaching piano and voice. She considered a career on the stage but changed her mind after the producer was "so rude", as she remembered. Manly had been selling fiction since 1927 and though the happy couple lived in Wichita, Kansas, Manly decided to move to New York to be closer to the magazine markets. He rapidly established himself and Frances joined him soon after. Their son, Wade, was born in November 1939. Frances had started to sell her own fiction by then, her first appearance being with "The High Places", about a haunted plane, in the April 1939 *Weird Tales*. She sold three more stories, the last being the following in the January 1940 *Weird Tales*, but then settled down to rearing their baby. She did not return to writing until 1979 when Stephen Jones lured her back with a story in his magazine *Fantasy Tales*, which had been launched in 1977 as a tribute to *Weird Tales*. Frances continued to sell stories to the small press magazines over the next decade, but the muse faded after her husband died. She published eleven stories in total, a modest output but every one of them memorable, just like the following.

When I had panted up the two flights of stairs and set down my suitcase, I saw that Father O'Neil was standing at the open door of my new flat. He was the very picture of chubby, priestly embarrassment.

"The place isn't ready yet, Miss Hampton," he protested. "We didn't expect you until tomorrow, you know."

"Yes, but I took an earlier train," I replied, "and the expressman's bringing up my trunk."

The good father looked at me thoughtfully. With his round belly, his black garments and comfortable warmth of nature, he reminded me of an old-fashioned depot stove. Even though his face was solemn just now, its rosy cheer was like a glow of friendly flame.

"Well, come in," he said at last. "I don't see how I can keep you on your own doorstep," and he managed a smile. "I promised to look after you, and I shall. I'm in charge here. Probably you think the arrangement odd."

"Oh, not at all," I made haste to say, though I burned with curiosity to know why a priest doubled as landlord. It was all because of Lola Knesbec, my old professor of boarding-school English, that I was taking the flat. She knew that I hoped to live and write in New York, and that I wanted the cheapest of comfortable lodgings.

Her old friend, Father O'Neil, was renting flats in an ancient house on the border of Greenwich Village. There was an exchange of letters, careful consideration of my financial and character references… and here I was, at once delighted and mystified by the situation.

I entered, and almost squealed in delight.

"You like it, Miss Hampton?" asked Father O'Neil.

"Tremendously!" I assured him, and I did. No tawdry stage-set this, simulating a crass dream of a Village studio with cushioned divans, batik hangings and conflicting colours; no, nor was it imitation Park Avenue, with mock-oriental rugs and plush over-stuffings. The huge living-room was papered in fawn brown up to the lofty ceiling, with heavy carved moulding, and the open fireplace—a real one, not a portable sham—had a white marble slab for mantel. The furniture, of massy wood with leather cushioning, bespoke unmodish comfort. A full-length mirror hung opposite the front door. The windows, set high in the front wall, had varnished maple shutters inside. To such a room might Washington Irving once have come to tea, talking of headless horsemen to his crinolined hostess; while, outside the half-open shutters, might have paced and shivered a beautiful, wretched man in unseasonable nankeen, hungry for the lunch he could not buy—Edgar Allan Poe.

"Miss Knesbec was sure you'd like it," smiled the priest. Standing close to a high-silled window, he was bathed from the knees up in grey light from the autumn sky. His shanks were darker and more indistinct, literally wading in floor shadows. He drew out a stubby briar pipe, already filled.

"May I smoke?" he asked.

"Please do."

And I remembered that I had something else to say, concerning a fascinating tale that Lola Knesbec had hinted.

"I understand that this house once belonged to Guilford Golt," I offered, and waited for a response. It came, and it was more intriguing than I had dared hope. Father O'Neil's face lost some of its pinkness, and the hand that held the pipe seemed to quiver.

"What do you know about Guilford Golt?" he demanded.

"Only that he was an eccentric scholar of the middle Nineteenth Century," I replied. "Miss Knesbec told our class that his character had been used by Fitz-James O'Brien in that story about the wizard who brought evil little toys to life, and by Nathaniel Hawthorne for the alchemical genius in *The Birthmark*—"

"Miss Knesbec was right," said Father O'Neil; "only those tales did not do Guilford Golt grim enough justice."

"And didn't this house once belong to him?" I pursued.

"It did," the priest nodded. "Golt conducted many experiments in it—experiments that escaped legal notice because legal men scorn to believe such things. But he and his works were baleful. A group of citizens visited him one night in a very vengeful mood—he had made himself too dreadful a figure, even for the strange and tolerant community that was New York nearly a century ago. And in the morning he had vanished.

"I doubt if he was to be frightened," continued Father O'Neil gravely. "He was the sort who had gone beyond fear. But—yes, he was driven away. And he had no heirs. And this house remained closed until recently, when we of the church, as trustees, were asked to put it to some profitable use. And so we are renting flats in it—having taken certain precautions."

As he spoke this last word, his eyes wandered, as if in spite of themselves, to a grey-painted door in the rear of the room. Then he spoke more brightly:

"I've laid a fire ready. Shall I light it?"

"Please," I said, slipping off my coat. The grey door to which his involuntary glance had directed me must be a clothes-closet. I moved toward it and drew down the latch, but it would not open. A great chest of dark wood, that at first had seemed a bar of the low-fallen shadows, had been shoved against the bottom of the door.

"Wait, don't open that door, my child," called Father O'Neil suddenly. He had crouched down to light the fire, but now, moving quickly for so plump a little man, he was at my side. His pleasant face was anxious.

"Not if you say so," I said, rather startled.

He smiled once more, in an obvious effort to reassure me. "The closet must never be opened. In fact it is to be plastered up—then it will be cut off permanently and can be forgotten."

"I doubt if I could pull that chest away, in any case," I smiled back.

"Don't even try."

I moved across the room, to the bedchamber, and laid my coat upon a stout old walnut bed.

"Now to get at my work," I said, coming back into the parlour. "I'm a long jump behind, as usual."

"Then I'll go. I, too, have work." Father O'Neil put his pipe into his mouth and took up his broad, black hat. "I'll be back later, if you don't mind. I'm expecting some workmen. I hope they won't bother you—interrupt your writing."

"It's quite all right," I assured him. "Don't give it a thought. Won't you have tea with me, around four o'clock?" I asked him on impulse. "I feel that we're destined to be friends."

"Thank you, I'll be delighted." And he smiled himself out.

Almost immediately came the expressman with my trunk and suitcase. I began at once to arrange my few possessions and as soon as possible got to work.

It was no inspiring job—merely a panegyric of a business man, even titled by my employer, the doting widow—*Truman Murdock, A Man's Man*. But I set out to do the best I could in a compromise between the canonizing taste of the man's heirs and my own idea of what a biography should be.

I had planned a good first chapter, at least—a widely imaginary pedigree. His patronymic suggested the dashing follower of Roderick Dhu, and I might even quote a few lines of Walter Scott. His mother's name had been Blake—perhaps this made him a connection of William Blake, perhaps even of that Sir Percy Blake who is supposed to have sat for Frans Hals as the *Laughing Cavalier*. All this could be whipped into good copy to get the book off to a readable start. Down I sat to the typewriter, drumming at it page after ambling page. "Each of us," I paraphrased something I had seen in *The Reader's Digest*, "is a great vehicle in which ride all the ghosts of his forefathers..."

What was it that stirred behind me?

I swung quickly around. No living thing was there; I saw only the room, the furniture, the fireplace in which the blaze had died to a ruddy scattering of coals, the grey closet door spanned by the dark chest. There was the noise again—or was it?

I rose, crossed the floor, and stopped just beside the forbidden closet, listening with both my ears.

Silence now. I might have been mistaken, nervous in a new house, excited by Father O'Neil's air of mystery. Who, and in what stodgy book, has said that an imaginative mind is bad for the nerves? Standing beside the closet, I wished that Father O'Neil had not been at once insistent and mysterious about my leaving it shut. My impulse to pry was natural and extreme, as with all women in such a situation, clear back to the wife of Bluebeard.

I examined the chest that did duty as obstacle. Heavy, dark, roughly carved, it looked at first like something out of the hold of a pirate ship; but undoubtedly it was only a modern imitation. The lock, for instance, was a new automatic one, and fast. I could not lift the lid.

The closet door, by contrast, was not locked at all. Indeed, it had not even a keyhole—only a heavy iron latch, painted dull grey like the rest of the panel, and once before I had lifted it.

Looking closely now, I saw that there was a mark in the paint above that latch, a line undoubtedly scraped when the paint had been fresh. A cross; no, it was more than a cross. At the upper end of the vertical bar was attached a sickle-like curve. I had seen such a device before, in my childhood, and had heard an old Irish cook call it the "God-have-mercy sign." What was such a sign doing here?

My mind turned again to Guilford Golt. The legend, so skimmed over by Lola Knesbec and now by Father O'Neil, had credited him with belief, if not power, in black magic. Did this closet have something to do with the tale? If so, why did not the priest bring such a knowledge into the light instead of plastering the door shut? The amateur-detective impulse, which surely makes up part of every human soul, became strong and insistent.

I bent, seized the handle at the side of the chest, and tried to drag it away. Who could have refrained from such an effort? But the weight momentarily baffled me. In the midst of my tugging, I let go and straightened up guiltily. A sharp ringing sound filled the room.

The telephone—I hadn't even noticed that there was one. It rang again, and yet again, while I walked toward it. The raucous summons angered me for a moment, and I snatched up the instrument with a needlessly sharp "Hello!"

"Hello," said a high, drawling voice, hard to classify as male or female, young or old. "I want to order a ton of coal."

"You have the wrong number," I replied.

"But I bought coal there last year," protested the drawl. "Isn't this Chelsea 3-0036?"

It was, as a glance at the instrument's foot showed me; but I could only repeat that I had no coal for sale.

"You used to sell coal," insisted the voice reproachfully.

"There's some mistake," I said, and somehow felt as if I were shirking my duty. "This is a private home." And I hung up.

Just like a telephone, I thought savagely; interrupting my work—but I hadn't been working. I had been about to investigate that closet.

I walked back to the chest. The problem, I felt, must be faced; Father O'Neil had not wanted me to open the door, but I must prove to myself that I did not fear that little scratching noise, if indeed there had been a noise. And I needed storage space.

Again I bent, seized the chest, and this time succeeded in dragging it slantingly back from its position.

Again sound—shrill now, and tuneful. It flowed in and filled the room, but from outside.

Mystified and intrigued, I hurried to the window. It was open a crack, and I lifted it all the way and leaned out.

The musical shrilling came from a penny whistle, and the ragged old man who played it was getting real melody out of his tawdry instrument. He was playing *Annie Laurie*, from which, as I peered out at him, he shifted to *Bonnie Doon*. Then he saw me, and ceased to play at all. Taking the whistle from his mouth, he gazed up at my window.

"Please, kind lady!" he bawled winningly.

My purse lay on that very sill, and I quickly opened it and fumbled out six copper pennies. These I flung down to him. They fell in a little rain about my serenader who, stooping quickly, retrieved the coins with eagerly darting clutches. In thanks he doffed the filthiest tweed cap I ever saw, played me a little chirpy flourish on his whistle, and tramped away.

A more pleasant dissuasion, that, from my attempt on the closet's secret... I frowned. Was Providence marshalling these telephones and whistles against me, to hold me back from flouting Father O'Neil's wish? I toyed with the fancy for only a moment, then told myself that it sprang from a falsely guilty conscience. I went straight and purposefully to the chest, once more clutched its handle, and drew it away with a mighty heave. Straightening up, I pressed down the latch and opened the closet door.

I looked into absolute blackness, a formless and spacious cave of it; it was as though there were no sides or back to the little nook, as though it were, instead, a vast and lightless valley. But close to me, so close that it must have dangled against the door when shut, hung something.

An old garment, was my first thought. I was about to step in and examine it, when my eyes were drawn to the inner side of the open door. It was covered with writing, crude, heavy writing as if it were done with a coarse instrument—even a human finger. I wondered what kind of ink could have turned such a rusty brown, and began to read:

> They are shutting me up in here to die. They think they are rid of me—but I'll live. Life, in some sort, will be mine forever. The rotting of my flesh and my bones will only make my spirit free.
>
> I write this in my own blood. They left me nothing else. I'm not done with this world. Whenever this prison is opened...

I was intrigued, and amused. Was this the bizarre legend that Father O'Neil had known of the place, and had hesitated telling me because it was so dreadful? The very fact of its being written in human blood was enough to discredit it with me. Melodramatic stuff from the paper-backed thrillers. I must chide him for judging me a simple, credulous child. I moved back, smiling, and saw a fluttery movement in the fabric-like hanging in the dark closet.

I turned to look again. There was a filmy openwork about it, like lace or net. Not a garment, after all; more probably a grubby grey curtain, stowed away here and forgotten...

But does a curtain hold itself erect, to the width and height of a human figure, without hook or rod to support it at the top? Does a curtain turn toward you an unshapen upper roundness like an ill-modelled head, that shows two black caverns like a mockery of eyes, and does a curtain lift slowly a pair of ragged trails so that they seem to gesture and grope like skinny arms?

Does a curtain drift slowly from its place, and come toward you, as if it wanted to catch and grapple you?

I fell back and away, my face gone all frostily dry and my legs suddenly bereft of stiffening bone, drained of living blood. The thing left its shadowed hiding, pausing for only an instant on the threshold. I had a good view of it. No, no curtain—no honest fabric at all. The cloudy mass of it, like a concentration of lint and dust and smoke, stirred in all its particles, yet clung to a filmy shape-travesty of a human being. The dull black eye-blotches narrowed themselves, as if the grey light were too strong. And then it drifted into the open, around the chest, and at me.

Its arms raised themselves to a level with the face. I saw, with an increase of disgusted horror, that its hands had no fingers—they flapped like dusty mittens, opening and extending, to take hold of me. My own hands drew up to fight back. My heart had become a giant fist, trying to batter free from my ribs. For by some fantastic telepathy, I knew what the creature wanted.

He intended to don me, as a human being puts on a garment, clothe himself in my flesh for his devil's doings. This was the thing that had been shut away from the world for so long—was now visiting its wrath and will upon me—once Guilford Golt, the sorcerer, now a fiend made stronger and ghastlier by death's change.

Something was blocking my retreat. I tried to scream at the touch of it, but achieved only a sigh. The wall, beside my writing-table, was at my shoulder-blades. Within reach of my hand lay my dictionary, bought last week for a dollar in a second-hand bookstore. I clutched it, hurled it with all my force. It struck, square upon the cheek, or where the cheek should be. The book did not make a noise, did not stop its flight. It flew through and past—into the inky blackness of the closet.

Where it had struck was a ragged notch. I could see the wall through it. The shape did not pause or falter. It drifted closer, I felt, like a crashing weight, its purposeful menace.

Its arms spread now, horizontally, to pin me against the wall. I thought to dodge away. Too late! I was caught in the angle of the wall and the table. The torn, musty head seemed to crinkle up its surface below the eyes, as though it were smiling for all its lack of mouth.

The window—could I reach it, lift it, scream for help? Jump out? Too late for that, too. The dirt-fluff mittens were soaring up before my face, fumbling to touch my neck. An aura of dust thickened in my nose and throat. A wave of cold passed over me like a shaking buffet, dimness weighted my eyelids, my head lolled upon my shoulders as if it were imperfectly fastened there. The round head, the dull eye-patches, were within inches of my face. I could not cry out.

But suddenly the creature shrank back, as shaken as I had been. Something had started, dismayed it. There! A noise, coming again to my rescue.

A knock, loud and free, at the door. After a moment, a voice: "Miss Hampton?"

Father O'Neil was outside. And the thing knew him. I had no doubt the thing had been outfaced by Father O'Neil, and feared him; so might a more forbidding creature fear what a priest could and would do... It retreated more swiftly, falling, almost, back on its trail through the room.

All at once I could breathe again, could hold myself erect without the help of the wall.

"Miss Hampton, may I come in?" asked Father O'Neil again.

The filmy greyness had gained the open door of the closet, drooping abjectly in its hurry to seek shelter there. It drew itself inside making itself small and dark, to match the shadows. I managed to hurry after, to throw myself across the dragged-away chest, to fall against the panel, swinging it shut with my weight.

My fingers groped to the latch, lifted it, and let it fall into place.

"F—Father O'Neil!" I found my voice at last. "Yes. Come in."

And my front door opened. Still sagging against the closet door, I turned to face that blessedly welcome visitor, all hearty girth and churchly blackness and rosy, beaming face.

"I'm afraid that I'm just a few minutes early for tea," he began, and then broke off, staring at me. "Why, Miss Hampton. What are you doing at that door?"

Quickly he hurried across to me.

I drew away, came around the chest once more and faced him.

"You weren't really going to open the closet?" he chided me earnestly.

I shook my head mutely and with absolute honesty. Not all the publisher's gold, the critics' acclaim, the reading public's patronage, would ever tempt me to put my hand on that latch again.

Father O'Neil bent. With a quick, solid shove, he moved the chest back into its sentinel place against the bottom of the door.

"Once more, I urge you never to look into that closet, Miss Hampton," he addressed me solemnly as he drew himself erect once more. "The plasterers will be here within an hour. Meanwhile I am forced to ask you for your promise."

"I promise," I assured him with husky eagerness.

The priest smiled approval, and helped me to set out the tea-things. My hands, deadened as though by injection of some drug, could not help but shake. And Father O'Neil noticed.

"I'm sorry if I frightened you, my child," he apologized gently. "Yet it is important—extremely important—that the closet door remain shut forever." He looked at me calculatingly. "I was tempted for a moment to tell you everything; but I doubt if you'd believe the story."

I nodded. I had learned too much already, ever to have complete peace of mind again. I had known the breath and face of a danger more dire than anything that threatens only the flesh. That danger had been averted. Father O'Neil had saved me without himself knowing how close a call it had been.

I made a sudden decision. Just now I held the priest's respect and friendship. He thought that he was protecting me by remaining silent. Why trouble him, worry him, by saying I knew the story of a horror that was now closed up again? Why shake his sturdy courage and mastery of the awful situation? And already the memory was becoming blessedly unreal, dreamlike...

"No," I agreed, as brightly as I could manage. "I might not believe it."

1949

THE UNDERBODY

Allison V. Harding

The identity of Allison V. Harding has long been a mystery, yet she was the most prolific female contributor of short fiction to *Weird Tales* with 36 stories from "The Unfriendly World" (July 1943), where a man fears sleep because he enters a world that proves too deadly, to "Scope" (January 1951), in which a scientist invents a telescope capable of seeing to the limits of the universe and witnesses something unimaginable. She also had six stories in the companion magazine *Short Stories*, but none of these issues provided any personal information and she appeared nowhere else.

It remained a mystery until science fiction historian Sam Moskowitz acquired the original purchase records for *Weird Tales* from publisher Leo Margulies. Margulies had acquired the rights to both *Weird Tales* and *Short Stories* in 1957 and was keen to revive both, but a blight had settled over specialist fiction magazines at the end of the 1950s following the collapse of the old pulps. A revival of *Short Stories* lasted only two years. Margulies delayed reviving *Weird Tales* until the magazine's fiftieth anniversary in 1973. Alas, that first revival lasted only four issues. Moskowitz was its editor and that was how he acquired the original purchase files for *Weird Tales* and *Short Stories*. He was able to identify that Allison V. Harding was the pen name of Jean Milligan, and a search of public documents identifies a Jean Milligan (1919–2004) who came to New York from Connecticut in the 1940s and worked as a secretary. In 1952 she married Lamont Buchanan, who had been the associate editor of *Weird Tales* from 1942 to 1949, years that match Harding's appearances. Unfortunately, the purchase files were destroyed after Moskowitz's death in 1997, so all essential data have been lost.

It may be that Buchanan had come to know Milligan through her submissions and that romance blossomed. Presumably it was Milligan who created the alias of Allison V. Harding but was she the sole writer, or did Buchanan write any of the stories, or were some or all collaborations? We don't know, so part of the mystery endures. What we do know is that she/he/they contributed some of the most memorable stories in the magazine's last decade.

There was a soft summer rain which meant "Stay inside," but with Mother away visiting, Jamie had run out the back door—Father was in the library reading and Cook was in the kitchen baking—across the lawn and down the path that ran into the meadow.

Dr. Holland sat in his favourite leather easy chair in the library, half reading but more interested in looking out the window. It was warm enough to be in shirtsleeves; he was glad that there seemed to be no patients who would need his attention that afternoon, for like the sparrows outside he felt a reluctance to move in the heat and humidity.

There was no sound except the soft hiss of the rain as it touched the griddle-hot earth still overheated from the morning's blazing sun. No other sound—except the occasional happy noise of Amanda in the kitchen whipping up cake batter. Amanda was one of those country prizes found in small towns. She filled in when needed and did just what had to be done, as on this occasion, for instance, when Albert Holland's wife had gone across the state for a two-week visit with her own folks.

It was nice to sit here like this not doing anything—the medical journal in his hand had an interesting article, but he didn't have to read it this afternoon. He wondered idly what kind of cake Amanda was whipping up, hoped it would be one of those thick white ones with chocolate icing and jelly fill.

And it was just then that he heard Jamie yipping and hollering, the sound of his small-boy voice coming from outside, getting louder as the little legs drove him closer.

*

Jamie had a secret. It was the biggest secret he'd ever had. Too big for its excitement to be contained in his small body dressed garishly in last Christmas' cowboy suit. After looking and looking to be sure, he ran away from it through the field and up the meadow hill, over the stone wall and across the lawn, his little feet splattering through puddles. He started to call before he reached the house, and his father met him at the back door.

"Young man, come in here directly and wipe your feet!"

"Daddy!" gasped Jamie, all out of breath.

His father marched him into the library. "You know perfectly well, Jamie, you wouldn't have been out playing Cowboy and Indian in this rain if your mother hadn't just gone away!"

"Daddy—"

"Young man, it won't look good for either of us if when Mother gets back, you're sniffling around with a head cold. I think you'd better go upstairs and change. Let me feel those shoes and socks."

"But, Daddy! *Daddy...!*"

"Yup, they're wet! Now march yourself upstairs."

"But there's a *man* out there in the field, Daddy, lying all in the ground looking up at me!"

"Now don't you try and get me in on your Indian games, Jamie."

"Really, Daddy, honest and truly—come an' see!" The little boy's voice rose to a crescendo and he pulled at his father's hand.

"You take yourself upstairs, young man, and change out of that costume. If you want to put on rubbers and a slicker, I'll walk out there with you. What did you say this was... an Indian chief?"

"It's no Indian chief, Daddy. Just a man lying there in a hole in the ground!"

"If you want me to go outside with you and help you hunt Buffalo Bill, you go upstairs and do as I told you!"

*

The little boy clattered away. A few moments later, father and son walked across the lawn over the stone fence and into the fields beyond. The drizzle was over, but mist had taken its place and clung with grey fingers to the meadow.

"Don't tug so, Jamie. Anyway, we want to sneak up kind of careful like! I don't want an arrow through me, pardner!"

Jamie's excitement increased as they reached the far side of the meadow. There between a boulder and a tree stump he stopped, he looked at the ground and then he looked up at his father crestfallen.

"Mister Mole was there, Daddy, right there!" He pointed.

There was some newly turned earth here, the top of it muddy from the rain, as though Jamie himself or someone else had used a spade. Dr. Holland poked at it with the tip of his boot. There was nothing.

"Guess the Indians got to him before we could, Jamie. Or maybe a mountain lion got him!"

"He *was* right there, Daddy!"

The physician laughed and put an arm around his son.

"Back to the house with you, youngster."

He liked the boy being imaginative. To him it signalled brains, and that in one's progeny never displeases a parent.

That evening at supper Jamie seemed unusually quiet, and Dr. Holland wondered if he'd made enough of the episode. To please his son he brought it up again.

"Why did you call that varmint Mister Mole, Jamie?"

"Because he was in the ground—stuck in the ground kind of, Daddy."

In the mornings the physician contrived to get their breakfast.

"I'm not much of a cook, Helen," he had confided to his wife, but she laughed and said, "Well, you men can't starve with Amanda getting two meals!"

Later this particular morning the schedule called for him to pick up Cook and she would spin her magic in the kitchen.

Dr. Holland was having a poor time with the breakfast dishes when Jamie came tearing into the kitchen.

"It's Mister Mole again!" in one great gush of air.

"Jamie... now look, you've tracked dirt in here. I don't mind, but you know your mother's told you not to do that and it means Amanda will have to clean it up. Maybe *we'd* better."

"Quick, Daddy!" The little boy was already pulling at Dr. Holland's apron. "Quick, before Mister Mole goes away!"

The Doctor went, something less than willingly, but forced along by his little son's urgency, out the back door again and across the lawn. And much nearer the house this time, just over the stone wall was a hole—funny, he'd not noticed that before; his son was getting to be quite the boy with the shovel—and in it... Dr. Holland stopped so abruptly that his hand in Jamie's pulled the little boy off balance backward.

"See, Daddy! See, it's Mister Mole, like I told you!"

There were two steps to be taken to the hole in the ground and Dr. Holland took them, instinctively pushing his son back a bit as he did.

The thing in the hole was... a man... or had been! He was dressed in nondescript brown jacket, shirt and trousers, shoes, and his skin had something of the colour of earth too, and there was earth coming from his nostrils and his ears and at the corner of his mouth.

His eyes were opened, staring upward—for he was lying on his back—as Holland knelt beside the thing, he noticed the quirk of the lips. The man, whoever he was, could not have been very pretty in life, and the leer turned the face into a distasteful grimace.

The Doctor reached for the wrist. As he lifted it to feel at the pulse, earth fell away from between the fingers. It was as he expected—no beat. He slipped a hand in under the man's jacket and felt over the heart region. There was not the slightest vibration.

He rose, and herding his son before him, hurried back to the house.

"You see, Daddy, I told you about Mister Mole! He comes out of the earth!"

"Now, son, I've got some things to do and I want you to stay here."

So there *had* been someone yesterday! Jamie must have become confused and led his father in the wrong direction.

Holland was due soon for a call on Mrs. Foster, whose nagging arthritis and irritable temperament demanded punctilious attendance by her physician. He thought of calling Ed Quinlan the next house away. Quinlan, aside from being town clerk, was also deputy sheriff of the district; but instead, professional curiosity made Holland first reach for his small medical bag and head out again to that grave across the lawn, unravelling his stethoscope as he went.

He was quite sure... well, positively sure, that the man was dead. The shock of the whole thing—his son, of course, didn't realize the dreadful significance of this gruesome business. He walked briskly—he figured afterward he could not have been in the house more than five minutes, and yet... yet when he returned and stood there where the spot was, the thing, Mr. Mole, was gone!

"Impossible!" Holland murmured half to himself.

This was the place, no mistake about that. The loose earth; he sifted it with his fingers. There was nothing! *Nothing!* He stood from kneeling and looked around, half fearful that he would find this man he had thought—no, he was sure—was dead walking somewhere away from his earthy grave. There was no one, and he could see a good ways in every direction!

He folded his stethoscope thoughtfully and returned to the house. It came to him that this might be some sort of outrageous joke played by persons unknown, like the time some of the high schoolers had monkeyed with the pipe on his birdbath and a firehose stream of water had come out instead of the usual graceful spray the birds welcomed.

But still it *had* been a body and it *had* been dead. That would mean either grave robbing or a corpse from some morgue or hospital laboratory.

He instructed Jamie to stay indoors "positively, and don't you dare disobey me" until he got back.

He made his call to Mrs. Foster as short as possible, picked up Amanda, and drove back at a great rate to find his son unconcernedly playing with his toy soldiers on the library floor.

Once, twice during the day the Doctor walked out to the plot of loose earth beyond the wall. Once he went out into the fields where Jamie had taken him the previous day. There was nothing to be seen except what looked like an area of spaded earth.

No more was said until that evening when Jamie brought the subject up just before being ordered to bed.

"Where does Mr. Mole go, Daddy?"

That was a stickler! If you presumed Mr. Mole existed, he couldn't just vanish without reason and to places unknown. If you presumed Mr. Mole didn't exist, then Dr. Holland should instantly fetch his son to an eye doctor and get himself to a psychiatrist!

For several days Dr. Holland thought a lot as he went about his doctor's tasks and as he puttered around the house being a father, and he found more than a few excuses to walk around the lawn and across the stone fence and into the meadows beyond.

In a few days the holes where Mr. Mole had appeared lost their freshness, lost their appearance of having been newly turned and again were reclaimed by the broad bosom of the earth.

It was one evening just before bedtime that Jamie said, "Mister Mole invited me to go for a walk today, Daddy!"

Holland almost dropped his pipe cleaner. He tried to keep his voice steady, for in the silence that had surrounded this subject for several days, it was as though that ugly dream had been swallowed up. The physician kept his voice even with an effort.

"Where was he, Jamie? Where was Mister Mole?"

The little boy indicated with a vague sweep of his arm and repeated again, "He asked me to take a walk with him. Down below, he said, Daddy."

"Jamie!" This thing had gone far enough. "I want you to tell me, when did you first see Mister Mole?"

"The time I told you. That rainy day."

"And, Jamie... honest to gosh now... he *talks* to you!"

"Sure, Daddy."

Holland rose to his feet. Something now would have to be done. This could not be set upon or dismissed with the hopeful conclusion that it was, after all, only a figment of the imagination.

"Let's go see Mister Mole, son, right now."

"But you can't! He's gone! He went right while I looked!"

"Which way? We'll follow him."

The boy crinkled up his brow as though even to his young and credulous mind, the event was unusual.

"He just kind of went. Down into the earth like. He said he'd be back."

The physician got his son to tell him the whereabouts of Mr. Mole's latest appearance and then bustled the six-year-old off to bed. He looked for himself later, and there about where his son had described it were the markings of freshly troubled and tossed earth. Precisely what to do was perplexing. His ordered scientific mind made Dr. Holland seek some definite, logical action, and yet there was none.

The thing—whatever it was, and it appeared to be a man—should be examined by the authorities. The first step in that programme, though, was to find Mr. Mole and constrain him from any more of his vanishings.

Albert Holland spent twenty-four hours thinking over a course of action and then the thought came to him that he should talk to his neighbour, Ed Quinlan, the deputy sheriff who lived across the long meadow that ran out back and down the hill apiece. Quinlan, a widower with a son about Jamie's age, was a nice fellow. He'd always appreciated that Holland had treated him without mention of a bill when things had been tough for the Quinlans a while back. And he showed his appreciation. But more, he was a bluff, realistic individual whose long suit was not imagination—though he was not stupid by any means—and would, therefore, bring a good slant to bear on this proposition, plus the weight of his official office in the county.

Holland was going to stroll over there this very evening, and now with Jamie bedded down, he was about to start when the knocker of his own front door sounded. It was, coincidentally, Quinlan.

"Hello, Ed!" the physician greeted warmly.

"Evenin', Doc. Sorry to bother you."

"Not at all. Come on in."

Holland saw immediately that the man was agitated. His broad, ruddy face looked worried and his big thick-fingered hands gripped at the somewhat worn panama he was never without.

"Missus still away, Doc?"

"Yup, another week, Ed."

They talked of things like this and that for some moments and then Ed got around to the point.

"Doc, if your youngster's safe in bed, I wonder if you could walk down toward my place apiece. Something funny has happened."

Holland waited, his own feeling of uncomfortableness increasing.

"My son, Eddie, Doc. Damndest thing you ever know. He came across a body lying out there—in the meadow back of our place. I thought the youngster was pulling my leg... you know the way these kids carry on. Kept after me all afternoon, he did. I went out with him just now, Doc. Seen *him* for myself. I did. All stained from the earth, kind of grinning like. Was the spookiest lookin' fellow you ever saw, Doc. I felt of him myself. Didn't have no more warmth any more than a tree. Sure he *looked* dead, although I can't really say if there's been some crime committed."

Quinlan stopped and took a deep breath, fiddled with his hat and then fixed his troubled eyes on the doctor again.

"Would you come along with me?"

"Why sure, Ed."

Quinlan hurried on, saying, "I think I saw the fellow move. It was getting kind of to twilight out there. I'd sent Eddie back to the house for a flashlight. To be honest, I couldn't see so good. But, Doc, he'd been lying on his back with the earth and all coming out of his mouth like, and when I looked again, I could swear he'd kind of rolled over. But there was still this grin on his face like he'd died smiling—only it wasn't a nice smile—or if he wasn't all dead, he was enjoying this."

The man rattled on, following the physician out into the hall as Holland went to the coat closet to get his own flashlight.

"I'll go with you, Ed."

"But here's the thing, Doc." Ed's hand held him just inside the front door as they were about to step out into the darkness of the summer evening. "I lost him. I must've been watching through the gloom for Eddie to come back with the light and all, but I turned around and he was gone—just like that as though he'd never been there 'cept that I knew he had 'cause the earth was all turned up new-grave like!"

The two walked then, the bobbing flashlight held in Holland's hand showing the way across the lush July countryside. The night with them and silence now between them, this lawman and the man of science, each with his thoughts and his puzzlement until they stood together, close together, brought there by Quinlan's sense of direction and the bobbing shaft of light that followed to its goal.

Ed's voice sounded small under the black archway of night as he breathed out and said, "There's where he was. Right there, Doc."

And Albert Holland stood and looked at the ground, the familiar look to it. Stood with flashlight beam steady, for there was nothing to do. They both were thinking what to do next and there was no need to say it. Finally Quinlan spoke.

"Guess you think I'm crazy, Doc."

And at that, the physician put his hand on the other's arm.

"No, I don't, Ed. You're not crazy. You saw something." And he was going to say, I saw it too, Ed. Out here in the meadow and then back nearer my house. Jamie called me just as Eddie called you. We've seen *something* all right—in God's heaven just what, I don't know and I'm a doctor and supposed to know what life and death look like.

But he didn't say it because Quinlan was talking some more:

"... claims he talked to him—imagine this, Doc, a corpse speaking to him—and invited Eddie to take a walk with him, although he couldn't be a corpse moving over onto his side, could he? People can't do things like that—if they're really dead, Doc, can they?" The deputy sheriff was plaintive.

Holland put his arm on the other's shoulder again, this time with more urgency.

"Ed, you say you shooed Eddie home before you came up to my place?"

"Why, sure... sure!"

Then the two almost automatically started walking towards Quinlan's small cottage just over the brow of the hill, and as they walked, though nothing more was said, their steps speeded.

It was the night that did it, Holland told himself, the night that puts fear into even the most unsuperstitious man, the most prosaic, the most unimaginative, but by rights they *should* feel that way, for this experience the two fathers shared with their two small sons was—poor weak word—extraordinary!

There was a light on the ground floor of the Quinlan house and they could see it through the gloom and it grew bigger as they walked hurriedly towards it. Quinlan, a tightness in his voice now, called as they went forward.

"Eddie! Eddie, lad? Are you there? It's your dad!"

And from the bigger bulk of house ahead of them through the night the small boy's voice came back.

"Gee, Pop, is that you? You been out there in the meadow talkin' to *him*?"

There was no need to answer. Almost simultaneously, their hurrying steps slowed. The crisis, not declared between the two men but appreciated by both of them, was over. Quinlan turned to face the physician.

"Thanks, Doc. Thanks a lot for coming over."

In the dark the two men shook hands. Fervently, it seemed. And then they parted to go their separate ways in the darkness—Quinlan to his home and Dr. Holland back across the night-grown meadow.

Holland sat up till very late that night thinking of the chain of events which were now more than the imaginings of one person or two.

Quinlan was his antithesis, his opposite and antidote, and yet the plain, good-hearted man had *seen*. The possibility of this being some ill-mannered joke was quite implausible. Aside from any other objections, people don't play that kind of joke on a deputy sheriff, even if the town physician is less immune. No, there was something out there... somebody. He was a man, or had been once, for he looked it and he wore clothes.

There were, Holland was well aware, cases of improper diagnosis. Persons have been declared dead who were not dead. There are diseases and conditions and states which resemble death and yet are not. The catatonic is one, for instance, and yet beneath his reasoning, beyond his speculating and his attempts to lay out at least in his own mind each possibility, and then rationally to plug these loopholes, he was certain as a physician that the man he had seen, the one Jamie had—so aptly wasn't it—called Mr. Mole, was not of the living.

He wished Helen were here for she was not only a good listener—and he needed such to parade his facts and suppositions before—but she had good suggestions. The night insects were quiet and there was a hint of light in the east when the physician retired to his room.

To explain to Jamie that he was not supposed to run small-boylike far and wide across the meadows necessitated the thinking up of a story about Indians on the move outside.

The little boy looked at his father closely, more wisely, the physician thought, than a child of his years should.

Holland went about his business glad that the days were six, five, four, then three until wife Helen would return. He could not in all conscience restrict his son to the house for there had to be a reason more than make-believe Indians and the danger to the small, towheaded boy was not proven, dwelling perhaps more in a father's mind than anywhere else.

As the days passed, the physician chided himself a bit. He became annoyed at the feeling of uncomfortableness that he experienced when he needs be, got the coupe with the physicians' emblem over the back licence plate, out of the garage to go on some necessary call or errand, and yet still felt uneasiness at leaving Jamie.

But the very passing of time gave strength to the hope that grew almost to conviction that whoever it was, whatever it was out there in the ground, moving like a mole from place to place, had gone back to whatever place from whence it had come, or had been stilled forever in some dark crevice beneath the earth's surface away from men's eyes.

Holland met Quinlan one day down in the village, and both men's spirits were good.

They didn't say so, but the meaning was clear. *I haven't seen him nor have you or we would have spoken of it.* The knowledge was between the two men and then they parted cheerfully.

The night before the good day Helen was to return, Holland's phone rang. Jamie was already upstairs, presumably asleep in his cheerful, wallpapered east room, and Holland had long since given Amanda a lift home explaining to her carefully that they'd "want her later on the morrow" because Helen would be coming back in time for supper and it would be nice to have something extra special for her homecoming.

"Hello, Doc," it was Quinlan when Holland picked up the receiver. "Eddie's seen him again!"

The doctor's hand tightened on the instrument.

"Out back in the woods apiece. Swears he moves around an' talks to him. Wanted Eddie to take a walk with him."

Holland tried to keep his voice even. "What's to do about it, Ed?"

"Tomorrow..." Quinlan added just as though he'd thought it out, "... I'll get a bunch of us together and we'll find out who or what this is! Maybe it's some kind of queer drunk." This last, hopefully.

"I think we ought to do something, Ed," the physician said resolutely. "Can't let this go on, you know!"

On that note the two men hung up, Holland to re-enter the library where he sat, the uneasiness with him again. In the last few days he had found the time and opportunity to peruse both the county clerk's and newspaper records. There had been no unaccounted-for disappearances or other incidents in this area which would explain this peripatetic "thing" which haunted the summer countryside. And in present-day society the hardest thing in the world to do is to disappear or get oneself killed or destroyed in any way without attracting considerable attention.

Yes, whoever heard of an unclaimed body or corpse? Try as he would, Holland could not dissuade himself from the nagging thought that here was something that did not fit in with the commonplace and, therefore, did not follow everyday laws of the workaday world.

Actually, it was a few minutes past seven the next morning when Holland heard his front-door knocker clattering. It seemed much earlier. The rain and mist across the land had held up the day. Jamie was just stirring in his room as his father clumped down the stairs muttering under his breath.

And then before he put his hand on the great knob that would turn the door to open it, a feeling of presentiment took hold of him, stiffened his arm, and touched his back with damp, cold fingers.

He pulled the portal open, and out of the early morning greyness stepped Quinlan, in his arms a bundle, his mute face wide-eyed, storm-streaked. He seemed to offer the thing cradled in his arms to Holland and Holland, seeing, suddenly became the physician.

He said gently, "Here, Ed. Let me take him," though he knew at first look it was no good.

There was dirt all over little Eddie; dirt turned to mud by the rain in his eyes and mouth and ears. The youngster had died, it was apparent, of suffocation—not from hands wrapped around his throat, but from going down deep, deep into the earth and being buried there.

The thought came back to Holland of what Quinlan had said over the phone the previous night, what his own son had said the last time the "thing" had visited over here—what was it?—Mr. Mole had invited him to take a walk *below*?

As the physician was thinking, Quinlan was talking brokenly, trying to hold onto himself with the will of a strong man, twisted and bending under the crudest tragedy of his life.

"I'm sure the youngster was to bed when I talked to you last night, Doc, but sometime in the night or early this morning, he must have gone out—God knows why—'cept that that devil has a power, a kind of fascination! I'm up early, you know, and Eddie was nowhere around the house this morning. I went out to look... and there was one of those holes not far from the house. You know... like we'd seen before. Seen little Eddie's footprints, I did, around this place like they went into the hole...

"... I got me a spade then, Doc, and I dug faster than a man's ever dug before... and after I got down a ways in that hole... I found him... like this. But there weren't a 'hello, Daddy' or a breath left in 'im at all."

Quinlan sank down on a chair, sobbing now, his head between his great, strong hands, shaking like a terrified child.

"Ed," said Holland quietly and sympathetically. "Ed, follow me into the medical room."

The physician led the way, carrying Eddie's body in his arms, and Quinlan dutifully lurched along behind. Jamie was a sensitive boy. Holland could find no use for having him look down the stairs through the banisters and see the scene in the front hall. Also, Quinlan himself needed some medication.

The doctor laid Eddie's body carefully on the examining table, made sure with his stethoscope what he already knew—that there was not the slightest flicker of life left in the earth-choked body, and then mixed the unfortunate boy's father a potent sedative.

"He's gone, isn't he, Doc?"

"I'm afraid he is, Ed. It's a terrible thing... terrible! And I know any words of sympathy now from me seem poor and inadequate."

Quinlan sat for a time, not saying anything, turning the glass that contained the sedative around and around in his strong fingers. He drained the medicine, and after a while, stood up.

"Well... thanks. Doc. I'll take my son, if you please. Take him home and then down to the undertaker's. I want to go quick, Doc...'cause I'm going to get after the devil out there in the ground! I'm going to get the men together. You'll join us, Doc?"

"You know I will, Ed. I'll come over to your place a little later in the morning."

"You got an axe, Doc? Bring it!" The deputy's teeth bared in a snarl. "We're gonna get this fellow!"

"Ed... don't you want me to go with you, or take little Eddie down to town myself?"

Quinlan shook his head determinedly. "What's done's done, Doc. Now we gotta get after the one who did this!"

He went out with Eddie again cradled in his arms, and the growing morning, as the light of it touched his face, showed it set in hard lines, the terrible sadness, shock and despair replaced with something else that was healthier in man.

Holland went for Jamie then and was steeled when the boy asked, "Daddy, what was Mister Quinlan doing here?"

"He had a very great problem, son," the physician replied carefully. "He came to ask me about it. How about driving into town with me,

Jamie, to pick up Amanda?" As they drove, the clouds scurried away before them and the sun came out to dry and heat up the wet, early morning world. Holland drove numbly and instinctively. He returned Amanda's greetings automatically. There was nothing to be said, but already, his son was looking at him curiously.

That was one of the curses of imagination. Amanda was old, good to bake cakes and make apple pie dumplings and filled with the desire to serve them and affection for them as a family, but she was too old to understand if he said, "Now look, Amanda. Something terrible has happened in this neighbourhood. There's a man loose... a dead man, and he's just killed a little boy. We have to be careful... we don't know from what direction danger may come. Maybe it won't come but there's the situation!"

He couldn't talk like that to her, or even if he could, not in front of his son.

They arrived back at the Holland house, and Amanda noticed at once that the physician had not gotten any breakfast. She insisted on getting something together. Holland ate poorly. Afterward, he must get over to Quinlan's as he had promised. The men would be gathering there for their grim task.

Jamie, from behind his glass of milk, said to his father behind his coffee cup, "I'm going over to play with Eddie this morning. We're going to fly the new kite, Daddy!"

Albert Holland swallowed with difficulty.

"No, Jamie, not this morning."

"But, Daddy—!"

What could he say? *What could he say?* Not "Jamie, I have something to tell you... Amanda's too old and you're really too young to understand the why of this, but the facts are, Eddie is... dead! He was pulled into a hole by a corpse and suffocated out there in the meadow where you and he have played so many times... where you were going to play this morning with your kite. He's dead, Jamie. No use looking for him out there."

How could he say that? What could he say? And all the time Jamie sitting there, tow-headed and wondering why.

"Daddy, we're going to..."

The boy's quick mind kept searching around his father's silence. "Is he sick?"

(That's a doctor's son for you.)

"That's what it is!" said the little boy, gathering momentum and sureness. "He's got measles!"

No, Jamie, that happened last winter and you don't get them twice, but you still remember how Helen and I wouldn't let you go over because Eddie had measles. This time, Jamie, it's something worse... oh, so much worse than measles.

"It's something catching, Daddy? Measles?"

"No."

No, Jamie, not measles, not something catching—not really. Or maybe it is! Maybe that's why I'm more frightened than I'd ever dare let you know. That's why in a moment I'm going to get the axe out of the woodshed and go over and join Quinlan and the rest of the men.

Instead he said, "No, Jamie, you can't go over this morning. Find something to do around here. And don't you disobey me! I'm going to tell Amanda to keep her eye on you, hear?"

Albert Holland walked towards Quinlan's, the axe in one hand, across the low stone wall into the meadow and towards the hillside. The sun was out now, accentuating the softness and the peace of midsummer. The fertile greenness soothed his eyes and made the unpleasant thoughts in the physician's mind seem incredible and implausible. That these things could have happened under the blueness of the sky, the brightness of the sun here in the softness of the land was surely not possible.

And yet as he walked farther, he saw the knots of men standing around Quinlan's house. From a distance they were short men and tall men, fat and lean. Here and there the sun touched a gun barrel. He recognized faces as he came closer—a drugstore clerk, several boys from the volunteer fire department, the assistant postmaster, others. They nodded to him and he nodded back. And there was one thing they all had in common, and that one thing was grim and unsmiling.

Men made suggestions and barked orders at one another, and finally they walked out onto the broad bosom of the meadow, taking their shovels and axes and clubs and guns with them, prodding at the earth, poking at it as though it, itself, had committed this awful crime.

Quinlan was everywhere, filled with a terrible rage that was the worse because it was silent except as it came out in the man's unquenchable energy.

The hours passed, and the men plodded across the fields, sloshed through brooks and tramped through underbrush. They had long since poked and spaded into the holes Quinlan and Dr. Holland knew of. Midday passed and afternoon. The sun slid towards the rim of the westerly hills, and Holland, consulting his watch, knew he should be getting back to get things all ready for Helen.

With the fatigue of walking, searching, there came a feeling of futility. What had they done... what could they do? What did they know, tapping their boots and steel instruments against the ground here and there for something that would not stand up fairly and say "Here I am!"

In relays some of the men came back to Quinlan's cottage where womenfolk were keeping coffee pots on the stove. Holland left his axe at Quinlan's and turned his steps towards home. He told himself that sooner or later they'd have to uncover this creature—whatever he was or it was. It was good, he thought with a physician's analysis, drat Quinlan had the direction of this posse on his hands at this moment of his so-great sorrow.

He made the house, went inside, the screen door slamming behind him. The noise of Amanda in the kitchen drew him there. She was "making something special" for the supper when Helen would be with them again.

"Where's Jamie?" he asked loudly. Amanda was a little on the deaf side and had to be bellowed at.

"He's around—playing in his cowboy costume, he is." She waved an old arm in a semi-circle. "Doctor Albert..." She always called him that, "... Doctor Albert, you look a fright! Whatever have you been doing?" Holland looked down at himself. Five or six hours of walking through thickets and looking at dirt holes in the fields had left him rather bedraggled. He'd have to clean up. The physician looked out the kitchen window.

"Where did you say Jamie was?"

"'Round somewhere," she repeated again. "Saw him not very long ago. Well, now maybe it *was* an hour. Had a friend, he did. Mister Somebody-or-other come to see him."

Holland froze. "Mister... Mister *Mole?*" His voice was much louder than necessary.

"That's it! Knew it sounded like an animal. Peculiar handle, isn't it, Doctor Albert? Said his friend invited him—this Mister Mole—to take a walk down below. Must mean out towards the meadow, Doctor Albert."

But Holland was gone, flinging himself out the door, running and trying to look in all directions, the inner hand clamped over his heart tightening, agonizing...

The house was behind and the lawn and the stone wall, and then in the woods in the other direction from the meadow, he found it. A new hole like all those others!

Holland went at it with his boots and hands, wishing he had something else, but there was no time to run back for a tool. He scooped and kicked the earth away as fast as he could. And by and by a corner of material showed and then he had it in his earth-coated shaking hands. It was a hat—a small boy's cowboy hat... from Jamie's outfit!

The doctor redoubled his efforts then frantically, clawing, getting down on all fours, and finally he found what he knew was there, and shaking away the earth covering and clinging, he laid it on the rim of the hole he had excavated with his hands... the same size bundle as Quinlan had brought to him the night before, equally lifeless and useless now.

Holland made a noise like an animal, and like that animal, he dug on, hollowing and scooping, for it was for him to do this thing. *He* would have to stop it. The old who had forgotten how to dream and who don't want to believe, like Amanda, and the very young who still believe in everything, like Jamie—they had caused this, unknowing.

He went on and on, a man in an earthen hole in the green countryside. And it must have been hours later that Amanda, wondering, came looking and heard the noises from that place in the woods. She got men from the posse over at Quinlan's, and they found him like that in an unbelievably deep hole of his own making, with the small earth-caked body of his son lying guard above.

It was Quinlan, himself, who pulled Albert Holland out, and later with Helen, who had arrived home again, tried to reassure and quiet the physician. Helen, whose shock, at finding this terrible tragedy in her own family, was only slightly more than the frightening condition of her husband.

*

For Dr. Holland was not a man of science any more, not a physician but a squealing, screaming, crying creature, stuffed with earth that came out of him when he talked. They sent for another doctor up at the county seat to come quickly, but there were miles in between, and meanwhile Holland had the time to tell over and over again how they shouldn't have pulled him out of the hole in the earth, for twice, three times, more, he had caught up with Mr. Mole down there. He had felt a trousered leg, an arm, a torso, and it had wriggled and twisted away from him like a worm in the earth. Yes—and it had leered at him!

"It speaks and it moves!" Holland ranted this over and over.

Sometimes in his horror he screamed so loudly that he frightened the birds outside in the twilight of the July evening, and even poor, old half-deaf Amanda far away in other parts of the house staying, with her kindly tear-streaked face, because "Maybe there's something I can do," would clap her withered hands to her ears to keep the awful sounds from them.

But Albert Holland's screams did not carry far enough, for later, not too much later, across the green land cooling in evening, a blond child named Janice ran across the spongy green ground—a child who believed in fairy stories, in everything—running and calling through the evening, filled to bursting with the secret as she ran.

"Mommy! Daddy! Guess what! Guess what *I've* found!"

THE END

1954

BRENDA

Margaret St. Clair

Margaret St. Clair (1911–1995) had ten stories in *Weird Tales*, all squeezed into the magazine's last four years starting with "The Family" (January 1950), but she had a letter in the June 1934 issue, revealing she had been reading the magazine since she was 12, which would be from the very start. Early efforts to sell her stories were without success until she acquired a literary agent when the floodgates opened. She was soon appearing in the sf and fantasy magazines starting with "Rocket to Limbo" (*Fantastic Adventures*, November 1946), where a wife considers a foolproof way of disposing of her husband.

She already had a busy life, studying, travelling and, after her marriage, turning her love of gardening into running a nursery. She also bred dachshunds. Her interests spread to astrology and witchcraft and it is a thread of ritual or an evocation of change that runs through her stories in *Weird Tales*. That debut story, "The Family", concerns the importance of sacrifice within a strange Addams-like family. "The Island of the Hands" (September 1952), which was included in the British Library volume *Queens of the Abyss*, deals with transformation. St. Clair revelled in the idea of otherness, and she was sorry when *Weird Tales* ceased but by then she had transformed herself into Idris Seabright and was writing very individualistic stories for *The Magazine of Fantasy & Science Fiction*. She continued to write throughout the fifties and early sixties but though she lived until 1995, her work is virtually encased in amber of the 1950s. A representative collection was assembled by Ramsey Campbell as *The Hole in the Moon and Other Tales* (2019).

Brenda Alden was a product of that aseptic, faintly sadistic, school of child rearing that is already a little old-fashioned. The vacationing parents on Moss Island liked her, and held up her politeness and good manners as examples to their offspring; the children themselves stayed away from her, scenting in her something waspish and irritable. She was tall for her age, and lanky, with limp blonde hair. She always wore slacks.

Monday began like all her days. She had breakfast, was told to keep her elbows off the table, helped with the dishes. Then she was told to go out and play. She sauntered slowly into the woods.

The woods on Moss Island were scattered clumps of birch and denser stands of conifers. There were places where Brenda, if she tried hard, could have the illusion of a forest, and she liked that. In the western part of the island there was a wide, deep excavation which people said had been a quarry. Nobody ever said what had been quarried out of it.

It was a little before noon when Brenda smelled the rotten smell. It was an intense, bitter, rottenness, almost strangling, and when it first met her nose Brenda's face wrinkled up with distaste. But after a moment her face relaxed. She inhaled, not without eagerness. She decided to try to find the source of the smell. Sometimes she liked to smell and look at rotten things. Sniffing, she wandered. The smell would be strong and then weak and then strong again. She was just about to give up and turn back—it was hot in the airless, piney pockets, under the sun—when she saw the man.

He was not a tramp, he was not one of the summer people. Brenda knew at once that he was not like any other man she had ever seen. His skin was not black, or brown, but of an inky greyness; his body was blobbish and irregular, as if it had been shaped out of the clots of soap and grease that stop up kitchen sinks. He held a dead bird in one crude hand. The rotten smell was welling out from him.

Brenda stared at him, her heart pounding. For a moment she was almost too frightened to move. She stood gasping and licking her lips. Then he extended an arm toward her. She turned and ran.

She heard the noise, she smelled the smell, as he came stumbling after her. Her lungs hurt. There was a stitch in her side. She tripped over a root, fell to her knees, and was up again. She ran on. Only when she was almost too exhausted to go further did she look back.

He was more distant then she had hoped, though he was still coming. For a second she stood panting, her narrow sides going in and out. He was still separated from her by some fifty feet. She blinked. Then her lips curved in what was almost a smile. She turned to the right, in the direction of the quarry, and began running again, though more leisurely.

There was a thicket of poison oak; she skirted it. She stooped for a pine cone, and then another one, thrust them into the waistband of her trousers, and went on with her steady trotting. He was still following. The light seemed to hurt his eyes; his head hung forward almost on his chest. Then they were on the edge of the quarry, and Brenda must try her plan.

She was no longer afraid—or, at any rate, only a little so. Exertion had washed her sallow cheeks with an unaccustomed red. Carefully she tossed one of the pine cones over the steep quarry side so that it landed halfway toward the bottom and then rolled on down. With more force she threw the second cone; it hit well beyond the first and slid toward the bottom in a rattle of loose stones and dirt. Then, very quickly and lightly, Brenda ran to the left and crouched behind a tree.

The noise of the pine cones had been not unlike that of a runner plunging over the quarry edge and down into the depths. Brenda's pursuer halted, turning his head from side to side blindly, and seeming to sniff the air. She felt a movement of intense anxiety. She was almost sure he couldn't catch her, even if he started after her again. But—oh—he was so—

One of the pine cones slid a few feet further. He seemed to listen. Then he went over the edge after the sound of it.

Brenda's heart was shaking the flat bosom of her shirt. While the rotten-smelling man stumbled back and forth among the dusty rocks in the quarry bottom hunting her, she waited and listened. It took him a long time to abandon the search. But at last the moment for which Brenda had been waiting came. He left his hunting and began to struggle up the quarry side.

He slid back. Brenda leaned forward, tense and expectant. Her eyes were bright. He started up again. Once more he slid back.

It was clear to the watching child much sooner than it was to the man in the depths of the quarry that he was imprisoned. He kept starting up the sides clumsily, clawing at the loose handholds, and sliding back. But his blobbish limbs were extraordinarily inept and awkward. He always slid back.

At last he gave up and stood quiet. His head dropped. He made no sound. But the penetrating rottenness was welling out from him.

Brenda got to her feet and walked toward him. Her pale lips were curving in a grin. "Hi!" she called over the edge of the quarry. "Hi! You can't get out, can you?"

The mockery in her tone seemed to cut through to his dull senses. He raised his greyish head. There was a flash of teeth, very white against their inky background. But he could not get out. After a moment, Brenda laughed.

Brenda hugged her secret to herself all the rest of the day. She was reprimanded for being late to lunch: her father said she needed discipline. She was not bothered. That night she slept soundly and well.

Early next morning she went to see Charles. Charles was a year older than she, and tolerated her better than anyone else on Moss Island. Once he had given her a cast-off snake skin. She had kept it in the drawer with her handkerchiefs.

Today he was making a cloud-chamber with rubbing alcohol, a jar, and a piece of dry ice. Brenda squatted down beside him and watched. After five minutes or so she said, "I know what's more fun than that."

"What?" Charles asked, without looking up from his manipulations.

"Something I found. Something funny. Scary. Queer."

The exchange continued. Brenda hinted. Charles was mildly curious. At last she said, "Come and see it, Chet. It's not like anything you ever saw before. Come on." She laid her hand on his arm.

Up until that moment, Charles might have accompanied her. The cloud-chamber was not going well, and he did not actively dislike the girl. But the dryness and tensity of her touch on his arm—the touch of a person who has never received or given a pleasant physical contact—repelled him. He drew away from her hand. "I don't want to see it. It isn't anything anyway. Just some sort of junk. I'm not interested," he said.

"But you'd like it! Please come and see."

"I told you, I'm not interested. I'm not going to go. Can't you take a hint? Go away."

When he used that tone, Brenda knew there was no use in arguing with him. She got up and walked off.

After lunch her father had her help him with the barbecue pit he was building. While she shovelled dirt and mixed concrete her thoughts were busy with the man in the quarry. Was he still standing motionless at the bottom, or was he once more stumbling back and forth hunting her? Or was he trying to clamber up to the sides again? He'd never make it, no matter how much he tried. But if he stayed there long enough, some of the other children might find him. Would they be more frightened than she had? She didn't know. She couldn't form any mental picture of what might happen then.

When her father knocked off work for the day, she lay down in the hammock. Her hands were sore and her back ached, but she couldn't relax. Finally, though it was almost supper time, she got up and walked off quickly toward the quarry.

He was still there. Brenda let out a deep breath of relief. The bitter, rotten smell hung strong in the air. She must have made a noise, for he raised his head and then let it drop forward again on his chest. Other than that, he was motionless.

Charles wouldn't come to see him. So... Brenda looked around her. Farther along the edge of the quarry, twenty feet or so from where she was standing, were two long boards. She measured their length with her eyes.

It was thirty feet or more to the bottom of the quarry. The boards were not quite long enough. But the zone of loose, sliding stuff did not extend all the way up; once the man in the excavation was past it, he ought to be able to get up easily enough. Charles had said that what she had found wasn't anything. Just some junk. Brenda began to move the boards.

Her hands were sore, but the boards themselves were not heavy. In fifteen minutes or so she had laid a narrow path from the bottom of the quarry to within a few feet of the top. *He*—the man—had done nothing while she worked, not even watched her. But underneath her shirt Brenda's narrow body was trembling and wet with sweat. She had to get closer to him than she had liked while she was putting down the second board.

She stood back. The man in the quarry did not move. Brenda felt a moment of anxious exasperation. Wasn't he going to do anything, after all her trouble? "Come on!" she said under her breath and then, more loudly, "Come on!"

The sun was beginning to decline toward the west. The shadows lengthened. The man below turned his head from side to side, as if the waning light had brought him a keener perception. One blobby grey hand went up. Then he started toward the boards.

Brenda waited until his uncertain feet were set upon the second of the lengths of wood. She could stand it no longer. She whirled about and ran as hard as she could toward home. She did not know whether or not he followed her.

Brenda did not go to the woods next morning. She hung around the house until her mother sent her out to help her father, who sent her back, saying that he had got to a place in his construction where she could be only in the way. Brenda went to the kitchen and got herself a sandwich and a glass of milk. When she came back with them her mother, pale and disturbed, was on the terrace outside the house talking to her father. Brenda went to the door and leaned her head against it.

"I don't see how it could be a tramp," her mother was saying. "Elizabeth said nothing had been taken. She was quite emphatic. Only the roast chicken. And even it hadn't been eaten, only torn into pieces." She hesitated. "She said there were spots of greyish slime all over it."

"Elizabeth exaggerates," Brenda's father answered. He gave the mortar he was smoothing an impatient pat. "What's her idea anyway, if it wasn't a tramp? Who else could break in her kitchen? There are only the six families on Moss Island."

"I don't think she has any definite idea. Oh, Rick, I wish you could have heard her talking. She mentioned the dreadful smell over and over. She said she was phoning the other families to warn them. She sounded afraid."

"Probably hysterical," he answered contemptuously. His eye fell on Brenda, standing in the shadow of the door. "Go up to your room, Brenda," he said sharply. "Stay there. I won't have you listening behind doors."

"Yes, father."

Brenda did not resent the order. She was afraid. Would Charles remember her hints of yesterday, connect them with the raid on Mrs. Emsden's kitchen (the man from the quarry must be hungry—but he hadn't eaten the chicken) and tell on her? Or would something worse happen, she didn't know what?

She moved about her room restlessly. The bed was made, there was nothing for her to do. She could hear the rumble of her parents' voices indistinctly, a word now and then rising into prominence. For the first time she felt a sharp curiosity about the man who had been in the quarry, about the man himself.

She got out her diary and opened it. But it wouldn't do; the volume had no lock, and she knew her mother read it. She never wrote anything important in it.

She looked at the scribbled pages with dislike. It would be nice to be able to tear them out and crumple them up in the wastepaper basket. But her mother would notice and ask her why she had destroyed her pretty book. No...

She hunted about the room until she found a box of note paper. Using the lid of the box as a desk, she printed carefully across the top of one of the narrow grey sheets: THE MAN.

She hesitated. Then she wrote: "1. Where did he come from?"

She licked her pencil. The idea was hard to put into words. But she wanted to see it written out on the paper. She began, erased, began again. Finally she wrote, "I think he came to Moss Island from the main land. I think he came over one night last month when the tide was so low. I think he came here by acci—" She erased. "By mistake."

Brenda was ready for the second question. "Why does he stay on the island?" she scribbled. She was writing faster now. "I think because he can not swim. The water would—" she paused, conscious that the exact word she wanted was not in her vocabulary. At last she wrote, "Would wash him away."

She got out another sheet of note paper. At the top she printed, "THE MAN Page 2." She bit into the pencil shank judiciously. Then she wrote, "What kind of a man is he? I think he is not like other people. Not like us. He is a different kind of a man."

She had written the last words slowly. Now inspiration came. She scribbled, "He is not like us because he likes dead things to eat. Things that have been dead for much—" an erasure—"for a long time. I think that is why he came to M.I. in the first place. Hunting. He is old. Has been the way he is for a long time."

She put the pencil down. She seemed to have finished. Her mother must have gone out: the noise of her parents' voices had ceased, and the house was perfectly quiet. Outside, she could hear the faint slap slap of her father's trowel as he worked on the concrete.

There was a long pause. Brenda sat motionless. Then she picked up the pencil again and wrote at the bottom of the page, very quickly, "I think he would help me to be born."

She picked up what she had written and looked at it. Then she took the two pages and went with them into the bathroom. She tore them into small pieces and flushed them down the drain.

*

Supper that night was quiet. Once Brenda's mother started to say something about Elizabeth Emsden, and was stopped by her father's warning frown. Brenda helped with the dishes. Just before she went upstairs to bed, she slipped into her parents' bedroom, which was on the ground floor, and unlatched the window screens.

She had trouble getting to sleep, but slept soundly. She was roused, when the night was well along, by the sound of voices. She stole out on the stair landing and listened, her heart beginning to thud.

The rotten smell was coming up in burning, bitter waves. The cottage seemed to rock under it. Brenda clung to the banister. He'd come then, the man—her man—from the quarry. She was glad.

Brenda's father was speaking. "That smell is really incredible," he said in an abstracted voice. And then, to Brenda's mother, "Flora, call Elizabeth and tell her to have Jim come over. Hurry. I don't know how much longer I can keep him back with this thing. Have Jim bring his gun."

"Yes." Flora Alden giggled. "You said Elizabeth was hysterical, didn't you? For God's sake keep your voice down, Rick. I don't want Brenda to waken and see this. She'd be—I don't think she'd ever get over it." She moved toward the telephone.

Brenda's eyes widened. Were her parents really solicitous for her? Were they afraid she'd be afraid? She moved down two or three steps, very softly, and sat down on one of the treads. If they noticed her now, she could say their voices had wakened her. She peered out between the banisters.

Her father was standing in the hall, holding the man from the quarry impaled in the stabbing beam of an electric torch. *He*—oh, he was brave—he kept moving about and trying to rub the light out of his eyes. He made little rushes. But her father shifted the torch mercilessly, playing him in it, even though his hand shook.

Brenda's mother came back from the phone. "He's coming," she reported. "He didn't think the gun would do much good. He had another plan."

It took Jim Emsden long enough to get to the cottage for Brenda to have time enough to shiver and wish she had put on her bathrobe. She yawned nervously and curled herself up more tightly against the banister. But she never took her eyes from the tableau in the hall below.

Emsden came in by the side door. He was wearing an overcoat over his pyjamas. He took a deep breath when he saw the grey, blobby shape in the light of the torch.

"Yes, it's the same man," he said in his rumbling voice. "Of course. Nobody could mistake that smell. I brought the gun, Rick, but I have a hunch it won't help. Not against a thing like that. Elizabeth got a glimpse of him, you know. I'll show you what I mean. Keep him in the torch."

He raised the .22 to his shoulder, clicked the bolt, and fired. Brenda's little scream went unheeded in the whoosh of the shot. But the man from the quarry made no sign of having received the impact. He did not even rock. The bullet might as well have spent its force in mud.

"You see?" Emsden demanded. "It wasn't any good."

Flora Alden was giggling gently. The beam of the torch moved in bobbing circles against the darkness. "What'll we do, Jim?" Rick asked. "I don't know things like this could happen. What are we going to do?—I'm afraid I'm going to be sick."

"Steady, Rick. Why, there's one thing he'll be afraid of. Whatever he is. Fire."

He produced rags and a bottle of kerosene. With the improvised torch they drove him out of the cottage and into the night outside. Whenever he slowed and tried to face them, his head lowered, his teeth gleaming, they thrust the bundle of burning rags in his face.

He had to give ground. Brenda was chewing her wrist in her excitement. She heard her father's higher voice saying, "But what will we do with him, Jim? We can't just leave him outside the house," and Emsden's deeper, less distinct answering rumble, "... kill him. But we can shut him up." And then a confused roll of voices ending in the word "quarry". She could hear nothing more.

Next day an atmosphere of exhaustion and cold defeat hung over the house. Brenda's mother moved about her household tasks mechanically, hardly speaking to her daughter, her face white. Her father had not come back to the cottage until nearly daybreak, and had left again after a few hours. It was not until nearly dusk that Brenda was able to slip out and try to find what had become of the man.

She made straight for the quarry. When she reached it, she looked about, bewildered. The sides were still sharp and square, but a great mound of rock had been piled up in the centre. The men of Moss Island must have worked hard all day to pile up so much rock.

She slid down the sides and clambered up the heap in the centre. What had become of him? Was he under the mound? She listened. She could hear nothing. After a moment she sat down and pressed her ear to the rock. It felt still warm from the heat of the sun.

She listened. She could hear only the beating of her heart. And then, far down, a long way off, a rustle within the heap like that made by a mole's soft paws.

After that, things changed. Brenda's father put the cottage up for sale, but there were no purchasers. He and Jim Emsden spent a couple of days piling up more rock in the quarry. Then he had go back to the office, since his vacation was over. He could visit the island only on weekends. Everyone, even Brenda, seemed to want to forget what was under the rock heap. Brenda's mother began to complain that the girl was getting hard to handle, no longer obeyed.

The children who had rejected her now sought her out. They came to the cottage as soon as breakfast was over, asking for Brenda, and she went off with them at once, deaf to all that her mother could say. She would return only at dusk, pale with exhaustion, but still blazing with frantic energy.

Her new energy seemed inexhaustible. The physical feats that had once repelled her drew her irresistibly. She tumbled, climbed, dove, chinned herself, did splits and cartwheels. The other children watched her admiringly and applauded. For the first time in her life she tasted the pleasure of leadership.

If that had been all, only Brenda's parents would have complained. But she drew her new followers after her into piece upon piece of mischief. They were destructive, wanton, irrepressible. By the end of the summer everyone on Moss Island was saying that Brenda Alden needed disciplining. Her parents complained bitterly that she was impossible to control. They sent her off ahead of time to school.

There the events of the late summer were repeated. Brenda's schoolmates accepted her lead blindly. The teachers punished and threatened. Her grades—for the first time in her life—were bad. She was within an inch of being expelled.

The year passed. Spring came, and summer. The Aldens fearing more trouble, left Brenda at school after the school year was over. She did not get back to Moss Island until late July.

The last few months had changed Brenda physically. Her narrow body had rounded and grown more womanly. Under her shirt—she still wore slacks and shirt—her breasts has begun to swell and lift. She seemed to have outgrown her tomboy ways. Her parents began to congratulate themselves.

She did not go at once to the cairn in the quarry. She often thought of it. But she felt a sweet reluctance, an almost tender disinclination, toward going. It could wait. August was well advanced before she visited the mound.

The day was warm. She was winded after the walk through the woods. She let herself down the side of the quarry delicately, paused for breath, and went up the mound with long, slipping steps. When she got to the top she sat down.

Was there, in the hot air, the faintest hint of rottenness? She inhaled doubtfully. Then, as she had done last year, she pressed her ear to the mound.

There was silence. Was he—but of course he couldn't be dead. "Hi," she called softly, her lips against the rock. "Hi. I've come back. It's me."

The scrabble began far down and seemed to come nearer. But there was too much rock in the way. Brenda sighed. "Poor old thing," she said. Her tone was rueful. "You want to be born, too, don't you? And you can't get out. It's too bad."

The scrabbling continued. Brenda, after a moment, stretched herself out against the rock. The sun was warm, the heat from the stones beat up lullingly against the body. She lay in drowsy contentment for a long time, listening to the noises within the mound.

The sun began to wester. The cool of evening roused her. She sat up.

The air was utterly silent. There were no bird calls anywhere. The only sounds came from within the mound.

Brenda leaned forward quickly, so that her long hair fell over her face. "I love you," she said softly to the rock. "I'll always love you.

You're not afraid of anyone, not even father. You're the only one I could ever love."

She halted. The scrabbling within had risen to a crescendo. She laughed. Then she drew a long, wavering sigh. "Be patient," she said. "Some day I'll let you out. There's a lot of rock, but I'll move it. I promise. Then you can make me a woman. I'll be alive for the first time. I'll love you. We'll be born together, you and I."

POSTHUMOUSLY PUBLISHED 2011

THEY THAT HAVE WINGS

Evangeline Walton

Evangeline Walton (1907–96) is best remembered for her series based on the Mabinogion tales which began with *The Virgin and the Swine* (1936). She also had a novel of witchcraft, *Witch House* from Arkham House in 1945. You might think she'd have had several stories in *Weird Tales* but she found the medium difficult. "My brain just does not work that way," she told bookseller Ben Abramson. So there was only one, "At the End of the Corridor" (May 1950), about an archaeologist who enters one tomb too many. But there could easily have been more. The following story was rejected by *Weird Tales* as being "too gory" and languished amongst her papers until rediscovered by researcher and editor Douglas Anderson. He managed to get it reprinted in *The Magazine of Fantasy & Science Fiction* in 2011 and included it in a compilation of her short fiction, *Above Ker-Is and Other Stories* (2012).

It was not the first time she had been rediscovered. Although the first book in her Mabinogion sequence had been published in 1936 the subsequent novels remained unpublished, though a British publisher had them scheduled for publication before the Blitz brought that to an end. It was only when the first volume, retitled *The Island of the Mighty* (1970), was reprinted in 1970 by Ballantine Books in their Adult Fantasy series, edited by Lin Carter, that they discovered not only that she was still alive but that there were three more books which they soon published: *The Children of Llyr* (1971), *The Song of Rhiannon* (1972) and *Prince of Annwn* (1974). Another early novel, *She Walks in Darkness* eventually saw print in 2013. She also wrote an historical novel *The Cross and the Sword* (1956), about the Viking invasion of Britain, and had completed a series about the ancient Greek hero Theseus, of which only the first volume, *The Sword is Forged* (1983) has been published. There is more work by Walton to be rediscovered.

May 29th: Bert Madden, Ronnie Lingard and I are in flight through the White Mountains. What will happen to us, God knows; we have become lost from the others, and there is no hope of succour. Nobody will come to look for us unless it is the Germans; nobody can come to look for us. We have known, ever since the attempt to retake the Maleme airdrome failed, that Crete was lost.

We could go faster if it were not for Ronnie. He is British, a flier, who was left behind hospitalized when what remained of our wrecked air force (not over a dozen planes, I think) was ordered out of Crete. He is slight, fair-haired, a boy not yet out of his teens, I am sure, though he casually told us that he is twenty. To say that makes him feel more dignified; I know boys. He has a leg wound that causes him to limp, and Bert and I take turns supporting him. Bert tries to do more than his share; he is a huge man, tough and burly, a stockman from western Queensland. But although I, John Ogilvy, was only a New Guinea schoolmaster before the war, scrawny and civilized and not used to using my muscles, I am as tough as he. As well able to help the lad.

If and while anybody can help him. There is still snow on the White Mountains. The winds cut like knives, and the barren rocks all about us rise to sharp points. Rocks that a man with two good legs can hardly climb. Not since yesterday have we seen any sign of human habitation, of other living beings. At first we did not mind; it was so good to get out of sight and sound of the Stukas, of the bombs and bullets that had been falling among us like a deadly, fiery hail. Little things that in a moment could change a man to a screaming, mutilated lump of flesh. Or leave no man at all; only a silent, bloody carcass.

But now we are beginning to be afraid. We must rest; we have stopped now; that is how, for the first time in days, I happen to be writing in this diary; it is easier to do that than to keep my hands still. But we cannot stay here; there is not an inch of dryness, of shelter, anywhere. Twice already Bert has helped Ronnie move. The boy does not want to; he wants nothing except to lie still. But if he does so for long at a time the warmth of his body (strange to think of warmth in our bodies!) melts the snow upon the rocks.

He is not strong, as Bert and I are. He will catch pneumonia if we stay here. And he must have food; none of us has eaten in more than forty-eight hours. Before too long we must all have food. A man can go only so long without—

A bird has just flown over us. Queer that the sight of a bird, the dark shadow of its wings upon the snow, should have the power to reduce three grown men to gibbering fear. But we all crouched and covered our faces, and Ronnie screamed; I dropped this book. Anything in the air above us still makes us think of a Stuka. And this was a very large, dark bird.

It has come back. It is circling low above us, as if curious. For a second, its dark, beady eyes met mine; more intelligent, more sinister, than I ever thought a bird's eyes could be. I cannot think what breed it is; I have never seen one like it, either in reality or in photographs. We cannot be frightened now; we know it is no plane; and yet something in the rustling of its wings, in that dark, moving shadow on the snow—

All of a sudden Bert turned over and fired at it, as it wheeled there in the air above us. I saw the revolver flash fire in his hand. The report, reverberating from rocky height to rocky height, was deafening. But the bird did not even seem frightened. It merely turned again, leisurely and lightly, in the air. Not hit; not disturbed.

Bert leaped to his feet, his face was convulsed with rage and fear. "Damn you!" he yelled. "We'll get you!—not you us!" He emptied his revolver into it, it seemed—I have never known a better shot than Bert.

Yet still the bird wheeled on, calm, graceful there, low in the sky. Not a feather fell.

Ronnie laughed. "If there's any eating done, it's going to do it, old man. Not us."

That is what we are afraid of, of course. Why our shot nerves did not quiet when we realized that there was no plane above us. The ancient danger, older than planes. The fate that, through the ages, has come upon unlucky travellers in deserts and upon men left dying upon battlefields. Rustling wings and tearing beaks.

I laughed, but it was not a good laugh. I said, "Shut up, Ronnie. It's not as bad as that, yet. Sit down, Bert."

Bert sat down. His tanned, leathery face looked queerly pale; a kind of yellowish, mottled grey. He licked his lips.

"I can't understand," he said. "I ought to 've hit that thing. I ought to have hit it several times over."

"It must be deaf," I said, frowning. "I never heard of a bird so tame it wouldn't run from gun-fire."

We were all silent a moment, digesting that. The unnatural thing, the thing that has bothered me from the beginning. Then Bert cursed.

"That—thing ain't no pet!" he said feelingly. "I'd hate to think who'd have it for a pet."

And somehow, at those last words, we all shuddered; I do not know why.

"It seems to be watching us," Ronnie said. "Look."

And we did. We are. The bird is staying near us. For the last quarter of an hour it has been flying back and forth, back and forth, between the two great, snow-rimed cliffs that tower above us. Sometimes it flies lower, sometimes higher, yet always I have the feeling that it is edging a little nearer to us, a little closer. I do not think it is healthy to watch it; its movements are like a queer kind of dance; they fascinate. And yet, somehow, I do not like to look away. To turn my back...

Soon the sun will be setting. We will not be able to see the creature so well then to know exactly where it is.

There is already a rim of fire above the western cliffs. And as I noticed that, the bird's small, beady eyes seemed to catch mine again; jewel-bright, night-black, like tiny corridors of polished jet leading down, down, into unfathomable darkness.

Perhaps Bert saw them too, for he caught my arm. "Give me your gun, Johnny! I ain't got no more bullets. And the light'll soon be gone!"

But I shook my head. I said slowly, "What's the use?"

Ronnie spoke dreamily. His eyes have become fixed, staring at the bird. "I wouldn't try to hurt it. I think maybe it wants to help us. To lead us somewhere, like in the old stories."

Bert laughed raucously; I was silent. I know the stories Ronnie means, the fairy tales he must have listened to, not so long ago, at his mother's or his nurse's knee; the old formula of the Helpful Beast or Bird. But I have never believed in those stories; I don't now. And this imperturbable creature of darkness is not my idea of a helper.

But it is true that the pattern of its movements is changing. It flies farther and farther toward the north. And then, every time we hope that it is really leaving, it will stop and turn and hang in the air a moment. Then it will fly back toward us, swift and straight as an arrow, and halt, circling low, just above our heads. The last time that happened Bert cried out and ducked, putting his hands over his eyes.

Twilight: It has happened again. And worse this time. The creature hurtled itself upon us almost as a dive-bomber might. Its flapping wings, its sharp, bright beak, almost raked my face and Bert's. Its beady eyes gleamed red as they glared into ours; demanding, commanding. But it only circled gently above Ronnie's head. Tenderly.

It has flown off to the north again now. But it will be back. It does want us to follow it. And the light is going. Dare we risk a real attack, in the dark? We cannot stay here anyhow; not unless we want Ronnie to freeze. After all, can the bird lead us to a worse place than this may be if we stay?

June 5th: I could laugh now, reading that last entry I made here. What queer tricks nerves can play men who are starving and sick and unbalanced by the shock of events no man ever ought to see! No doubt there was a bird that had been deafened by the din of the Stukas, or by some natural cause. No doubt its failure to be startled by gunshots startled us and set our diseased imaginations off. Certainly it was blessed chance, no bird, that led us to the peace of this little house on the heights. Indeed, only Ronnie claims that he saw any bird during the last half of that terrible night-journey. Bert and I, sick, stumbling, holding him up as best we might, saw only low-hanging clouds about us; mists through which sometimes gleamed two tiny, luminous red points, like eyes.

But all troubles, real and imagined, seem far from us now. We need not fear that the Germans will ever find us, in this little place above the clouds. It is high enough to be a bird's nest, guarded by almost impassable slopes of rock and ice. And the two women here are themselves like birds; they have the same light swiftness of motion, the same high, sweet voices, the same bright, dark eyes.

Aretoúla, the younger, has also a face that might have been carved on some ancient Greek coin. Her grandmother has the same delicate profile, grown beaky now, so that it reminds one a little of a bird of prey. Just as the thinness of her brown, wrinkled old hands sometimes makes one think of claws. But forty years ago I imagine that her body moved and curved with the same singing grace as Aretoúla's.

They are very good to us. They are forever feeding us, continually bringing us tempting little trays because they knew that, at first, our shrunken stomachs could not hold much at a time. Forever apologizing for the poor quality of what they have. They do not know how good their bread and honey and olives taste after the days of battle and flight and fear. When we try to tell them how good the old woman only shakes her head and says, almost fiercely, "There is no meat!" a hungry gleam in her black eyes.

It is natural, especially at her age, that she should crave, need meat. When I am a little better I will go out and set traps, as I used to do as a boy in New Guinea. We must give her meat; she has done a great deal for us.

Aretoúla never seems hungry. Aretoúla only holds out her little trays and smiles and says softly: "See the sweet honey, *kyrie*. The honey and the good bread and the strong olives. The *kyrios* must eat, eat all he can, and grow well and strong again. Well and fat and strong."

She has smiles enough for all of us; they bring out the dimples around her lovely mouth just as the sun brings out the unfolding petals of a flower. But the smiles in her eyes are warmest and deepest for Ronnie. Sometimes they make her dark eyes truly soft, take the hardness out of their brightness. I never realized, until this last week, that bright eyes are always hard.

But I am talking like the poet I always wanted to be. The poet very few poor school-teachers get to be. Aretoúla makes a poet of a man. I only hope she is not going to make a lovesick fool of Ronnie. It would be a great pity to repay old Kyra Stamata's hospitality with any kind of hurt. Too bad that the women speak so much English; I am the only one of us three who knows Greek. Perhaps young people do not need a common language.

They are very lonely up here. No neighbours ever seem to visit them; which, perhaps, is not too strange, considering at what an almost inaccessible height their little house is perched. Yet it seems a little queer that nobody ever comes.

Bert said so once, to the old woman; I would not have. And she looked down at her hands and said sadly:

"We are considered unlucky. My man died when we were both young, leaving me with but one child, a girl. And Aretoúla's mother, too, lost Aretoúla's father early. People are afraid to come, lest our ill-luck reach out to them."

A strange thought, that. Of ill-luck as a dark, cloaked presence brooding above the house and ready to stretch out long, invisible arms to clutch anybody who may enter. And how cruel, that such a superstition should isolate two women.

Bert and I were both awkwardly sympathetic. We told old Kyra Stamata that when the war was over she ought to take Aretoúla and go down to some town or village. Where both of them could live nearer other women; where Aretoúla could meet young men.

But she shook her head. "No. In this house I was born, and in this house I will die. As my father and mother died, and my four brothers. My four tall, strong brothers. And after them my husband and my daughter's husband."

Bert said: "That's hard on the girl. Never getting anywhere, never meeting any other young people."

The old woman smiled. A sudden broad smile, so deeply amused that it lit her dark beady eyes, the few yellow teeth still showing under her jutting, beaklike nose, with a red glow oddly like evil. Like a secret, gloating greed.

"If a young man is meant to come to Aretoúla, one will come."

*

June 6th: I am afraid that Aretoúla thinks that young man has already come. And so does Ronnie. Tonight I heard them whispering together, out on the mountainside. Traces of snow still showed beneath their feet, but around them—so clear and fragrant that even a dried-up, prosaic codger like myself could catch it—was the breath of spring. Their arms were round each other, and his head was bent close to her dark one. I heard him saying:

"There must be a priest we can get to come up here, Aretoúla. My friends can go for him, even if I can't, because of this blasted leg; I don't know why it doesn't mend."

It is true that Ronnie's leg is the only one of our ills that this rest here has not mended. He is lamer now than he was when we wandered on the hills. But no doubt the strength of desperation bore him up then.

Aretoúla's voice came, tender, velvety as a caressing hand: "Your leg will be well. All of you will be well. Wait, my Ronnie; only wait. With me."

"I can't wait much longer, Aretoúla. Not for you. The fellows'll be glad to go for a priest. And it'll be safe. Your Cretans are a good sort—they don't betray allies."

She laughed and nuzzled her cheek against his. "Foolish one, my golden love, you do not have to wait! Not for Aretoúla. She is yours. As much so as any priest could make her. We will not ask your comrades to risk their lives among these mountain passes that they do not know. Among, perhaps, the Germans."

He said stubbornly, very low: "I can't do that, Aretoúla. What would your granny think? I can't take advantage of you and her like that; not after all you've both done for us."

She threw back her head then, looked up into his face. Even from where I stood, around the corner of the hut, I could see how the stars shone, reflected in her eyes.

"Listen, my Ronnie. Granny will understand. I see that I must tell you of sad things—things that I had hoped need not yet trouble us. No priest would come here, if your comrades went for him. They hold this place accursed."

"But why—what—"

"You cannot understand, you who are English and so not superstitious. You do not know how the mother of my grandmother died raving mad, after she had tried to kill my grandmother, whom she called a *striga*, the murderess of her brothers. For three of them had died indeed, of some wasting sickness, and grief had turned the old woman's brain, so that she remembered a legend of our people—one that is old, very old, among us. Of how sometimes a girl-child is born with a craving for food that is not meant for man. And with other gifts also—a *striga*.

"Yes, she would have killed my grandmother, her own child. Her husband and her remaining son had all they could do, strong men though they were, to drag her off her only daughter. And that night she died, raving. And soon they themselves died also, of the same sickness that had taken the others. But the words of the poor mother's ravings lived, and my grandmother was left alone. None of the neighbours (for we had neighbours then, here on the mountain) would enter this house; none of her kin would take her in. All hated and feared her; all shunned her. Until my grandfather came climbing this way from another village in another valley—tall and strong and laughing, such a man as her brothers had been. And he laughed at the tales and loved her. All might have been different if he had lived—or if my father had lived. But now the curse has settled here, like a black bird brooding above this house forever. No man will ever marry Aretoúla."

"I will—some day." Ronnie's young face was exalted. "I'll take you away from here. To England, where people are civilized and don't do things like this to women. We'll always be together."

His arms tightened around her, and his head bent to hers. Her mouth plastered itself on his; she pressed herself against him, seemed almost to press herself into him, as if her body might melt, cloudlike, into his.

I came forward then. I said, "Good evening," casually, before I came round the corner, and Ronnie jumped back, out of her arms. I stayed with them until she went in, and later, after he was asleep, I got Bert out of the house and talked with him:

"We'll have to leave, Bert. Things are getting too thick here; the kids are falling in love."

I told him everything; everything, that is, except those fantastic nightmares of old Kyra Stamata's mother. Bert, like many Queenslanders, has seen a good deal of the aborigines; and although he pretends to scoff at their dark beliefs and practices, they have left their mark upon his mind. I was afraid he might be too much impressed.

As it was, he was not enough impressed. He laughed.

"Me, I'd let the kids have their fun, Johnny. This is wartime; it may be all they'll ever have. But that's the schoolmaster of it, I suppose; you've got to have everything proper and respectable. And maybe it would be just as well to clear out. The longer we stay the less chance we'll have of getting picked up by our own boats; they may be all gone already."

I was so surprised that I was startled into an undiplomatic honesty. Undiplomatic since I wanted, suddenly and desperately, to get away.

"You know very well there's no chance of that, Bert. Any Englishmen that are left on this island are stranded—without a dog's chance of getting out, unless it's on a Cretan fishing-boat."

Bert looked sheepish. "I know. But, nice as they've been to us here and all, I'd just as soon get out, Johnny. The old lady makes me feel funny; I can't help it. She looks like somebody—or something—I've seen somewhere else. And how do she and the girl both come to know English so well when they've never either one been down off this mountain, and when there's not a book—not even a Greek bible—in the house?"

I said testily: "That's nonsense, Bert. You sound as if you suspected them of something. You know Aretoúla's father had been to America— was educated and progressive, quite different from the superstitious peasants around here. Kyra Stamata has talked about that. He must have taught her English."

He said doggedly: "Maybe. But it's queer she learned it so well— and remembered it so well all these years. And it's queer how she knew every last thing that was going on in the war up until we came here—and now she never hears a thing. Nobody ever comes up here; nobody's supposed to have come up here in a long time. How did she get her news then—and what made it stop? If it did stop. I'm not accusing her of anything; I just don't like the whole lay-out. It's too queer."

I laughed at him; there can be no doubt of these good women's friendliness. But some of his points were shrewd and well made. More shrewd than I would have expected of Bert. I am more glad than ever that I did not tell him the wild parts of that story of Aretoúla's. In the morning we will ask her grandmother about the mountain passes, about the best way to leave.

June 7th: They were hurt and grieved, as I was afraid they would be; our two hostesses. They say that Ronnie's leg is not well enough for any journey—too much truth in that, I fear. They ask us if we are not happy with them—safe? If they have not done everything they can for us? They have; the trouble is that I am afraid that if we stay Aretoúla will do too much. Perhaps I can find a chance to talk with Kyra Stamata before the day is over; warn her of that danger. We cannot leave till tomorrow anyway; that is clear.

Midnight: I have had horrible dreams; I could almost think that I am going mad. Perhaps it was my failure to get a chance for private talk with Kyra Stamata that made me restless, unable to sleep soundly. Yet I was very sleepy when we went to bed; we all were, for, in honour of our last night, Kyra Stamata had brought out her last bottle of wine, one that she had brewed with her own hands, according to an ancient recipe of her family. A strange wine, tasting of honey. And of something else, something to which I cannot put a name.

It went to all our heads, and we were glad to go to bed early; I remember thinking hazily that that would be better, anyway, when we men were to start out early in the morning. But in the dead of night I woke; in a sudden sweat of fear, though I did not know what had roused me.

And then I heard it again: the creak of a door, the door of the inner room, where the women slept. They were coming out, into the room where we lay, and as I realized that my heart leapt with relief—and then stood still.

For Aretoúla was carrying a torch, and in her grandmother's hand was a knife. A long, thin knife. The torchlight shone brightly on the blade and redly in both women's eager eyes.

Aretoúla said softly: "All is well, Grandmother. They sleep."

The old woman did not answer at once. She came a little farther into the room, her head thrust forward, slightly bent. Like a bird's, when it hunts food. Her neck looked long; longer than a woman's neck should be; her jutting nose was like a beak, her beady eyes blazed with greed. And in that instant I knew her! Knew her for the bird that had flown above us in the mountains, the bird that had danced and menaced us as the sun set!

She came and stood looking down at us. And though I strained every muscle to rise, though my throat swelled with a shriek, I could not! I lay as if paralysed; even my lips were locked.

Aretoúla said nervously: "You will not touch the young one, Grandmother? You had Grandfather awhile before you ate out his vitals; Mother had Father awhile before you and she ate his out. I, too, want my time of love."

The old woman grunted. "You shall have it, little one; never fear. We will take the big one first; he should be the richest and most savoury. Give me the dish now."

Aretoúla bent and lifted it from its place beside the hearth. A pot that I had often seen them cook in; a fine old copper pot. It gleamed now as the torchlight touched it.

Kyra Stamata came a step nearer; stood squarely above us. Above Bert...

I tried to cry out; I tried, as hard as any man ever tried to move. But I might as well have tried to lift a stone wall as my own body.

I saw the knife flash, swift and bright as lightning, as the old woman's arm shot down. I saw it rip Bert's whole chest open; heard him groan and saw his body lift convulsively and then stiffen. There was another hollow groan. And then he lay very still, with a bright red ribbon seeming to stretch between his throat and chest.

But not for long. The old woman still bent over him. She thrust the knife back into the wound, turned it... thrust in her whole hand... I think I must have swooned.

After that I had only brief glimpses. I saw her straightening up again, with Bert's heart in her hand; Bert's heart, red and dripping. I heard her telling Aretoúla to stir the embers of the fire. Once after that, I was roused from another spell of unconsciousness by the smell of burning flesh.

But I will not tell what I saw after that. I cannot. Only one thing: once Ronnie stirred and moaned in his sleep, and Aretoúla came across to him and laid her hand gently on his face, her own face as tender as a young mother's.

"Sleep, my golden one," she murmured in her soft, singing voice. "Sleep."

And he did sleep. Thank God, he is still asleep.

Before they went back into the inner room they came and leaned over Bert again. They ran their slim hands gently over his body. And they laughed; their sweet, shrill, birdlike laughter.

"Beware! Beware, O squeezed sponge, of running water!"

And then again, I seemed to swoon. And when I awoke, a little while ago, Bert was breathing peacefully. There was no sign of any wound upon his chest. But I dare not try to sleep again; I dare not dream again. I will sit up for what is left of this night.

June 8th: I will steal a few minutes to write in this journal before we leave. To write something sane and sensible in it, after last night's vagaries. It was a dream; all a horrible, fantastic dream.

And yet Bert seems a little pale this morning; not quite his hearty, vigorous self. He has not joined in the laughter and talk about the breakfast table as he usually does. And I wish Kyra Stamata were not polishing her copper pot. Polishing it carefully, as if it had been used. And I wonder why Aretoúla is so gay and laughing; I had thought she would be sad for Ronnie's going.

But they are calling me now; Bert himself is calling me. We must start.

Night again: We are back in Kyra Stamata's cottage. That is, two of us are back. Bert is dead.

We walked all morning, down the steep mountain roads that Kyra Stamata had told us of. And he complained of hunger, of a queer feeling of emptiness. "Like as if I was hollow inside," he said once. He, the strong man, was as ready as Ronnie to rest, when we sat down at noon.

We did not dare eat much; we did not know how long the food Kyra Stamata had given us might have to last. And Bert was ravenous.

After he had eaten he rose and walked over toward a little mountain stream that foamed about a hundred yards from us.

"Water ain't my choice of a drink, but maybe it'll fill me up some. I don't know what ails me, anyway. The old lady's wine must have given me a funny kind of hangover."

He drank. I was beside him; I saw his throat move as the water went down. And then I heard him gasp; saw the red ribbon spring out again, across his chest. He fell forward, with his face in the torrent. Ronnie and I pulled him out together.

Ronnie thinks it must have been a haemorrhage; some lesion caused by all the fatigue of our wanderings, begun again too soon. There was a little blood on his mouth; Ronnie thinks it must have fallen from there to his chest, that shows no wound. But there was not much blood anywhere. I cannot help thinking of a sponge that has been squeezed...

And while we were dragging the body up the bank Ronnie's leg crumpled under him. I had to go back to the cottage and get the women to come and help me. With Ronnie; with Bert's body. So we are back here—back, I had almost said, where it all happened.

But there is no danger. There can be no danger. What I saw last night was a dream. Bert's illness and death were a coincidence. I will not insult, even in thought, women who have been kind to me; who have risked their lives to help me, as all Cretans risk their lives when they help Allied soldiers now. I will not let myself go mad.

I will not remember blood running down the sides of a copper pot...

Aug. 15th. I have let the weeks pass by as in a trance; I have not even written in this journal. I was ill for awhile, and Kyra Stamata nursed me as tenderly as if she had been my mother. And sometimes Ronnie and Aretoúla would tiptoe in, hand in hand, and smile down at me... They are happy. Perhaps Bert was right, and one should never try to prevent happiness. It may indeed be all that these war-united youngsters will ever have.

I do not sleep well. Kyra Stamata has noticed it, and has brewed potions of herbs for me to drink. I try to throw them out when she is not looking, for somehow at night I am afraid to sleep. Full of fancies; not sane and reasonable as I am by day.

But she watches me too closely; it is becoming harder and harder to get chances to empty the stuff out. I suppose she thinks I do not like the taste of it, and has a womanly determination to help me against my will. So often I have to fall into sleep as a man might fall over a precipice; passing blindly, in blind terror, into oblivion.

Aug. 16th: Morning again, the good, bright morning, wholesome as fresh bread. It shows one how foolish are night terrors, the grisly shadows childhood leaves in every man's brain. Ronnie and Aretoúla are laughing outside the window; young wholesome laughter. Her laugh is as tender as any woman's could be, and yet it never loses that shrill sweet note that is a little wild; the note that sounds like a bird...

There! He has caught her, and they are kissing. Their lips are too busy for laughter now. Too sweetly busy. Her arms are tight about his neck, with that hungry, enfolding tightness they seem to have at times. She loves him.

I do not know why I am afraid, even at night. For Bert knew nothing; he did not wake. And I will never see that happen to Ronnie. They will take me before they will take him, because Aretoúla still loves him. And when his turn does come he, too, will know nothing. We will not suffer; men die far worse deaths on the battlefield.

And yet—

I will tear this page out. It is lunacy, madness as great as Aretoúla's great-grandmother's.

*

Aug. 17th: Today Kyra Stamata said that she was feeling ill and sent Ronnie and me out onto the mountain to look for more of a certain herb she wanted to dose herself with. Aretoúla, she said, must stay with her. Ronnie and I wandered far afield; we were never able to find any herb to match the sample she had given us.

When we came back there seemed to be tension between the two women. Kyra Stamata looked well enough, but Aretoúla was white and her eyes look red, as if from weeping. All evening she has been very quiet. Ronnie is much concerned; he makes more fuss over a cut finger of Aretoúla's than he would if he broke his own arm. All trivial, no doubt; women's squabbles. The best of them will do it. And yet my nerves respond to any tension now, like race-horses to a cut of the whip. I can feel them tensing; feel fear shooting through them, as electricity shoots through wires.

One good thing: When Kyra Stamata gave me my nightly sleeping-draught, she forgot to look at me. She was staring at Aretoúla, who was staring at Ronnie, and I poured the drug quietly into the embers of the fire.

Kyra Stamata remembered me after a moment. She looked at me and smiled. "An empty cup already? Good. You will sleep well, soldier. You must sleep very well and grow strong again; very strong. We have all been worrying about you long enough, soldier. Long enough."

Aug. 18th: This may be the last entry I shall ever make in this diary; I think that probably it will be.

I did not sleep last night. I closed my eyes and lay still; I breathed regularly, as I have trained myself to do, when Kyra Stamata bent above me. I could see her through my eyelashes as a shadow, as a black vulture's shadow, when she bent...

But then perhaps I did fall asleep. For the next thing I knew I heard Aretoúla's voice:

"See, I have the knife, Grandmother. Let us eat; let us eat and drink tonight."

My eyes opened; saw the flash of the knife in her hand. And shut again; faintness took me. Once more I could not move.

Then I heard the old woman laugh; shrill, cackling laughter.

"As you will, granddaughter. As you will."

I felt the cold chill of steel as Aretoúla set it, ever so gently, against my throat.

"Surely he will be enough for this time, Grandmother. Let us eat of him, let us eat and drink of him tonight. Let me show you how well I can cut his throat. I have never killed before; I have fed—yes, feasted—but I have never killed."

Kyra Stamata laughed again, more loudly; harsh shrill laughter like the screech of a bird.

"You think that will show me your strength, girl? You think I will feed on that weakling, who cannot grow strong again, no matter how well I nurse him? No! He dies only that we may be rid of him. It is your lover that we will feed on, child. Tonight, or tomorrow night, as you choose."

There was silence a moment. Then Aretoúla said eagerly: "He is not so strong, either. He has been hurt; and he is slight—as slightly built as this one." She did not move the knife from my throat.

"But young and healthy, girl; healthy enough to please you. You have made him happy, you have made him strong. And we have kept him long enough; I am hungry."

Aretoúla did not answer at once. For a second the knife pressed closer against my throat. Then she lowered it. Slowly, I could tell; reluctantly. Her grandmother's derisive cackle came again.

"What! Have you lost your taste for your first kill, girl? Will you let him live?"

Aretoúla said sullenly: "You have promised me one more night. And if he should see this man dead tomorrow my Ronnie would grieve. He would not think only of me. Tomorrow night, before the dawn comes, I will kill him; I will kill them both, if you wish it. But not tonight."

She went away then. Back to the inner room that she shares with Ronnie now. Kyra Stamata fell asleep again; I heard her deep, regular breathing; I thought of creeping toward her quietly, there where she lay curled on her pallet by the hearth. Of putting my hands about her skinny old throat.

What a pity that her father and brother did not let her mother kill her—put out of the world the monstrosity she had brought into it! But they saved her—saved her to be their own destroyer, and now ours! No doubt they thought, poor fools, that they were protecting innocence; no doubt she was young and lovely then, like Aretoúla.

Like Aretoúla!

Twice I did creep toward the hag. But each time she woke and stirred; each time I dropped back quickly. Her senses have indeed the sharpness of a bird's.

Through the rest of the night she lay in peaceful sleep, and I lay thinking. Thinking and fearing, hating and shuddering, and trying to plan.

And at last, toward dawn, the idea came. Like white light.

It may not work. I think it very unlikely that it will work. But it may win us death in the open.

At dawn I rose and walked out of the house. I walked on and on. Up the mountain; to its crest and over.

From this high rock where I am writing I can look down upon the little ledge where the hut stands; that vulture's nest that we all thought was salvation, paradise. It lies there black under the red morning light; still in shadow. Shadow less black than what it holds.

If Ronnie does not follow me I will go back tonight. I will watch and try to surprise them; I will do whatever man may do. But Ronnie will follow me. He will be worried and come in search of me. And then, with my two sound legs, it ought not to be hard for me to keep ahead of him. With luck—incredible luck!—I may lead him on such a chase that we will fall into the Germans' hands. A prison camp would seem like heaven now.

But will he follow me so far? Or will he turn back—to Aretoúla? He would only think me mad if I tried to tell him what I know.

He is coming. I see him clearly, down there in the morning sun. Climbing the mountain, shading his eyes with his hand as he looks about him. For me...

5 p.m.: I am very tired. All day I have played this ghastly game of hide-and-seek with Ronnie, here in the mountains. Without food, without any more rest than I knew we had to take. For if Ronnie's leg crumples under him again we are done. This game in which our lives are the stakes will be over.

He must think me mad indeed, the boy. Deranged, after our hardships and my long, low fever; by the shock of Bert's death. But he keeps after me with a blind, sweet stubbornness; he will not desert a comrade.

He is resting now, on a ledge some three hundred feet below me. He has not the strength, I think, to climb up to this rock where he must know that I am hiding; I moved once and let him see me. I wish, desperately, that I could see some house, some sign of man. But there is nothing. The peaks press close about us, like enemies; dark and implacable now in this failing light. Great masses of spiky, barren rock at best indifferent, alien to man.

What will happen when night falls? But it was not night before, when—

God, I dare not think of that! If only we can stay alone, in the darkness and among the rocks, meet no dangers but those that nature planned for these terrible, desolate heights!

The sun is setting. The clouds above the peaks are as red as fire, as red as blood. The sky itself gleams like a vast sheet of white light. No speck of darkness on it anywhere.

No, no! There are two specks, far to the north. Two black specks, blotting the shining red-and-whiteness of the heavens. They are coming closer, growing larger—and my heart is tightening into a knot of terror in my breast!

Birds!

Later: It is over. It all happened very quickly after that. They came and flew low and circled over Ronnie's head. I was scrambling down toward him as they came. I do not know what I thought I could even try to do; I knew he would believe nothing that I said.

I was in time to see his face as they circled above him. To see its first puzzled look fade and turn into a smile. A very gentle, very boyish and trusting smile.

"Two of you this time, you little beggars! What is it? Do you want me to go back—to her?"

For a little while he lay watching their weird weaving, the pattern that their black wings seemed to be making in the air above him. And then slowly, his eyes still fixed upon them, he rose—like a man entranced, not moving by his own volition.

He turned back—back the way we had come.

I showed myself then. I sprang up and called to him—loudly, desperately, in anguish.

"Ronnie! Ronnie!"

He hesitated. He turned again, and looked at me, and in his eyes there was a strange struggle—bewilderment and friendliness and recognition, all fighting with a strange charm that moved him as if he had been an automaton, no longer in control of his own limbs.

I called him again: "Ronnie—Ronnie!"

He took an uncertain step toward me; then another and another. He said, "Johnny—old John!"

And then the birds swooped. With a terrible, shrill cry of rage one of them leapt at me, her long bright beak aiming at my eyes. I saw hers as she came, and knew them, for all their red fierceness—the eyes of Aretoúla!

Then my hands were over my face, and I could feel her savage beak tearing them, biting through muscle and flesh and bone. Could feel her claws slashing at my chest like knives, while her great wings beat my shoulders and head.

I heard Ronnie give a cry of horror—and then another cry, a long-drawn, horrible cry of pain. And knew that the other bird's swoop had taken him.

I forgot my own danger. I lowered one hand and looked.

She had him by the chest and throat. Her long claws held him by his shirt-front, and by the flesh beneath it, and her beak was in his throat. He was reeling, staggering, trying to fight her off, but that beak was sawing ever deeper...

And then I heard another shriek, the most terrible of all. The fiercest sound of rage and hate, surely, that ever came out of any throat, human or beast's or demon's.

The bird that had been attacking me had left me. Had launched herself through the air, a black, whirling missile, straight for the other's throat!

Her beak closed just beneath that other beak, which was set in Ronnie's throat; sank deep into the black feathers just below that savage, red-eyed little head. And the bird let go of Ronnie. He staggered back, blood streaming from his throat and chest, and fell.

I ran to him. I worked to staunch his wounds while the battle raged above us.

And not only above us. Over the ledge and over the heights above it they fought, sometimes breaking apart and staring at each other, red-eyed, and then springing back upon each other, with mad, savage cries. Sometimes they fought almost over our heads, so that bloody feathers fell on us and I covered Ronnie's face and my own eyes; and sometimes they flew so far away, a whirling, battling black ball of awful, self-destroying oneness, that we lost sight of them, and hoped that they were gone.

But always they came back. Always we heard those shrill, deadly cries again, saw the beating of those black, threshing wings.

They whirled in battle above the depths below the ledge, shrieking and biting, clawing and tearing, pounding each other with their wings.

And there one of them fell. Sank down slowly, softly, like a dropped ball of down, into the depths below.

The other staggered in the air, then turned and flew back toward us, its wide wings black against the shining heavens.

I crouched over Ronnie, shielding his head with my body, peeping through the fingers that I held before my own face.

Which had won—*which*?

The bird reached the ledge. Swung in the air six feet above us. I could see its head quite clearly against the darkness of the great, outspread wings. And the reddish-black little eyes were glazed and queerly glassy; no longer menacing. Its beak was red—red as the wounds that covered its body.

It looked down once, as if seeking something it could not find—Ronnie's face, that my body hid. And then its eyes closed and it fell.

But as it struck the earth it trembled and spread out as water spreads. It quivered and changed and grew in a strange, transforming convulsion. And then, where the dying sun had glistened in a bird's black feathers, it glistened on a woman's black hair. Aretoúla lay there, pale and torn and bloody, her mouth redder than the wounds that disfigured her lovely face.

With a great cry Ronnie tore himself away from me. He ran to her. And as he came she lifted slim, dripping fingers and tried to wipe the blood away from her mouth. She seemed ashamed.

When he dropped to his knees beside her she smiled at him, and once again her mouth was lovely and tender, a woman's mouth.

"I—loved you, Ronnie. I could not let her kill you—when the moment came. I was—more woman than *striga*."

He could only gasp, "Aretoúla—Aretoúla!" and hold her close. He could not understand.

I came to them, and she looked up at me. "Is—my mouth all right now, Johnny? Not—ugly? I would like him to remember me as—beautiful. As beautiful as—any of your English girls."

I knelt and wiped the last of her grandmother's blood from her mouth. Ronnie kissed her, sobbing. His grief-stricken eyes were dazed.

She said gently, explaining, "My grandmother would have killed you, Ronnie. She did kill Bert. And now I have killed her—for you. And I—am dying. But there is a village—yonder—beyond that peak—to the west." She tried to raise her hand, but could not. I had to raise it; with a great effort she pointed the shaking fingers.

"They will—hide you there. From the Germans. They are—clean. No *strigas*—there. And no—woman who will love you as much as—I—" And then the words stopped, and the breath rattled in her throat. She never spoke again.

She has been dead since moonrise. Ronnie and I have dug her grave. We will not go down into the abyss and try to find the other; the birds of prey, her kin, may clean her bones. We will rest here tonight, and in the morning we will go on. To the village. To another day.

1953

FOXY'S HOLLOW

Leah Bodine Drake

Leah Bodine Drake (1904–1964) was one of *Weird Tales*'s most prolific contributors, almost entirely of poetry. Her first, "In the Shadows", appeared in the October 1935 issue which also printed her letter supporting the covers by Margaret Brundage. She would continue to appear in the magazine until her final, twenty-fourth poem, "Out!" (March 1954). When the magazine folded, she continued to place poetry with *The Magazine of Fantasy & Science Fiction* but she died of cancer just before her sixtieth birthday in 1964. August Derleth published her first volume of poetry, *A Hornbook for Witches*, at Arkham House in 1950, though it was at Drake's expense, and it has become one of the rarest of all Arkham House books.

Drake was a theatre and music critic—she was a devotee of jazz—and a great collector of children's books. She had only two stories published in *Weird Tales* and one, the following, in the short-lived magazine *Fantasy Fiction*. Recently David Schultz compiled a collection of her work, *The Song of the Sun* (2020).

Burke Bennett was out with the Peddingham one wet day in autumn when his mare took a fence in the worst possible manner and threw her rider seven feet away.

When Burke tried to rise he found he had a sprained ankle and that the mare was nowhere to be seen.

Now isn't this dandy? thought Burke. Isn't this just dandy?

He didn't know where he was or how to get to Bewley Hall where he was staying, from here or how he'd walk there if he knew. Why couldn't he have stayed with the field instead of streaking off by himself in strange country?

Burke Bennett was a large young American with a red face and bad manners who wrote fiction of a sort about tanned young men who met beautiful young women on beaches. He was much beloved by bookies and loan-sharks and was a great hand with the girls, none of whom he intended to marry. Lord Bewley, who collected Americans, Irishmen and Toby jugs, had asked him down for the hunting in a part of England that Burke didn't know very well, and here he was in the middle of Hawkshire with a sprained ankle. He was sitting in the mud, cursing splendidly, when he saw a little wooded hollow nearby from which smoke was curling lazily. Now to Burke, who was no Boy Scout, smoke in the woods meant just one thing—a house. He hoisted himself painfully to his feet and limped off towards the trees.

When he got closer he saw he'd guessed right. There *was* a house there—big, half-timbered job, all sloping eaves, dormer windows and little leaded panes. It was set in a formal garden of rose arbours, dark yews, and privet trimmed in the shapes of ships and peacocks. For a minute Burke had the idea that there was something odd about it. Then he realized what it was: the day had been misty, but now the sun was shining brightly on the golden beeches and glossy holly-trees. Must have cleared up in a hurry, he thought briefly. The house had a great many little twisty chimneys, two of which stood up on each side of the main building like the ears of some animal. Quaint as hell.

Thud! Thud!... Burke at the door-knocker, which was a fox's head in brass, and grinning. Nobody answered. Burke hadn't known he could swear so colourfully. He gave the door a kick and it swung open, so he walked in. There was a low-ceilinged hall with the usual things found in English country houses—good, heavy, old-fashioned furniture, crossed hunting-crops on the walls under foxes' masks, a stuffed otter (very dusty) on a side-board, and a fire blazing away on the hearth. Burke yelled, "Hey! Anybody home?"... Nobody. So he made himself cosy before the fire, pulled off his boot and decided to wait it out. Someone was bound to show up sometime.

The day waned. Dusk fell. Burke was nearly asleep when there was a noise at the front door, it was flung open and slammed shut, and a loud feminine voice said, "Beat 'em again, by gad!"

Burke took one look at the owner of the voice and forgot about his ankle. She was a slim, red-headed girl as beautiful as any of his own heroines. Instead of a bathing-suit, she wore russet tweeds, and she was breathing hard, which did interesting things to her chest. She didn't seem surprised to see Burke, and as she came over to the fire observed pleasantly, "What a run! Jolly good, though that last bullfinch is all that saved me! Please don't get up—I know you've hurt your foot." She added, "I'm Clarinda Foxer."

Burke, wondering how she knew about his ankle, explained who he was, and so on, and so forth, and said, "I'll have to ask your hospitality,

Miss Foxer, until word can be gotten to Bewley Hall for somebody to drive over here and pick me up."

He really had no intention of leaving yet, and he turned on the charm that had devastated blonde Hungarian countesses. He was pleased to see that it worked here, as the young woman said, "Oh, not so fast! I haven't enjoyed a good-looking man's company for ages and I'm not giving you up so soon! Old Bewley can wait a bit. I like you—even if you *were* out with the Peddingham, blast 'em."

"Oh, you've been watching the hunt?" asked Burke.

The girl gave a sharp laugh. "Watching, hell! I'm the fox."

Ha ha to you, too, thought Burke, think you're funny, don't you? Aloud he said, "Well, that's a new way of seeing hounds work, I guess," which his hostess seemed to find unaccountably funny, for she gave a series of short, sharp laughs. Burke joined in, and soon they were chummy as all get out, with Miss Foxer bringing in a bottle of champagne and some cold chicken. Burke outdid himself in charm and whatnot, and it wasn't long before the two of them were making love together, and Clarinda told him (they'd gotten to "Clarinda" and "Burke" by this time, as well they might) that he was at Foxy's Hollow. The estate had originally been called Faux Air, the same as her own name, the family having come over from France a long while back.

"Faux Air... that means a kind of make-believe, doesn't it?" said Burke, and Clarinda told him not to get personal, and bit him playfully on the neck.

The morning came, and Burke said he didn't feel up to moving about on that ankle, and Clarinda said she should think not, and for him to lie up at Foxy's Hollow until it improved. Burke wondered aloud feebly what his host would think of his absence and Clarinda replied that he'd probably suspect the worst, and Burke was too sleepy to try to figure that one out. In mid-morning Miss Foxer told him she was going out for a while, and that there was a cold rabbit pie in the boot-cupboard if he got hungry. Burke lolled about the big empty house all day, wondering where the servants were, if any. He examined the portraits of former red-haired Foxers, peering at the signatures to see if they'd been painted by anybody worthwhile; poked around the dining hall and calculated how much, at a pinch, could be raised on the plate, and finally resigned himself to reading some poems of his hostess's which she'd dug out of an old hat box and left for his perusal, after learning he was a writer. They were terrible.

About three o'clock Clarinda came in, very sweaty and with twigs in her hair. She threw herself in a chair before the fire, and said briskly, "Saw some of your friends today. I'll bet they're wondering where you've got to! This is Saturday country for the Peddingham, you know."

"Good Lord, I almost forgot about Bewley! What did you tell 'em, baby?"

"Tell them! I can't talk to anyone when I'm out! I've told you, Burke—I'm a fox."

"Oh, sure," nodded the American. "O. K., you're a fox. How could I have forgotten?" (Could this babe be a looney? But a gorgeous job, at that!)

"I am, too, a fox," insisted his hostess, facing him suddenly and looking so alert that Burke almost expected her ears to prick up. "Quite likely you find that hard to believe, but I've *been* a fox, confound it, since 1789! I've been running before Peddingham hounds and old Bewley and his ancestors for two hundred years, almost. And though it's been devilish close at times I've never been caught yet—and won't be, as long as I can get back to this house. Not that it looks like a house now to 'em," she added oddly.

"Why don't they ever chase a real fox?" (This was crazy talk, but kind of cute.)

"Why, they do! Been a good many tods around here that haven't gotten clean away like myself. Friends of mine, too." She sighed. "Poor little devils."

"Well, why do you let 'em run you? Should think you'd just hole up here." (If she wanted to keep up this screwy conversation Burke was her boy.)

Clarinda carefully pulled a thorn from her right thumb. "Can't—against Rules. You see, sweetheart, it's my Doom. Have to let 'em chase me. And I get a kind of kick out of it." She giggled. "And I *do* rob their hen roosts."

She grew solemn. "You see, Burke, I used to dabble in witchcraft when I was a girl. Runs in my family. And I got mixed up with a wizard. Big, black-eyed fellow from Sligo. We got into a bit of a hum one night at a Sabbat. He claimed I kicked him while we were dancing—maybe I did—God knows I was stinking drunk. Anyway, he was furious! Black Irish temper. He turned me into a fox. On account of my red hair and my name, naturally." She stared dreamily into the fire. "He was a romantic old beggar."

When she found out she was a fox (she continued) she hid out in the woods. She was ashamed of letting the servants and her father see her. She had hung around the house at night and old Mr. Foxer used to put out dead pheasants and small animals for her until she got accustomed to foxy ways. But he died soon afterwards—"I'd ruined his huntin', you see. He never knew if he were chasing his own daughter. Deuced awkward."

Then it seemed that the servants started leaving, Faux Air was empty, so she moved in. But the country people claimed it was haunted and one night they burned it down...

"*What?*" shouted Burke at this point. For a minute he'd gotten quite a shock, she sounded so serious!

"Oh, yes! They said it was a very mischancey place," she went on cheerfully. "So I just moved what had *been* the house into another dimension, bag and baggage. I can always move it back—temporarily—for various reasons." She leaned over to Burke, smiled and patted his knee. "And it hasn't been at all bad, being a fox. I get exercise with the Peddingham, and I've kept up with current styles and all that sort of thing, by sneaking around Bewley Hall during week ends. Bewley always has had a very *tonish* crowd. And of course that wizard permits me to keep my own shape while I'm in here. Has to—in the Rules, you know. He even keeps an eye on me to see I don't really come to any harm. Always was a bit of a cake about me."

"After two hundred years that guy still gets about? Some wizard!"

"Oh, yes! Dashed good one. Sociable fellow, too. Likes huntin' and all that."

"You're nuts, baby, but I love you," said Burke. (She was a screwball, all right! Might be able to use some of this in a story, though.)

Crazy or not (Burke forebore to say "crazy like a fox") Clarinda was a gorgeous job and he stayed on at Foxy's Hollow. The days passed, all pretty much alike. When Clarinda wasn't out in the hunting-field they'd doze together in front of the fire. At dusk his companion would rouse herself and get lively as anything. They'd drink champagne and snap wishbones, or play piquet, or argue about breeds of foxhounds, or make love, and then Clarinda would slip out of the house and stay for all hours. The next day they'd have chicken for dinner.

It was after Burke had been at Foxy's Hollow for about a week (as he reckoned it) that he began to notice things. Although he seemed to be as drowsy as Clarinda in the daytime now, he still spent less time in bed than she did, and in his prowls about the silent house he noticed quite a lot. Item: the little leaded windows with their painted panes of purple, red and amber cast a peculiar light in the room that was exactly like that in an autumn wood when the sun is shining. Item: although nobody came to the house and neither his hostess or himself lifted a hand to clean the place, the beds were made up daily and the dishes washed. Item: one of the Foxer portraits, a young woman in lilac lutestring and patches, bore a remarkable resemblance to Clarinda and the date on it was 1786. Item: however freely he could walk *in* the house, he couldn't seem to open any doors to go *out* of it, although its owner popped in and out at will. Item: its owner's nose was really very pointed and her teeth very white and sharp, and she cracked goose-bones with them. She also had a damned foxy laugh. Could it be possible...? Was she really a...? Burke began to wonder.

One night he had a disturbing experience. He'd gotten up for a perfectly natural reason and happened to glance out of the bedroom window. Instead of the formal garden with its well-trimmed shrubbery and autumn-brown lawns, he saw something quite different. There were no lawns, only wet leaves, and brambles and docks growing all over. The privet peacocks were indistinguishable, and there certainly were a lot more hollies and yew-trees about than he'd thought. And what was that heap of rocks doing over there where the stables should be?

Burke was thoughtful as he went back to bed.

The next morning he looked at Clarinda, who'd come in about dawn, lying curled up in a ball amid a tangle of red hair, and uncommonly foxy she looked, too. I'm getting out of here, he said to himself.

But he didn't. He wouldn't admit it, but the poor fellow was spellbound. Doors wouldn't open to let him out. Those curious little windows seemed to be glued fast. Of course there was no telephone. It looked as if he really *was* stuck in the fourth dimension or whatever it was, ha, ha, ha, ha, with this awful doll, this witch, this... this... *fox!* Burke now spent all his time, while his companion was asleep or outside, in roaming the house looking for a way out.

The Peddingham was due around again one day and Clarinda left about noon—"to have another go at the little bastards," she told him—and Burke roved about in desperation. First, however, he locked the front door against her sudden return, muttering bitterly as he did so, "I can shut myself in, all right, but I can't get out."

All at once he heard a terrible baying and barking and yapping coming nearer and nearer, and then a wild scrabbling at the door. He knew what *that* was—it was Clarinda. There was a frenzied squalling and vixenish squawking. He knew what *that* was, too. It was Clarinda saying, "Let me in, Burke, and be devilish quick about it!"

Burke stood a moment pulling at his jaw and listening to the noises. Then he walked to the door and drew down the big old-fashioned bolt. Now the door was locked and bolted.

"Just try to get in now, Miss Foxy Foxer," he gritted.

There was more scrabbling and fumbling, then a regular pandemonium of sounds—doggy noises, hooves, and the high, hoarse note of a horn. Then some more hubbub, a cheer, and the sounds moved away. All was quiet.

Very quiet. Burke felt cold and a little dizzy. He thought he heard a small voice, high above him and growing fainter, say, "All right for you, Burke Bennett!" Then the walls of the house gave a shake, and then they weren't there. He was standing in a wooded hollow, full of wet leaves and brambles. There was no house. There was some crumbled masonry, a great many hollies and beeches and overgrown privet, but no house.

At his back was a hole in the stones of what had probably once been a cellar, almost hidden by nettles and vines. In front of it were some bones and reddish fur, or hair, with blood on them. The hole had been neatly stopped up with stones—from the inside.

Burke shuddered. Man, what a dream he'd had! Must have knocked himself out when he took that spill in the morning! And still in the middle of Hawkshire with this damned ankle... He heard hooves and looked up. A man on a big hunter was looking down at him. With a sigh of relief, Burke recognized him as one of Lord Bewley's house guests.

"Gillegan! Am I glad to see you!" Burke lifted a hand in greeting. He felt an unpleasant shock go through him. He looked at his hand.

Hard! It was a paw. He looked down at himself. He was a large red fox.

He heard Gillegan give a whistle, and then a whole pack of hounds could be heard coming towards them, giving tongue happily.

He looked up. Gillegan was smiling down at him in a very nasty way. His eyes were black and shining.

"Start running," said the Irish wizard.

1953

THE CRYING CHILD

Dorothea Gibbons

There's a puzzle regarding Dorothea Gibbons. She had three stories in the final year of *Weird Tales*, and it has been suggested that she may be Stella Gibbons (1902–89), author of *Cold Comfort Farm* (1932), chiefly on the basis that that author's full name was Stella Dorothea Gibbons. She had written several supernatural stories, most collected in *The Roaring Tower* (1937), but her final collection, *Beside the Pearly Water* (1954), published after the stories that appeared in *Weird Tales*, does not contain any of them. Moreover, Reggie Oliver, who was her nephew and biographer, makes no mention of them. Even though all three stories are set in England I'm inclined to think these are two different writers but with the magazine's purchase records having been destroyed, we may never know.

I t had happened again. In the dim maze of half sleep, Tamar Forrest had thought it a dream, the restless imagining of an overtired mind. But now it was different, and she was fully awake and conscious of the sounds of night. The light wind barely moved the stifle of leaves near the window, an owl hooted in the woods below the garden and there were the creaking sounds which an old house makes at night.

But from among those faint sounds it came again and it stabbed her brain for all it was such a little noise. Thinly and far off she could hear the crying of a child. She sat up in bed, every sense alert while she fumbled for the switch of the lamp, but when the light flooded her room the crying had ceased.

She thought she knew each room in the house, every cupboard, and the only other living thing in it beside herself was her West Highland terrier, Flora, who lay on the bed, her eyes fixed on the door.

There it was again, and Flora growled softly. A cold feeling slid into Tamar's heart for surely something, someone must be trapped here in this house, for the crying had an insistent and heartbreaking quality.

But a search of the old house brought no solution. Tamar looked into every room and cupboard, every corner. Her torch roamed emptily on dust and disuse, but nothing human could be found, and she had to own to herself that she was afraid.

She returned to bed. "An owl in the wood," she said aloud, "they often sound like people, like a child crying."

But she was not comforted and fell into uneasy sleep.

"The house is in a bad state of repair but I intend to work at it until it's fit to live in. I do admit, however, that it will be very difficult with things as they are today."

Tamar's voice had echoed drearily in the forlorn room, empty of everything but dust and cobwebs and the hot slanting rays of the sun on the dirty floor. Without lay the sad parched garden, untidy and derelict.

The man who was looking out of the window had turned his head.

"It will break your heart," he had said sourly, "as it has broken mine."

Tamar had laughed. "My heart," she answered, "is fairly well toughened against heartbreak. It will take more than Abegale to do it."

The dark sullen face opposite her half smiled, and something like appreciation had come into the man's eyes for a moment. He had lit a cigarette, throwing the match out of the window before he answered her.

"I sold you Abegale because I was hard up and because—of other things. Why an attractive young woman like you wants to live in this old place beats me." His voice was quite impersonal. "That, however, is none of my business," he went on, "and now you'd better ask me any questions about the house, which is the reason, I gather, that you asked me here today."

"I want to know quite a lot of things," said Tamar, notebook in hand, "and among others I'm interested in Abegale itself, its history. I want the house to be happy so that I can have people here who aren't," she ended bravely, flushing under the man's derisive grin.

He threw his cigarette on the floor, crushing it under his heel.

"You'll never succeed at Abegale, never," he said. "Do it up, fill it with your friends who like drinking parties. That's the only hope for the place. Never give it time to think or to remember—"

"To remember what?" cried Tamar sharply.

The man turned away as if he was tired of the conversation.

"Oh, I meant nothing. Now is there anything else you want to know?"

"I want to know everything, Mr. Montfichet," Tamar had said.

But Simon Montfichet left Abegale five minutes later and strode off down the drive in the sweltering heat and Tamar had watched him go, a frown between her eyes. She pushed back the hair from her hot brow, staring down at her notebook, open at the front page which was blank.

The hot August days drew on towards September and still the weather showed no sign of breaking. Plumbers and decorators arrived and the air was filled with the noise of hammering and Tamar measured and sewed and gradually the spacious rooms of Abegale became inhabited with furniture, old and lovely. But for all the outward show that Tamar put up, both to herself and to other people, something quite outside her own personal affairs was making her uneasy.

Simon Montfichet found her one evening sitting in a chair by the open window, her hands idle in her lap and her little dog beside her.

"Are you sleeping better?" he asked abruptly, which was his usual way of speaking. "You told me the other day you lie awake a lot."

"Not very well," she answered him sighing. "The heat doesn't help."

"Some weeks ago you told me also a ridiculous story that you heard a child crying in the house and you mentioned it again a few days ago," said Simon irritably. "Is your imagination still playing you tricks."

Tamar turned on him with a hot anger which surprised her.

"You wouldn't tell me anything about Abegale, not about the things I wanted to know—the history of it, things you could tell and which are not in the guide books. You could have told me and you wouldn't. Why?"

Simon looked at her flaming cheeks and angry eyes with an odd expression. But he merely said, "You know as much about the history of Abegale as I do. As for my own personal experiences while I lived here, I hardly feel you can expect me to tell you those. You know I was married and that my wife died here. I must admit I find your curiosity rather vulgar."

His curt words cut her and she bit her lip. "I do assure you I'm not in the least vulgarly curious, as you so aptly put it," she answered coldly. "Your affairs are nothing to me, Mr. Montfichet. Naturally I'm very sorry for the trouble which came on you here. But there's something in the house, something I don't understand. I keep on thinking about it and I can't sleep because I hear it, you see. I'm always listening for it—it grieves me so that I should hear a child crying. It's so horrible!"

Simon made an exclamation of annoyance. "Oh for heaven's sake!" he said. "Look here, you must be fearfully overwrought or something. D'you usually get like this? I mean, do stupid things prey on your mind, things which aren't there?"

A tinge of concern had crept into his voice but Tamar didn't notice because she was crying. She cried in a brave way, letting the tears run down her face and not trying to wipe them away.

"There, you see what you've done!" she said angrily, "I never thought any man or woman either, could ever make me cry again."

"Oh God!" said Simon Montfichet and he turned sharply away and was gone.

All the next day the heat was worse than ever. Not a breath of wind stirred the tired trees and the late summer flowers drooped, too dispirited to raise their heads to the burning sun. Wasps and flies buzzed ceaselessly against the windows and from the overloaded apple trees the fruit thumped to the earth. They seemed to fall with infuriating frequency and Tamar waited for the thud which she knew was coming, wincing when it came. The apples should be picked, she thought feverishly, but the initiative to see to it had left her.

The evening light crept into the airless room and still Tamar sat there, the sweat running down her face, though her hands were clammy. The shadows took shape behind the chairs and tables. The gracious colours of the rugs and cretonnes faded to grey, and as the light faded, so the heat and the silence grew.

Little Flora climbed up beside Tamar to lick her hands and then through the heat a sound came, faintly and far away. From beyond the woods she heard it, sullen and menacing. Presently the still air was rent with noise, as a roar sounded much nearer and a gust of wind tore past the house, taking Abegale in its grasp, shaking her old timbers till the bricks and tiles chattered like teeth in an ancient face. Enormous drops of rain were hurled against the windows with the noise of a thousand hailstones and a terrific crash outside brought Tamar to her feet. Evidently a branch of a tree had struck the side of the house.

With a noise louder than the thunder something banged to the floor of the room, and in the weird half-light she saw that an old corner cupboard had been wrenched from its fastenings and was lying face downwards in clouds of dust and rubble.

An odd lethargy stole over Tamar, in spite of the spattering rain and roar of thunder. The light faded to blackness which was lit by greenish flashes of lightning, and the dust settled quietly on everything in the room. Though she had eaten nothing all day she felt no thirst or hunger, but just a sorrow, deep and penetrating, and a fear as she waited for something which she knew she would hear.

The storm grew louder and the old house bowed its head before it. Within it the wind raised sounds as boards creaked where a light foot might have pressed; a curtain flapping could have been a woman's dress moving as she ran terrified across the hall. What was her fear and who pursued her? Then in a lull of sound came the thing for which Tamar had listened and it jolted her into stark terror.

From away up near the roof tops came the thin, high cry of a child. Tamar screamed, but a deafening roar of thunder drowned the noise so that she scarcely knew she was doing it, and she called out something without knowing what she said.

She ran, still screaming from the room. She wrenched open the front door and seizing the little dog cowering beside her, staggered out into the drive. The sheets of rain stung her face like a whip and the winding whiteness of the way before her flickered wetly in the ghastly light of lightning. The thunder roared above her head and flashes of light tore the sky in half in gaping wounds. The sweet smell of the grateful thirsty earth was all about her, but she heeded nothing. With her dog in her arms she ran, leaving Abegale behind her, its ancient head bowed before the storm.

The rain and her hair streaked wetly across her eyes prevented her from seeing, and so unknowing she bumped into something which held her fast. A flash of lightning revealed who it was.

"Simon! Oh Simon!" sobbed Tamar, and her wet arms still clutching poor little draggled Flora were held up to him.

Presently at Abegale a certain normality took shape. Simon lit a fire, fetched dry clothes and produced whiskey for Tamar and a towel for Flora. The storm was gradually abating.

"You'd better change by the fire while I fetch some logs," he said, "go on, don't mind me, I shall be quite a while. I'll boil up some coffee—yes, I know what you were going to say, but I've eyes in my head and can find it. Lucky I discovered these candles, because the electric light has fused."

When Simon returned with cups of steaming hot coffee, he found Tamar huddled in her dry clothes rubbing Flora with a large towel, but her eyes were on the cupboard lying on the floor, the rusty nails sticking out of its back like ancient claws. They were of a pattern which had not been used for perhaps two hundred years. Dust lay everywhere and still wreathed round the room where the candle flame caught it.

"Now," said Simon, leaning forward to throw another log on the fire, "now that I've saved you and Flora from drowning, I think we shall have to talk to one another, not just say things which we've done up to the present."

His voice was different and very kind.

Tamar caught her breath. "Have you heard—the crying?" she asked him quickly. Simon looked at her queerly, then gave attention to his pipe which needed filling.

"It cries at night," Tamar persisted, her hands clasped together, "It cried sometimes in the day as well. It—did it tonight in the storm. That's why I ran out of the house. I'm ashamed, but it was awful. It's—as if it were unhappy and neglected and alone."

A sudden gust of wind blew open the long doors into the garden, driving in the wet leaves like little creatures coming in to shelter from the rain.

Then from away upstairs they heard it, plaintive and thin, a thread of sound which chilled their hearts.

Tamar gave a shuddering sob and Simon was beside her, his arms holding her.

"Don't listen," he said urgently. "Don't listen. It can't hurt you, it can't and—wouldn't want to." He held her tighter and again it came, but fainter now and emptied itself into the air. The rain hissed against the window and a log fell spluttering to the hearth. Simon bent to put it back and then drew Tamar close to him again.

"Stay still and listen," he said, and his voice had some of the rough urgency which Tamar remembered so well. "I ought to have told you something before, but I tried to think you were imagining things. Part of it's an odd story and some people might think I was mad to attach any importance to it. I've never wanted to believe these sorts of tales but the war taught me something—about things you can't account for—and I've no option but to wonder whether what I'm going to tell you is possible, to say the least of it."

"Tell me, Simon," said Tamar.

"The Montfichets have mostly been an evil lot," said Simon. "Several hundred years ago they had a bad reputation for theft and rape and even witchcraft. Latterly they haven't gone to those extremes, but there's usually a few rotters in each generation. I don't know in what category you'd put me," he added grimly. He sighed sharply and held Tamar still more tightly.

"There's a story—about a child," he said, picking his words with difficulty. "I rather hate telling it because I loathe it so. I'm afraid there was a small girl who was delicate and hadn't kind parents. She'd got a mother who was no good and a father who was an evil fellow. It happened about two hundred years ago and the poor little kid was supposed to have lost something—at least that's the story, a plaything of some kind I should imagine, and no one would look for it.

"She died and I know there's always been a story of a child crying. I never heard it till I got married and then I thought I was imagining things. I was—blown up at sea during the D-Day business and it made me jumpy. But I hated the story, hated thinking I heard the crying, particularly as my wife was going to have a baby. She didn't want it and she never heard the crying, I'm sure of that or I'd have taken her away. Avice—my wife, died. I think she hated children."

Simon cleared his throat. "I like them and I wanted the baby. I don't know exactly what this part of the story has to do with the little girl of two hundred years ago—only that I think the crying has been worse since Avice lived here. She—tried to get rid of the baby. That's why she died. There was an awful woman living in the village who'd been a nurse, a gaunt ghastly woman who used to tramp the damp woods that autumn with a pack of half-breed wolfhounds as raffish as herself. I met her in the clearing below the house just after Avice died. The doctor had told me why she was so ill and I accused this woman of having been the cause of it. She denied it, of course, but I knew it was true and that she was afraid. I can see her long viperish face now, with the rain running down it and those damned wolf dogs snarling round my heels. I love dogs but these were awful. It seemed that more evil had come to Abegale when there had been so much."

"Can't you forget that woman and the evil, Simon?" asked Tamar gently.

"I always wanted a son," he answered hardly, "and Avice cheated me out of it."

"No good can come out of bitterness," said Tamar gently.

Simon put his mouth against hers. "It's like this with me," he said as if he was exhausted. "I've tried not to let it because I'm a hard man and very bitter, and you'll think I want to marry you because you've bought Abegale. That's not true, I love you and not Abegale. I hate it."

In the flickering candlelight the white face and soft brown eyes of Flora peered at them as she rested her two front paws on Tamar's knee with something in her mouth.

Taking it from her, Tamar held it out to Simon.

"It's a doll, isn't it?" she asked and her voice was awed. "It must be very old. The cupboard, you see. It must have been pushed behind it many years ago, and when the cupboard came down it must have fallen out. And now Flora's found it."

The odd little painted thing lay in Simon's large hand, its garish face smiling at him. The crude colours were blotched and worn but here, they knew, lay the plaything which had been lost two hundred years ago, and for which a little child had cried in an evil house where no one cared.

They also knew, each of them in their hearts, that because the beloved toy had been found that the child was comforted and would cry no more. Where the evil of Abegale had been, the two of them would build something grand and good in its place.

1994

MIRROR, MIRROR

Tanith Lee

Tanith Lee (1947–2015) was born too late to be a contributor to the original series of *Weird Tales*, but she made up for it with many contributions to the subsequent revivals, starting with "When the Clock Strikes" in the first of the Lin Carter edited series in 1981. She published 28 stories in total in the magazine, with two of the issues (Summer 1988 and Spring 1994) being special Tanith Lee numbers.

She had a rather peripatetic childhood, due to her parents' work, but read voraciously and gradually overcame her innate dyslexia. She had a small booklet, *The Betrothed*, published by a friend in 1968 and a tiny tale "Eustace" in *The Ninth Pan Book of Horror Stories*, edited by Herbert van Thal, also in 1968. Neither were representative of her later work, some of which included stories for children, starting with *Princess Hynchatti and Some Other Surprises* (1972) but mostly massive stories of exotic fantasy, starting with *The Birthgrave* (1975) and its sequels. She was immensely prolific with well over a hundred books, mostly vivid, spell-binding fantasy or dark horror. She was nominated for and won many awards including the World Fantasy Award twice, and she also received the World Horror Grand Master Award in 2009 and the World Fantasy Lifetime Achievement Award in 2013. After her death her husband published *The Weird Tales of Tanith Lee* (2017) which includes all her contributions to the magazine.

In the early winter a vampire began to call at our house. What made it so terrible was that my mother, who was wise and lovely and perfect, was infatuated with her. Inside a week she was calling the vampire "Miriam", and they would sit overcast afternoons face to face, on the long backless couch, which caused them to lean together like two dark tulips in a vase.

Both wore black, my mother because she was still in mourning for my father, though he had died five years before. The vampire because, presumably, she favoured sombreness, just as she liked the night and the winter days when the sun was hidden in a cloud. Miriam the vampire's dresses were long, with tight boned waists and flounces. She wore black hats with veils fixed to her hair with an enormous ruby pin. When she came in the house she would draw out the pin and take off the hat. She would then play with the pin as if with a red berry or a drop of frozen blood. She was eccentric, and did not put up her hair as my mother did. Miriam's hair hung to her waist like the black cloud that kept the sun in. She was extremely beautiful, in an awful way, her face so white and smooth without a single line, so it was like the face of a child turned to marble. Her eyes were black and rather dull but large enough they must be called beautiful too. Her lips were the pale pink of a faded sugared almond kept in the dark.

All the children on the block knew that Miriam was a vampire. The moment we saw her we knew. The way she came from nowhere as soon as the sun was obscured, and vanished again if it chanced to escape. The way she walked in her black clothes and now and then looked at us with soft hatred, as if we were flowers she would uproot. Adults passed Miriam often with a second look, but without an inkling of what she was. We were aware, sadly, we too would move eventually into that realm, where we would be half-blind and half-deaf. It was the fee that must be paid for losing our half-dumbness. So soon as we had learned to speak fully, to control language, our other senses would be mutilated.

But for now, we saw the vampire and we recognized her. We understood it was only a question of time. And then, as in a horrible game, it was my gate she approached, and our narrow patterned steps she ascended. On my mother's door she knocked, and my mother fell in love with her at once and let her in.

I have no idea what excuse Miriam made for coming to the house. Perhaps that she was looking for some lost relative. It did not matter really. Within minutes, seconds, she had won. And I, returning from play, found her there on the long couch, her hat beside her, the pin twirling in her fingers, and her other hand uplifting a smoking cigarette in a long holder of bone.

My mother introduced her by some foreign name I could not assimilate and have forgotten. In any case soon it was "Miriam".

Soon, too, I came to know the particular grey afternoons, like dusks, when I would enter the house and find my lovely mother in the thrall of the vampire, on the long couch, with the long windows and long ruched blinds behind them.

"Look, here's Miriam."

And the table would be piled with dainty cakes and jugs of home-made lemonade, and the mat lacquer teapot, none of which Miriam, of course, could ever be persuaded to sample, although my mother would beg her: "You're so slight, Miriam. And with the winter coming... I must try to fatten you up a little, darling."

When Miriam's leaden eyes would go over me, there would come the soft flicker of hatred once again. How easy I would be to pluck. When Miriam gazed at my mother her look was quite unreadable and dense. Yet in it my mother seemed to find irresistible magic. My mother had once stared into my eyes like that, but no more.

There was another reason too why the vampire had come to our house, beyond my mother's loving and marvellous nature.

Just as she must avoid the sun, and all holy things, sacred wine and bread, the cross, Miriam must avoid a looking-glass. And in our house there were none. The night my father had died of pneumonia, my mother had veiled all the mirrors, and later she had sent them away like wicked servants who had stood by and coldly watched her husband's final struggle and defeat. In rather the same way, maybe, she had locked up a drawer in the bureau which contained all his treasures, things I did not know about, as if no one must be permitted to look.

For Miriam, naturally, a house without mirrors, which would refuse to reflect her and so would give her away, was a wonderful piece of luck. How had she known? But then, everything about her was mysterious and foul. Where for example did she come from and return to out of the twilight? Probably a graveyard, but none of us had dared to follow. The very swish of her skirt warned us we must not.

"Oh, Miriam," said my mother adoringly, "do try a little of this raspberry cake. I baked it just this morning."

But Miriam did not touch the cake, only smoking her pale cigarettes in the ivory holder, and fiddling with the strange fruit of the ruby pin.

How long would it be before she could delay no more, before the exquisite foreplay could no longer be drawn out, and she pulled my mother into her rustling embrace and pierced my mother's human neck, and drank her blood?

Every night, when I kissed my mother good-bye before the journey into sleep, I examined her throat closely. Once she had scratched herself with a little brooch she sometimes wore, and my heart stopped. But it was not the mark of teeth.

I had never tried to *tell* her the truth, for I knew infallibly that despite her wisdom, because of the blindness and deafness of her adult state, she either would not hear or could not grasp what I would say. And if she found that I was Miriam's enemy, she might keep us apart. Probably my presence in the room, or the possibility of my arrival there, were part of the reason Miriam had held off from her deadly kiss.

In the monosyllables of our dumbness and lack of language, I conferred with other children. What could I do?

"If only there were a mirror," said Dorothy.

Then Dorothy hung her head and made her confession. "The vampire came to our house once. I saw her in the hall. There's granny's old green mirror there like a pond. And my mother saw in it. I couldn't see in the mirror, only my mother did, but she blinked, two or three times, as if something had got into her eyes. And then she said to the vampire, 'No, I can't help you.' And she shut the door."

Dorothy and I realized that Dorothy's mother, being partly blind, did not comprehend what she had glimpsed—Miriam's invisibility in a reflecting surface. But nevertheless some preserving instinct had been activated.

It seemed to me that, since my mother was special, she, seeing or not seeing Miriam in a mirror, would know the truth fully. For my mother had beheld a fairy woman once in the park when she was all of seventeen. She had told me, solemnly, about the tinsel antennae and the tiny wings. So she had more sight left than most adults. It was only that Miriam had put a spell on her.

How then to bring Miriam to a mirror and to let my mother see?

In a way it might be easy, for when Miriam was in the house, my mother paid me scarcely any attention. I could have eaten all the cakes on the table. Then again, Miriam was subtly conscious of me, as one would be of an animal one did not like prowling in the room.

Dorothy ran up to me in her big old garden. It was a sunny wintry morning, but by two o'clock the cloud in the east would have swallowed up the sun, turning it from gold to smothered silver.

In Dorothy's hand, a misty foretaste of that silver sun.

"My shell mirror," said Dorothy. "It's all I've got."

We considered the mirror, staring down into each of our faces, puzzled to see ourselves so different from what we knew we were.

"There's a little loop," I said.

"Yes, I hang it on the wall. Then when I sit my doll on the chest, she can watch her face."

Dorothy and her doll were making a sacrifice for my sake, and I took the mirror carefully. It was the size of a small pumpkin, and the shells which decorated its edge hardly hid any of the surface. Yet it was light too, and would hang from the loop.

I took it home quickly. My mother was busy in the kitchen, sifting flour and stoning summer damsons, sensing of course that darkness was coming, and so, Miriam.

I wandered about the room where Miriam would sit, looking for a spot to set the mirror. Normally Miriam would surely detect such a thing at once, but I sensed that she was by now so involved with my mother, the clean scent of her, cologne and brushed hair, my mother's delicate skin with the tiny fairy antennae lines about the mouth and eyes, that Miriam's vampire cleverness was slightly dimmed. If I could only find a place that she avoided, perhaps she would not realize.

Ultimately it was simple. The area of the room which Miriam intuitively did not care for was, not unnaturally, the two long windows. She would seat herself on the backless couch, turned away from them, and would not look in that direction even if my mother went through this part of the room. My mother also had taken to pampering Miriam's aversion. When she guessed that Miriam would be coming, my mother let down the ruched yellow blinds, and today, already, they were in place.

Going upstairs I took a large safety pin from my mother's pottery bowl. Returning with it below, I stood on a chair and attached the loop of the mirror to the yellow ruched blind of the second window. Something useful occurred. The reflected yellow folds of the blind shone into the mirror, like a buttery sun into a pond. It was not easy to see. I got down, crossed the room and stood in my usual position, just beyond the table where the cakes and tea were laid. It seemed to me that Miriam, sitting on the right of the couch as she always did, would now be reflected from the back into the mirror. Except there would be nothing to show.

As the sun moved low over the sky and the cloud rose after it like a bank of fog, the light died from the windows and the mirror too turned dull.

A glorious smell of baking drifted from the kitchen. But I felt sick with hope and rage.

At two o'clock, as the cakes were lifted from the oven, cloud absorbed the sun and all down the block grey dusk breathed out into the day. The sun was pale at first as a lemon, and then it melted entirely. And as I glared out from my bedroom window, I saw the black figure of the vampire walking up the street. About her slender ankles her black skirts bounded like little dogs, and in her hat the red pin smouldered like a coal.

I ran downstairs, and as I stationed myself behind the table, our front door was knocked upon.

My mother came, washed and powdered and sweet, with combs in her hair.

"Oh, Miriam," she sighed, "oh, Miriam. How good to see you."

The vampire glided into the room as she had so often done, and as so often over me her dead eyes glimmered, and with her colourless tongue she licked her lip, thinking, I suppose, of when she could pull me up and throw me on the compost. How aggravating for her that I was always here, always about. How she would have liked to cut off my head and be done with me. Her hatred was so vast, so cushiony, she could not catch sight of mine, nor of my excitement.

She drew out the ruby pin and let fall her ghastly hat. She lit a cigarette in the bone holder. But she did not sit down.

I would not let my eyes go to the blind. Not yet. She must not have a hint. I squinted instead at her black buckled shoes and her nasty flounced yipping dog of a skirt.

My mother entered with golden cakes and the steaming teapot. Putting them on the table, she added the frosted decanter of sherry.

"Something to warm you, Miriam?"

But Miriam gently shook her head. What could warm her after all, but one thing only?

"It seems so long since I saw you, darling," said my mother, and she sat down on the long couch, to the left. I would not glance at the mirror on the blind. I stared at Miriam's ruby pin spinning in one set of her fingers, and the other set with the smoking bone of the cigarette holder.

She gazed at my mother, and seduced, Miriam also sat.

Then I looked straight up into the mirror.

What I saw was so ludicrous, so terrifying, that it produced a spontaneous and unforeseen reaction.

I had forgotten, or never thought, that while Miriam would not be caught in any reflective surface, her clothes were still corporeal.

And so I beheld a corsetted black dress sitting upright on the couch, straight as a rod, and in the air there flashed a turning jewel, and then, floating some four inches free of the black cuff, an ivory holder and a cigarette, which was borne higher up into the headless space where the collar of the dress ended, sparkled with sudden life, and out of nothing came a gush of smoke like a cloud.

Never before or since have I known the sensation, but at that instant my blood ran cold. Cold as liquid ice beneath a river at midnight.

And I screamed.

From the corner of vision I noticed my mother's head jerk up. What Miriam did I could not see, but in the looking-glass her clothing did not shift.

My mother spoke to me sharply, but I was beyond response. My eyes were wide and fixed, glued to the image in the mirror, the headless dress of the invisible smoking woman.

And then my mother was beside me. I felt her kneeling, staring into my face. I wanted to shriek that she must turn round, look there, *there*—but no further noise would come out of me and I could not seem to move.

My mother stood up abruptly.

"How foolish children are," she said, quietly.

These terrible words loosened all my limbs, and I flopped down on the floor. I was able to look about now, and saw my mother go over to the bureau. She was unlocking the drawer with my father's treasures in it.

"But then," said my mother, slipping in her hand and taking something out, "here's a thing I'd like to show you, darling."

From my mother's hand depended a golden crucifix which shone and burned brighter than either the coal of the ruby or the cigarette.

The vampire started up. She snatched on her hat and drove the pin into it, as it seemed right through her skull.

"Oh, must you be going? What a shame."

My mother saw Miriam to the door. Miriam opened and slipped round it like a puff of smoke, already perhaps vanishing.

My mother shut the door. She held the crucifix in her hand, and slowly her gaze settled on me.

"Silly child, not to have told me. Did you think I wouldn't believe you?"

I stammered something.

"Or did you only suddenly see?" asked my mother.

"The mirror!" I cried.

"What mirror?" inquired my mother.

I babbled that surely she must understand, she must have seen into the mirror on the blind—though how?—for why else had she fathomed what Miriam was?

"Oh, yes," said my mother calmly, "of course I saw. Her dress without anyone in it. But not in a mirror." I gaped at her miraculousness. She smiled, and said, her voice trembling slightly, "I saw the reflection in your eyes."

STORY SOURCES

All the stories in this anthology are in the public domain unless otherwise noted. Every effort has been made to trace copyright holders and the publisher apologizes for any errors or omissions and would be pleased to be notified of any corrections to be incorporated in reprints or future editions. The following gives the first publication details for each story.

"The Rat Master" by Greye La Spina © 1942, first published in *Weird Tales*, March 1942.

"The Withered Heart" by G. G. Pendarves, first published in *Weird Tales*, November 1939.

"Leonora" by Everil Worrell © 1926, first published in *Weird Tales*, January 1927.

"Ode to Pegasus" by Maria Moravsky © 1926, first published in *Weird Tales*, November 1926.

"Mommy" by Mary Elizabeth Counselman © 1939, first published in *Weird Tales*, April 1939.

"Daemon" by C. L. Moore © 1946, first published in *Famous Fantastic Mysteries*, October 1946.

"More Than Shadow" by Dorothy Quick © 1954, first published in *Weird Tales*, July 1954.

"The House Party on Smoky Island" by L. M. Montgomery, first published in *Weird Tales*, August 1935.

"Forbidden Cupboard" by Frances Garfield © 1939, first published in *Weird Tales*, January 1940.

"The Underbody" by Allison V. Harding, first published in *Weird Tales*, November 1949.

"Brenda" by Margaret St. Clair © 1954, first published in *Weird Tales*, March 1954.

"They That Have Wings" by Evangeline Walton © 2011, first published in *The Magazine of Fantasy & Science Fiction*, November/December 2011.

"Foxy's Hollow" by Leah Bodine Drake © 1953, first published in *Fantasy Fiction*, August 1953.

"The Crying Child" by Dorothea Gibbons, first published in *Weird Tales*, November 1953.

"Mirror, Mirror" by Tanith Lee © 1994, first published in *Weird Tales*, Spring 1994.

ALSO AVAILABLE EDITED BY MIKE ASHLEY

It is too often accepted that during the nineteenth and early twentieth centuries it was the male writers who developed and pushed the boundaries of the weird tale, with women writers following in their wake—but this is far from the truth.

This new anthology presents the thrilling work of just a handful of writers crucial to the evolution of the genre, and revives lost authors of the early pulp magazines with material from the abyssal depths of the British Library vaults returning to the light for the first time since its original publication.

Delve in to see the darker side of *The Secret Garden* author Frances Hodgson Burnett and the sensitively drawn nightmares of Marie Corelli and May Sinclair. Hear the captivating voices of *Weird Tales* magazine contributors Sophie Wenzel Ellis and Greye La Spina, and bow down to the sensational and surreal imaginings of Alicia Ramsey and Leonora Carrington.

ALSO AVAILABLE

"Mother!" she called. "Will I help you, mother?"
The woman did not answer... Suddenly, disturbed, she looked over
her shoulder, and Mary saw that it was not her mother at all.

The fabric of Dorothy K. Haynes's weird fiction is truly the stuff of nightmares, where horrors cruel and mundane are interwoven with threads of dark fairy folklore, orphanage miseries, twisted witchcraft and uncanny timeslips to deliver heady supernatural thrills.

In this new collection, Haynes expert Craig Lamont presents the essential classics of her strange storytelling alongside rarities from obscure anthologies and magazines—and five stories exhumed from the family archive which have never been published before.

With appendices featuring an illustrated letter by Mervyn Peake and typescript images, this volume knits the irresistible pull of Haynes's unique brand of the uncanny with a rare opportunity to discover new material from one of the great weavers of Scottish horror.

ALSO AVAILABLE

'These stories have all had their origins in dreams... Terrifying enough to the dreamer... I hope that some readers will experience an agreeable shudder or two in the reading of them.'

A malignant entity answers the call of an ancient curse on the coast of Brittany; a traveller's curiosity delivers him to an abominable Hallowe'en ritual; the curious new owner of a haunted mansion discovers something far worse than ghosts in the night.

Randalls Round has long been revered by devotees of the weird tale. First published in 1929, its stories of ritualistic folk horror and M. R. James-inspired accounts of ancient forces terrorising humanity are thoroughly deserving of wider recognition. This collection includes a new introduction exploring Eleanor Scott's impact on weird and folk horror fiction, and two chilling stories by N. Dennett—speculated to be another of the author's pseudonyms.

For more Tales of the Weird titles
visit the British Library Shop (shop.bl.uk)

We welcome any suggestions, corrections or feedback you may have,
and will aim to respond to all items addressed to the following:

The Editor (Tales of the Weird), British Library Publishing,
The British Library, 96 Euston Road, London NW1 2DB

We also welcome enquiries through our Twitter account, @BL_Publishing.